Dancing
with
Strangers

Nadia Samar

NEVERLAND
BOOKCLUB PUBLISHING

Published by Neverland Bookclub Publishing

Dancing With Strangers

For permissions requests, please contact

Nadia Samar at nadiasamarauthor@gmail.com

ISBN 979-8-9922407-0-2 (paperback)

ISBN 979-8-9922407-1-9 (ebook)

For those who find comfort in an unlikely beginning,
a *spicy* middle, and a happy ending.

This is for us.

Playlist

These songs and artists were paramount in shaping the heart and soul of this story. From various parts of the world and eras in history, they carried me through every pivotal moment. From the first dance on page one to the closing credits in the imaginary film adaptation I dare to dream of, these songs brought to life the characters you're about to meet.

1. La Femme de mon ami by Enrico Macias

2. No Hay Problema by Pink Martini

3. El Farol by Santana

4. Quizas Quizas Quizas (feat. Storm Large) by Pink Martini

5. Spanish Guitar by Toni Braxton

6. Un Beso by Carla Morrison

7. Bamboléo by Gipsy Kings

8. Compagnon disparu by Enrico Macias

9. Che vuole questa musica stasera by Armando Trovajoli & Peppino Gagliardi

Listen on Spotify:
DWS – (Official Book Playlist) by Nadia Samar

Prologue

Three Years Ago

The first thing I see is her back. Freckles dust across slender shoulders. Muscles tense as she lowers herself onto the edge of a plush chaise lounge, ankles entwined. A plunging back and messy updo of dark curls cast a spell of their own. The slope of her neck and curve of her shoulders on full display, save for the thin straps holding up the fabric. Her toned thigh and calf peek through the high slit of her black dress. A cigarette sits precariously between two fingers, its sweetness swirling into the surrounding air.

Her face remains the only mystery.

The music of the underground club is slow and intimate, mild conversations mingling through the haze. The dim glow mimics candlelight, a lyrical guitar blanketing the room in anonymity. Sweat and smoke fill my lungs in a cocktail of lightheaded delight, my senses on edge, tasting the air combined with remnants of tonight's poison. Amidst swaying bodies, the wine in my belly gives me the nerve to put one foot in front of the other.

"Care to dance with a stranger?"

Her head of loosely pinned curls whips around at the sound of my voice. I tighten at the idea of her obedience. *Her face*. My thoughts run away with the wicked visage before me—the part of her lips, the arch of her thick brows, the delicate nature of her nose. All wrapped in a heart-shaped face that comes to an elegant point at her chin. I want to see her express joy, hatred, pleasure.

I want to see it twisted in ecstasy.

"Oh, I prefer it." She stamps out the lit cigarette and slips slender fingers into my outstretched hand.

Only then do I notice the broad man beside her, occupying more space than necessary. He leans back in his seat and gives me a challenging look. The rolled up sleeves of his thin, white button-down reveal ink-adorned arms. Unchallenged, I return his expression with an indulgent nod, relishing the lady's eagerness to leave his side and take my hand.

I guide her to the dance floor, flicking my arm into a question mark, directing her to turn and face me. Her weight falls gracefully into my arms as her scent hits me like a memory of clean sheets and evening light. Her free hand finds its place on my shoulder, mine on the curve of her back. My thumb fits idly in the divot of her spine. The low plunge of her backless dress spares no heat between our skin as the music moves us in place. We sway to the rhythm of the light drums accompanied by a serenading guitar. A song I've played many times before, familiar with every turn and pause.

From across the room, I mistook her dress as black. It is the color of a field after heavy rain, a dark green reminiscent of the peace found in an old forest. The fabric plays like shadows against her tan skin, hugging every delicious curve, and almost as soft as what's hidden underneath. My hand slips lower and back up, exploring her further with every sway. I caress the dip of her back and up her spine once more to curl around the nape of her neck. She arches into my touch, stretching and relaxing. Her hips move against mine, agreeing with the music.

A woman takes the stage and begins singing an unfamiliar melody. The singer is beautiful, in a long flowing red dress, bearing a striking resemblance in body and shape to my dance partner. Dark hair draped across slim shoulders, features both sharp and delicate. Yet this stranger with her temple resting against my chest, her neck upturned in welcome, seems familiar somehow.

The music flows from one song to the next as our bodies become a moving sculpture of entangled limbs. With confidence in her step, she anticipates the movement between each bar. *She can handle me.* I play with the stray strands of hair behind her ear, wrapping my arm tighter around her back as I pull her closer still, leading her motion to respond to mine in turn, as a sorcerer conducts the wind.

This strange woman does not feel strange in my arms. She fits. Our bodies oblige with every passing note, every trill of the singer's song, like two strangers dancing a practiced choreography before taking the stage.

I palm the small of her back, my hand spanning the width of her body. Her chest presses tight against mine and her breathing hitches as I push one leg between her thighs. She's hot to the touch as I lift her into a full turn. With one hand supporting her weight, she braces an arm around my neck and regards me with the point of a toe between my legs. She lifts a shin. I trace her length from ankle to knee to thigh, finally gripping her waist in another abrupt turn. Her brows lift in acquiescence, our indolent swaying now a full-on performance.

Honey eyes meet mine, and I still at their hungry recognition. She bends at the knees suggestively, one leg pointing out to support her weight, and warm fingers skate down to my navel. I grab both wrists and haul her back up. Without missing a beat, she uses my own force to push me away, lifting the skirt of her dress to display strong legs. The music pours through her like wine through the curve of a bottle, decadent and slow, as her hips rise and fall with every beat of the drum. With every strum of the guitar, her body builds the music up from foot to fingertip in one triumphant pose after another. I circle her writhing form like a predator, unaware of those around us as we continue our show. She pauses with an outstretched hand, and I grab her wrist and spin. Her back crashes hard against my chest. A breathy sound escapes her, and she reaches back, fingers finding the thickness of my hair. I skate one arm across her stomach, the other up her lifted arm to find a trail of pebbled flesh. Holding the point of her elbow, I stretch her body further along my own.

Her head falls back to rest in the crook of my neck, dark eyes gazing up at me through thick lashes, pulling on something deep within. Her face is a spell, moonlight on still water. Unwavering and ethereal, yet graceful. Lips parted, she leans further into me. I lower my head to the arch of her shoulder and wrap my arms around her in a lover's embrace, my lips touching the skin of her collarbone as I move my head from side to side, gliding across her softness. Her scent envelops my senses, and I am lost in a land of sweat and skin and pounding pulse. She sinks into my touch, against my hardness pressed against the base of her spine.

Her breath tickles the hair around my ear. "Do I know you?" Her voice is sinful, breathy. It carries a familiar accent I can't quite place. *I want to hear it sing my name.*

I tighten my grasp, eliciting an intoxicating noise from the back of her throat. Avoiding the swell of her breast despite myself, I lift my grip up to her neck, where her pulse thrums in rhythm under soft skin. Her hand finds mine and our fingers entwine.

"Not yet, love," I say.

She grinds gallantly against me, never missing a beat. Barely aware of our public display, I turn her to face me again, and there they are. Those eyes. Hooded under deep, thick brows. *Wicked*. Watching me like an old movie. Her hair comes undone and I smell traces of coconut in the air between us. Liquid heat runs down my spine at the intensity of her stare.

My mind flips through all the imaginable possibilities of her face. A future. A thought so fleeting, it's gone with the next beat of the drum. She feels small in my hands, her presence transcending her size. I don't notice the music stop as chatter fills the room, and her countenance changes.

Her brows pinch together, shifting from hunger to question.

"I do know you," she says.

She lifts a hand to brush a strand of hair away from my face. I open my mouth to answer but hold my breath instead as her fingertips make contact. A flash of beckoning want rushes through my chest at her light touch as I'm rendered speechless. This stranger, with whom I've exchanged no more than ten words, has captivated me in a memory. Something destined to persist until it fades with the passage of time.

Her eyes widen with something like recognition before the crowd parts behind her. The singer in the red dress races through the now still and bemused bodies and grabs this dream of a woman by the arm. A slew of French words swirl in the air. Her gaze searches my face again before she turns and flees. The man with the tattoos stands at the edge of the dance floor. He watches me for a moment before following the two women into the darkness of the stairwell. The air is heavy with unspoken words and an unfinished dance.

Left alone on the dance floor of an underground speakeasy nestled on a Spanish island's coast, I can't help but feel akin to Romeo, exiled from Verona.

I

Enzo

I hate flying. The suffocating cabin air, turbulence that rattles my nerves, the disorienting sensation of being suspended thousands of feet above ground. Yet, here I am, gripping the armrest with white-knuckled vehemence as the plane pierces through a layer of clouds.

The seatbelt sign dings on, and the island comes into view. The olive groves are beautiful from above, with orderly rows of lush trees. Their tops sway in the breeze, as if pointing to the coming sunset. *How much of this will soon belong to my brother?*

My first emotion after complete elation when Cyrus asked me to be his best man was a slow groaning fear. Cyrus has always been an authoritative older brother. Reliable as he was stoic in his ideals and practices. He always held steadfast to his principles and rarely saw things from a perspective other than his own. Disappointing him will forever be one of my greatest fears. Even more so than flying.

Cyrus encouraged my decision to move to America. Or so I let him believe. I used an opportunity to teach at NYU and the prestige that came with it as an excuse. I could have easily continued my career at any university close to home. I would have probably been tenured by now. Of course he knew—there was a girl. But he wanted better for his baby brother than a string of meaningless years with meaningless women to look back on. The disappointment in his eyes every time I returned home was beginning to cut too deep. A wound I kept open, fearing what such a scar would look like if left to heal.

Which was why when a certain American student crashed one of my classes, I followed her home like a lost puppy.

Cyrus saw the subtle differences in me when she was around. My change in posture, my shift in tone. And, as often is the case regarding women, Cyrus was right. Such was the case with Ana. And so, I left my home. Not only in pursuit of a career and a woman, but a life. Now, here I return, just like all those years before. With empty hands and a heavy heart. Continuously lured into the depths, time after time. But the guilt was too much—after that dance three years ago, I never saw her the same again. She forgave me for that night, and for the day that followed. But in the end, it was far more than a dance that led to our demise. It was no longer Ana I pictured when I imagined what I wanted for tomorrow. It was *her*.

Engines roar as the plane descends toward Spanish soil, the cabin trembles as the wheels touch down on the tarmac below. My grip tightens, seeking peace in this temporary chaos. Recycled air thickens around me, and it becomes difficult to breathe.

As we come to a rest, the cabin stirs with eager passengers waiting to disembark. I swipe down on my phone screen to turn off airplane mode and a slew of messages flood my inbox, my phone practically vibrating out of my grasp. Messages from Cyrus expressing his excitement at his baby brother's arrival. Emails from students inquiring about deadline extensions. I scroll through them and give a quick reply first to Cyrus, then to Lily, my top PhD candidate. I let her know I intend to review her dissertation edits upon my return in a week.

Setting boundaries with those who look up to you is something for which I was never prepared. I remember being her age, eager to begin down the path laid ahead. Hopeful for the future and the changes I might bring through my work.

I swipe back to my inbox and scroll a significant amount before reaching my text thread with Ana. Months rolling back as far as last year. Before the courage slips from my fingertips, I snap a shot of the Spanish sky through the plane window and send it to her. A lonely red "!" stands beside the photo. No service. Saved from myself.

I sigh, both in relief and disappointment.

I miss her.

No, you don't.

I'm not entirely sure if I miss the woman or the company. Or perhaps the comfort of familiarity she brings, even now. And I suppose that is a good enough reason to release her from such a shallow grasp. Despite how I felt on my first plane ride to America with Ana's hand in mine, she wasn't the love of my life. Though the allure of adventure was definitely a factor when pursuing her all those years ago. That and impatience for my own happy ending. Chasing the idea of love, slighting all questions and hesitations. And yet, even then, my thoughts would wander.

My mind reaches for *her* as its respite. I haven't been this close to her in over three years. I try to will the guilt away and allow myself her image. The corner of her mouth, which always seems to hide her intent. The curve of her neck as it meets the arch of her shoulder. The roundness of her ear and the freckle that darkens her left cuff. Her eyes, which always in my mind, hold an air of defiance. These are my favorite parts of her. The only parts I can recall, conjuring her face in a misty memory. I've never been sure if I made a fantasy out of her. If I'm imagining these musings enough to crawl into the idea of them when the pain of my failed relationship creeps in too deep.

It was easier on a different continent, with an ocean and another life between us. The truth, a simple matter of omission. But now, as the plane calms and a muffled voice announces we're ready to deplane, such fantasies wander without the tether of guilt holding me to another woman. The feel of her in my hands as we move. The smell of her hair as it whips past me from one fluid motion to another. The damp coolness of the small of her back against my palm. These thoughts have plagued me ever since. Now, I indulge in as much of her mirage as my curiosity will allow before seeing her in person for my brother's wedding.

Unlike myself, Cyrus waited as long as it took to find the right woman in Katia. A single mother with fire in her heart and molten chocolate in her eyes, a dark brown speckled with honey and sunrise in her daughter's.

Attempting to steady my pulse, I breathe deep as a sea of bodies make their way toward the plane's exit. I stay seated, praying time will stop for a moment before having to face the trial of willpower this trip will demand.

One last thought of her. That's all I'll allow before facing the flowing sands. Her hands. Their freckled wrists and long fingers. The expressive way they flex and move as she speaks. Oval shaped nails, rounded and trimmed on the lesser side of too-long. Calloused pads at the base of her fingers yet knuckles smooth and tanned. Her grasp wrapped tight around my wrist, clutching the backs of my arms. Fingers entwined in my hair, gripping the back of my neck. Those nails clawing at my back, my chest, my throat...

A young woman stumbles, breaking me from my reverie as she rights herself with the help of my shoulder. She smiles with an apology on her lips and adjusts her luggage before continuing down the aisle. My gaze travels the length of her from behind as she walks away. She turns to see me watching and brushes a strand of hair away from her face, trying to hide a smirk of confidence.

Why can't I be free to think of this stranger instead? To think of anyone, man or woman, instead of the one that curses my psyche with her Lorelei song of a laugh. A laugh I know, if given the chance, I would blindly follow.

With my jeans now well and tight from my indulged memories, I try to steer my thoughts away from *her*.

I finally rise from my seat, wobbly legs finding their strength as my heart flutters, palpitations I know will pass after a few practiced breaths. The back of my neck pricks with sweat, my palms soon to follow, and I close my eyes, focusing on the wind moving in and out of my lungs. My phone pings in distraction, another message from Cyrus telling me to hurry the hell up. I chuckle at the eagerness of my brother and am overrun with a feeling of excitement for all the right reasons. His name on the screen calms my racing heart, and I rub my palm against the back of my neck, the anxiety dispelled for now.

My brother is getting *married*. He gets his happily ever after. Even this late in life, now well into his fifties, he found her. He found the woman of his dreams and has created a life around the two of them that is so picture perfect it's hard not to feel a twang of envy. A hint of green in a sea of sky blue at the misfortune of my love life.

Not only because of my separation from Ana, but because of the one I know I veritably want and can never have. The forbidden fruit dancing in front of my outstretched, starving hands.

A bright sun and welcoming sea breeze greet me as I step outside and onto the tarmac at the Palma de Mallorca Airport. The sound of the ocean is distant yet constant. I shield my eyes from the sun and search for my brother's rugged face. After seeing passengers enter welcoming embraces, I find a massive man in a black suit and bowler hat holding a sign that reads, "Lorenzo Alarcon."

My cheeks hurt as my face widens into a smile, and I run into my brother's arms. He drops the sign and hugs me so tight my feet lift from the floor. We sway once, twice, before he lowers me back to the ground, kisses both cheeks, and holds my face in his hands.

"Lorencito!" My big brother holds back tears as he looks at me with all the pride in the world for doing nothing but show up for him.

I grab the hat off his head. "What the hell is this for?"

He snatches it from my hand and makes a performance of putting it back on his head. "A chauffeur has to look the part, no?"

We laugh like children. The sound reminiscent of mischievous brotherly adventures as though no time has passed at all. A longing for family and summer rile in my heart.

The woman from the plane passes us with a smile and a wave, and Cyrus nudges me with his elbow, twitching his brows. I return the woman's smile and flick the rim of Cyrus's hat.

"How is Ana? I'm sorry she couldn't make it, *hermanito*. Going stag to your own brother's wedding."

"She's doing well. Just busy with work," I lie. I have no idea how Ana is. Though I do know, come this fall, she will be joining the staff as a fellow professor of engineering. A fact I am not particularly excited about upon my return.

"I'm sure. She's still young enough to be excited about the work. Unlike you, old man. Tell me, how are your forties treating you?"

"You know I have three years left before making it to forty." My head falls down toward my feet, and I try my best to give off an air of nonchalance. He buys the performance, picking up my luggage and ushering us to the car park. The mention of my age with my lack of companionship stings more than ever at this moment.

I can't tell him about losing Ana. Not yet. This week is not about me, it's about Cyrus and Katia. It's about love and patience and family. I have a duty to my brother. To be his best friend as well as his best man. The problem which seems to persist every time I remind myself of this truth is my own self-control. My own resolve to restrain from taking *her* body in my hands the moment I see her and tasting every inch of her regardless of our tabooed kin. Of giving over to temptation and damning myself forever as the one who ruined his brother's wedding. Despite this, I still doubt myself. Will we fall back into step as though we were never interrupted that night? I still cannot say for certain what I will do when I see her.

But, God forgive me, I'm not sure I care.

2

Mia

A shes fall three flights down, burning summer air before meeting the ground. Chattering voices echo from below as I sit perched on my terrace overlooking the courtyard, one leg tucked beneath the other. Dangling over the edge, my back sits cool against the stone wall. Frantic workers maneuver across the courtyard as the wedding week looms ever nearer, the air thickening with a foreboding charge. Cyrus should be back within the hour, though I plan on disappearing for the night by then. I take a deep breath before sucking another drag from my Marlboro.

This balcony, a haven of retreat and ritual, serves as my sanctuary. A place to survey the crashing waves in the distance as well as our vast sea of olive groves. I find myself in this corner quite often. Both hiding from and running to a feeling of peace and stillness. However fleeting it may be.

Despite having an entire wing of the house to myself, I seldom feel lonely. I don't mind sharing my space with an occasional guest now and then, though this week brings much uncertainty as to who exactly I will be sharing my smoky haven with.

"*Ayuda me,*" my mother calls as she and my young brother burst through my bedroom door without knocking, both of them with a mess of fabric cradled in their arms.

"*Ayuda me, hermana,*" my baby brother mimics, his three-year-old voice bird-like.

I put out my cigarette on the stone ledge and hurry to help collect the clothes from my mother's arms. The cool tiles against my bare feet run a chill up my legs, and I toss the bundle onto my bed as my brother struggles to do the same. His tiny arms reach out, urging me to lift him up. I oblige, cradling him in the crook of my arm. He wraps himself around my shoulders and blows a raspberry on my cheek.

"*Basta*, Marco," I say.

He giggles in such a way that brings sunlight back into the room.

"What's all this?" I ask.

"Options," my mother responds, hands on her hips.

"For?"

"Your dress, of course. You're my maid of honor and my only bridesmaid. You're lucky I'm giving you *choices*. Any one of these will do."

I sift through the array of fabrics, examining the colors and materials. Pastels and lace, a nest of tulle and spring. I crinkle my nose and cast my mother a pleading glance.

"You cannot look like a mourner at my wedding, Mia."

"Mourners are tasteful and flattering," I whine.

"You're twenty-six years old. You're tasteful and flattering no matter what you wear, I made sure of that," she says with a hint of pride, "but please, indulge the bride anyway."

A sigh of defeat escapes me. I can't deny her when she takes that tone.

"Thank you," she says, and gestures for me to hand over Marco.

I reluctantly pass him to her welcoming arms.

"Where is Matteo, by the way? I could use his help setting up the tables outside."

"He's helping Simone at the club tonight. I should head over soon. I'll be there quite late, actually," I say.

"You're leaving?" she asks with surprise.

I suppress an eye roll. We don't want Marco to emulate any unsavory habits. Although I have explained many times my obligations to Simone and the speakeasy, the question in her voice still thrums a string of guilt in my chest.

"Yes, Mama. I promised Simone and Matteo I'd go over their expenses and finish the payroll for this month. The club sees a lot of tourists this time of year." No matter my best efforts to maintain a professional air, my mother will always see me as small as the child in her arms, mesmerized by her dangling earring.

"Is our meeting with the new vendor at the grove confirmed? I don't want to work more than I have to this week."

"Yes," I say with a heavy nod, "I returned his call last night, the agreement will be signed by tomorrow. It's handled, Mama."

"*Bien, bien,*" she says. "You'll miss Enzo's arrival tonight, then? Is his room all set up?"

I steel myself at the mention of his name. The reminder of his inevitable closeness.

"Yes, I checked this morning. The cleaning crew did a thorough job preparing the room, and I've tidied the shared bathroom," I confirm.

"Good, good. Well, that leaves me to be the sole woman of the house for the evening, I suppose." Her attempts at adding further guilt to coerce my compliance are clearly a jest.

I make an effort not to take it any deeper than such.

She points with her chin toward the dresses on my bed and says, "Give the pastels a chance, Mia. Your complexion was made for a blush pink."

My face twists in disgust at the thought of myself in a puffy pink dress, and Marco giggles.

With her son in one arm, my mother places her hand on my face and kisses the top of my head before rushing out of the room. Marco waves goodbye, his feet swinging from her deft hips. She moves like the dancer she used to be, the one I aspire to become.

In my solitude, I survey my "options." My mother wasn't exaggerating with the pastels. Some pieces I've never seen before, while others I recognize as old outfits she's been trying to push on me for years. Amidst the colors of spring, a contrasting dark emerald green catches my eye. I hold it up against my body to examine it further. A modest yet alluring design with simple straps and a square neckline. Is this a silk slip? Meant to be worn underneath something more extravagant? The crossing design of the straps on the back suggests otherwise. I stagger out of my clothes and immediately bask in the fabric's feel against my bare skin. The dress slides on with little resistance, and I rush to the washroom to examine myself in the floor-length mirror.

Flooded by a familiar feeling of confidence—I remember.

This is *that* dress. The dress I wore that night. A dress riding on the edge of simple and bold. Where did my mother find this? I haven't seen it since the night Marco was born, and yet here it lies, soft and indulgent against my nakedness. The sensation reminiscent of the last time I wore the simple garment to Simone's club. When I thought dancing with a stranger was an innocent enough pleasure.

Was this thrown into the pile by mistake? Does it matter? I want to turn heads with my chin held high, pretending I don't notice those noticing me in this dress. I want to tease, to test, to see how far the silk on my skin could convince one to throw all values of family and allegiance out the window and fall over the edge of temptation.

I want to see *his* face when he sees me in this dress again.

3

ENZO

After being away from Cyrus for over three years, I don't realize how much I've missed him until we climb into his convertible and head for the villa. His enthusiastic storytelling makes the forty-five-minute ride fly by. He speaks of his son Marco with such endearment and pride, describing his first words, fiddling with his phone to show me videos of his first steps. I watch my nephew wobbling from one end of the carpet to the other and my heart lurches, tears threatening to prick behind my eyes. He'd sent this video to me years before, but I'm truly seeing it now for the first time. My brother. A father. And soon to be a husband.

He drives with one careless hand hanging out the window, interrupting himself to point out neighboring orchards and vineyards as we make our way through the town. We pass the speakeasy, and I can't help but notice how much smaller it appears in the light of day. How inconspicuous and innocent the building stands, and yet, only a few feet below ground, you're transported to an entirely different world.

A familiar looking man with tattooed arms carries a case of wine while a dark-haired woman directs him into the building. The scene resembles a polaroid snapped from decades ago. A moment of mundane beauty in the scenery and stone of the surrounding architecture. I blame the island for this feeling of nostalgia. As though it's playing a beguiling trick on a mere visitor. The sky becomes a watercolor of blushing pinks and purples as the day ends and the bartender's work begins.

We drive through the city, witnessing the everyday lives of the island's residents, and I let myself daydream of a potential life here, surrounded by family rather than strangers. Ocean and earth and orchards rather than buildings of glass and concrete. As if by some cosmic acknowledgment, my phone pings with another insistent email from Lily. I ignore it, taking pleasure in the intention to be here, with my brother, in a car with no roof, in a town with family-owned restaurants and stores, traveling toward a villa of paradise, where everyone I love is in one place, no matter how small that number may be.

I'm unsure when Cyrus ceases his story, but the ensuing silence is neither awkward nor unwelcome. We've never felt the need to fill the space between us with shallow conversation or uninteresting anecdotes. We simply enjoy being near one another. As children, our shared bed always came with an understanding of space despite the lack of room. Wordless conversations, glances across the room filled with gossip and inside jokes at the lift of a brow.

When our father left, Cyrus filled that void for both our mother and me, assuming the masculine role of the house. And as he matured, my mother felt her own necessity dwindle, leaving us as our father had, seeking more thrilling exploits than motherhood. Despite our tumultuous upbringing, Cyrus never made our childhood feel less than in his pursuits of normalcy. He took to raising me, tending to my schoolwork, always making sure I was nurtured in more ways than just food. For that, I love him. And that, I know, is why he has waited so long to live himself. Only now, at such an age, is he finally thinking of his own happiness, while still prioritizing the women and son in his life.

My heart swells again, and I rearrange my thoughts to avoid becoming a blubbering fool. I take out my phone and scan through more student emails, and Cyrus clicks his tongue at me. Compelled by the smile on his face, the mien of pure bliss behind his dark sunglasses and thick beard, I put my phone away and enjoy the rest of the ride. The sound of wheels on dirt and the heartbeat of distant crashing waves serve as the only company needed.

"One bag is all you brought?" Katia asks by way of greeting. Flowers of varying shades of pink and red teem within the courtyard, vines of jasmine climbing the three stories of every wall. People flow by like dancers among the tables and tall heating lamps, decorating and transporting assorted items from here to there.

As we approach, Marco jumps out of his mother's arms, nearly tackling Cyrus to the floor. He stumbles a few steps back before grabbing Marco under both arms, hoisting him up in the air and catching him in a spin.

"Can you say *'Ciao'* to Tio Enzo?" Cyrus asks in his high pitched I'm-Talking-To-My-Son voice.

Marco plops his head on his father's shoulder and raises a sticky hand toward me.

"*Ciao*, Tio Enzo."

"Good boy," Cyrus praises.

I give him a firm, yet playful handshake. "*Ciao, Marcito*. You don't know who I am, do you?"

Marco shakes his head, our hands breaking free. Cyrus explains our relationship in loud, enunciated Spanish, and Marco lights up with understanding as he looks from his father's face to mine. Acceptance from a child is a feeling like no other.

In customary greeting, Katia holds my face and kisses both cheeks. The pain in my chest seizes yet again at the picture before me. A picture I would give anything to be a part of instead of the feeble brother of the painter himself.

"Hello, Katia," I say.

Katia smiles at me and swipes a stray lock of hair from my forehead. "You're not eating, Enzo," she says in the most motherly tone possible.

Movement from a balcony up above catches my eye, and a flash of black hair stills my breath.

"Cyrus, show him the room and help him put his *one* bag away," she says with a hint of sarcasm. Katia places a hand on my shoulder, retrieving my attention, and I give an awkward chuckle. "Get freshened up and come down for dinner, *si*?"

Nodding and giving her a genuine smile, I gather my things, kiss her on the cheek, and head for the open glass doors behind Cyrus.

"Don't take too long, you must be starving," she calls out.

She's right. I am starving.

We walk through the house and into a vast kitchen. The open layout and conservatory ceiling bathe the entire space in bouncing light. The most comfortable looking sofa I've ever seen sits in front of an alcove fireplace large enough to walk into. Cyrus whisks us toward a hidden stairway nudged between the large rooms. We make our way to the second floor, passing open doors revealing their secrets.

Unable to help my curiosity, I poke my head into a room filled floor to ceiling with books on dark wood shelves. Binders and loose papers lay strewn across a massive desk. "Yours?" I ask.

"Katia's. Though she hasn't worked here in ages since Mia stepped up at the grove. Our office now comprises a changing table and a crib." His voice is light, happy.

We continue up to the third floor and down another corridor. Cyrus opens a heavy oak door into a room filled with golden evening light. The smell hits me first—a blend of clean linens and jasmine. A modest bed sits in a dark wood frame, dressed in pristine white and gray accented sheets. Two tables with mounted gold lamps flank the bed. On the right, a seating area with a chaise lounge and a set of armchairs creates a cozy nook. A coffee table with artfully arranged candles brings this section of the room together. On the other side, a simple antique writing desk with a matching chair stands beside a wardrobe. Heavy, dark wood forms every piece of furniture, creating a feeling of strength, steadiness, and peace in the room. Another door faces opposite the bed, presumably the washroom. Across the room, a row of open glass doors matching the ones downstairs let in the evening air, sheer white linen curtains pulled back to expose a massive terrace.

Cyrus places my bag on the long, padded bench at the foot of the bed and gestures to the room before putting his hands on his hips and smiling at me, eyebrows raised as if to say *Nice, huh?* But of course he doesn't need to say anything. I nod in return, *Very nice indeed*, then walk over to the bed and feel the soft sheets under my fingertips. It isn't until this moment that I realize how tired I am. How much I would love to wash the anxious sweat from the flight off my skin, crawl under the soft cotton, and find a blissful dreamless sleep. I set the yearning aside, instead making my way toward the glass terrace doors.

A summer sea breeze kisses my cheeks as I step onto the terrace, a wide space with cool clay tiles and stone walls that box you in, perceiving the world as if through a window. The view is remarkable. Beyond rows and rows of olive trees and green fields, a sparkling blue stretches in the distance. I imagine myself sitting out here from dawn to dusk, drinking in this view and never tiring of its beauty. Watching the changing color of the sky without worrying about trivial things such as recommendation letters or staff scheduling. A good book, a hot cup of coffee, *her sitting in my lap.*

"*Papa!*" Marco cries from the courtyard floor.

"*Marcito!*" Cyrus walks up to the stone ledge beside me and waves down at his son.

To my left, the terrace is much wider than the length of my room. An outdoor lounge sits in the far corner with a used ashtray on the balcony ledge. A few cigarette butts huddle in the middle of a crystal bowl. Another identical set of doors glare against the setting sun. They stand closed with the same linens drawn.

"Are you and Katia my neighbors? Because I would really rather not hear your wedding night, *hermano.*"

Cyrus gives a halfhearted laugh. "That's Mia's room."

I stiffen. No. *No.*

"This is her side of the house, really. Katia, Marco, and I are across the courtyard right there." He points to another wide balcony mirroring the one we stand on now. "We enjoy the morning sun while Mia prefers the evening light. And this way, she gets her privacy."

I grip the ledge, my knuckles threatening to split.

"*Date prisa,* Cyrus, Enzo, hurry up!" Katia calls to us, picking up Marco. She makes an impatient gesture with one hand and walks off to tackle the next task.

I hear the distant creak of the iron gate but see no one enter or exit where Cyrus and I came in.

"I'll leave you to get settled. Don't make my fiancé wait, Lorenzo. I need her happy."

I laugh at his commanding use of my full name and nod in compliance. He leaves me on the terrace, and I hear the heavy wood swing shut behind him before turning to examine the closed set of glass doors. She could be standing only a few feet away, holding her long fingers above the latch, waiting to greet me on the other side.

Wishful thinking clouds with intrusive thoughts of lust and desire. A storm in my head. My heart flutters again, and I will myself to close my eyes, breathe deep, and step back into the room.

Zipping open my bag and retrieving a small parcel of toiletries, I take my things to the door opposite the bed and find a washroom. Another door glares at me from the opposite end of the room. I gently grasp the copper knob and turn. Locked. Of course. Why would it not be locked?

I survey the rest of the room with two framed mirrors above his-and-her sinks, a standing shower, and a claw-foot ceramic tub. Colorful Spanish tiles adorn the backsplash and accents of the shower and tub. The room is intimately lit with gloaming light cascading through a circular window above the open tub. I must not have noticed this hidden eyelet while out on the terrace. The tub is still wet, drops of water scattered across the basin. *So, she prefers a bath to a shower.* I imagine she fills the porcelain with steaming water, salts, and oils before lowering her naked body into the suds. She fights the bite of hot water against her skin, slowly adjusting to the temperature. Her muscles relax, accepting the heat. Using the washcloth hanging on the waterspout, she scrubs away the day from her sun-dark skin. No doubt a cigarette sitting between pouted lips, ashes falling into the water as she moves. What music does she listen to while she bathes? Does she listen to music at all, or does she prefer to sit in silence? Does she read a book until the water grows tepid and her fingertips wrinkle?

I need to stop.

Stop thinking of her in this way. It's bad enough I've allowed myself to get this close to her, even if only in my mind. With her room being this close, I must be disciplined if I am to survive this week. This is the last time. No more daydreaming, no more longing, no more pining over a woman who will never be mine. This masochistic game I'm playing with myself must end now, because the only one who will end up hurt on the other side is me.

Marco's giddy laugh in the distance breaks me from my inner monologue of sweeping declarations. I splash some cold water onto my face in the basin closest to my room and unpack my toothbrush and toothpaste, laying them neatly on the countertop, claiming my side of the shared room for the time being.

After giving my mouth a quick rinse, I change clothes and make my way downstairs. The sun has finally set, leaving the courtyard dark save for the twinkling lights hovering above in geometric strips.

In the middle sits a dining table; the edges of the tablecloth dancing aloof in the summer breeze. Alone, I admire the table setting and the view of the space at night. The air here is different. I can almost taste a hint of tang in the sea breeze interlaced with the olive trees nearby. It smells clean. It smells like a home I wish to return to.

I think of my apartment back in New York, the smell of the subway and the damp sidewalks, not a moment of silence as is here, now. The most serene silence only broken by an occasional crashing wave. A gust of wind carries another set of delicious scents from inside the house.

Cyrus approaches the glass doors, hands full with trays of food, and uses his back to push the door open. I run to take the food from his hands, but he brushes me away, insisting he has it. I help him set the table as Katia and Marco trail behind with their hands full as well. Marco is holding a pot almost as big as he is, expressing a great deal of effort on his tiny, determined face.

We take our seats around the table, and I try not to notice the empty chair beside me. No plate to announce an inevitable arrival. Cyrus seems to notice this as well.

"No Mia tonight?" he asks.

"She's with Simone and Matteo. Some business with the club," Katia explains while scooping food onto Marco's plate. "She just left, actually. Said she'll be home late."

I remember Simone from Marco's baptism. The man with the tattoos must be Matteo. Today wasn't the first time I'd seen those tattoos as we passed the club. I had victoriously eyed him in a dimly lit speakeasy once upon a time ago. A ping of envy pierces through my chest as I imagine those inked arms around Mia. Caging her to his body as they dance in an office, closed off from the rest of the club. The loud music vibrating the floor beneath them. Bitter jealousy spoils the food in my mouth as I picture the drawn curtains, the locked doors. She's shutting me out before even seeing me after all this time. She's running from me before I have an opportunity to give chase. Do I even want to chase her? Am I such a narcissistic ass to think her choices have anything to do with me in the first place? But then, how can I not? After what happened all those years ago, how can we not see one another in a certain light? Am I so delusional to think there may lie some silent string held taut between us, waiting to be thrummed alive?

Ana never instilled so much doubt. So much envy and rage, as if my skin were stretched too thin above my bones.

Just *her*.

I eat in silence while the family before me treats the evening as they would any other. A fly on the wall observing my own kin. An outsider who inevitably chose the comfort of solitude rather than risk the possibility of happiness. I ruined it with Ana the moment I led a stranger to that underground dance floor. I've just been too afraid to admit it to myself. It isn't until now, seeing all the potential I've wasted, that it hits me. I never loved Ana. Do I even love teaching or anything else about my constructed life?

As if hearing my self-pitying thoughts whispering across the table, Katia asks me about my work back in New York. I give her the same generic answer I always give when asked such questions, throwing in a bit of scientific engineering jargon with every other answer to make myself feel better, feel more important while the interviewer looks on in wonder. I did love my work in the beginning, but the magic has faded. I've peeked behind the curtain, the illusion no longer a mystery. After all your goals have been met, what's left is the pursuit of meaning. Longing to fill the days with something worthy of what little time we have left.

The conversation flows away from me—thank God—and we discuss a recent deal with another overseas shipper for the olive groves. Katia's back straightens as Cyrus roughly maps out the trees that will produce the best olives for this vendor. She places a hand over her fiancé's and gives him a light squeeze. A silent gesture of adoration I would give anything to experience in its honest nature.

"Oh, before I forget." Cyrus stands from the table, his chair screeching against the floor, then he runs into the house, and I raise my brows at Katia in question. She shakes her head, appearing just as bewildered as I. Cyrus returns with a guitar in hand. A simple yet master-crafted instrument with blond wood accents and a deep maple neck. A Spanish guitar I don't have to hear to know will sound as crisp as the night we are sharing.

"For you, *hermanito*." Cyrus holds the guitar out to me, and I tentatively reach for the neck.

"Where did you get this, Cy?"

"Don't worry about it. I knew you wouldn't want to travel with your own, so this one can stay here, for when you visit. But it's yours all the same," Cyrus says.

I take the instrument in my hands and let it sit naturally in my lap. It feels expensive. The weight of the body, the opening in the center yawning in invitation. I place my fingers around the neck, holding each fingertip to the right string, and strum a delightful G chord. It needs tuning, but the strings are clean, free of dust and oil. The voice elegant and light.

"*Bravo!*" Katia says.

I hum a low E note in the back of my throat, then strum the first string, turning the tuning pegs first higher and then lower to match. I do the same for the A string, then the D, G, B, then finally the higher E. I give the strings a preliminary strum once again. *Much better.*

Marco claps, his parents following suit. My audience of three. There's one missing.

I play a simple tune, riding the high of my family's approval as my fingers dance across the neck of the instrument. My right hand expertly strumming and plucking, music filling the courtyard. Music I rarely play for anyone but myself. Slowly, my self-doubt melts away with every pass of my thumb on the strings.

I still have this. A family to come home to, even if they are on an island far, far away. There is a room upstairs for me, despite its unfavorable location. There is a place for me at the altar with my brother on one of the most important days of his life. Where once it was just him and me, it is now me and them. Although, if this first night on the island has taught me anything, it's that a simple instrument placed in the right hands can turn a silent courtyard into a concert hall. And what pride I feel, knowing those hands are my own.

In my new state of slightly-less-self-deprecating-than-usual, I lay my new guitar across my chair and help Katia clear the table. Cyrus picks up Marco and mumbles about getting him bathed and ready for bed as Katia and I gather the dishes and bring them inside.

The kitchen is similar in style to the rest of the house, though on a grander scale. Details I hadn't yet appreciated come into view. Dark oak cabinets and white marble countertops give the room an air of expense without seeming ostentatious. Arched doorways to every room, with additional arches over the hidden staircase and the stove which sits in a large alcove. Mosaic glass tiles adorn the back splash, giving the room a godly feel.

Based on the meal we just shared, I wouldn't doubt God's presence in a kitchen such as this.

Katia scrapes remnants of food off each plate and hands them to me to rinse and load into the dishwasher. Another appliance hidden behind oak cabinetry. I wonder if they open the fridge by mistake while looking for the coffee mugs. We finish loading the dishwasher and turn it on, the sloshing water inaudible—an expensive brand, no doubt. We continue clearing up the kitchen, putting glass containers filled with leftovers away in the fridge, playing Tetris with the various random items. When we're through, Katia reminds me to grab the guitar before heading up and kisses my cheek goodnight. She makes her way across the yard to her own wing of the house; I retrieve the guitar, get myself a glass of water, and turn off the lights.

Upstairs, the veranda doors of my bedroom are still open, bringing a lovely crispness to the air. I go to shut them and see Cyrus on the opposite side of the courtyard holding Marco. They're both in pajamas, Cyrus bouncing him on one arm while the other rubs his back. He catches sight of me and we both wave goodnight. I glance at Mia's set of doors, hoping against logic that they may be open.

They're not.

I retrieve the rest of my toiletries along with a set of boxers; the tiles cool against the soles of my feet. The roar of the shower fills the room as I undress, leaving my clothes in a heap on the floor to collect later. Warm water pounds against my skin, the pressure beating down on my back and shoulders, and I close my eyes and tilt my head back, allowing the water to fully embrace me. I lather the soap in my hands and run the slick foam across my chest, my shoulders, arms, stomach.

When I reach the base of my pubic bone, I think of this same bar of soap lathering her body in its clean scent. Bubbles gliding without friction across her skin. I imagine her standing in this same shower, letting me make her dirty body clean again. I tug on my length as it stands at attention, soapy water cascading around my hunched shoulders as I run my hand up and down myself again, again, again.

No. Stop.

I groan at this voice of reason and turn the shower knob to freezing to finish washing the rest of my body and step out of the shower. The closed washroom door on her side tells me she hasn't been home and likely won't be until tomorrow.

I dry myself off, climb into bed, and let sleep take me.

A sound wakes me. Not words, but a voice. At first, I think someone might be in pain or discomfort. I sit up in bed and the thin sheet falls from my torso, exposing my bare chest. Faint at first but louder now, I can't tell if this is a trick of my sleeping mind or if the voice is gaining tone. Staccato breathing. First short, then long moans.

And then I see it.

Moonlight spills from the windows, revealing open washroom doors.

Mine. And Mia's.

Her locked door is now open, her bedroom visible in the blue glow of night. The foot of her bed is half draped in shadow, but there is no mistaking the movement causing her sheets to rustle this way and that.

The nature of those noises registers and my cock responds, tightening in my boxers. My ears flex and I try to listen further. Raspy breaths rise and fall between each desperate sigh. Each little whimper that tapers off at the end in question. I picture her pleasing herself in bed in the middle of the night, ignorant to the presence of another next door.

Unless. She knows I'm here. She must. Her doors were locked. *She knows I can hear her.* She propped her door open ever so slightly to make sure of it.

She's putting on a show for me. Not a complete invitation. No. For that, she would have crawled into bed with me, and I would have thrown all hesitation regarding loyalty and duty out the veranda windows and fucked her until the sun rose and set again. Until those little sobs of pleasure morphed into the sound of my name deep in her throat.

Those moans are for me.

Fully hard now, my cock aches to be touched, to be ridden, to fuck. I pull down my boxers just enough to free myself, and without hesitation I run my palm over the blunt tip, trying to stifle a groan of my own. I wrap my hand around the shaft and tug gently, teasing myself. In the other room, her breathing quickens with sharp inhales. She's close. A bead of moisture appears at my tip, and I use my thumb to spread it across the taught head. This slight lubrication makes my hips jerk, my breath catch. I keep going, grinding into my fist, listening to her sweet cries.

My breathing grows heavy, and I will myself to slow down. I haven't decided yet if I want to get caught. If she's playing this game, I can't stumble in the first round and lose my queen to a pawn. But that doesn't mean I can't have a little fun of my own. I prop a pillow behind my head, keeping a tight grip on its edge while my other hand methodically pulls at my length. Stretched out on the bed, my chest and stomach flex and relax as I torture myself. As *she* tortures me.

I imagine her slickness coating me, the ease she would bring, and the harsh pull of my hand is almost a punishment for these actions. But I am too far gone to stop now. I pull and pull, twisting at the top to give my head an extra lip of attention. The sheets in the other room rustle loudly, and I picture her moving from her back to her stomach, riding her own fingers with her face pressed into the mattress. Legs sprawled, the balls of her feet digging into the bed, reaching for more, more, more friction. Her soft cries grow wild. Wicked.

I hear a word. One word repeated again and again in anguish. *Please.*

This one word, recited like a prayer in that breathy voice, unravels me. Sweat pricks at the back of my neck, and my hips buck hard as I fuck my hand in wild strokes. I bite into the pillow to stifle a yell and grip the headboard as every muscle in my body snaps and I release into my fist. I'm not exactly quiet. And neither is she. We tip each other over the edge, and she comes in the most exquisite song I have ever heard.

At the sound of my own steady breath, a terrible thought comes to mind that hadn't occurred to me until now.

What if she's not alone?

I peer through the doors, still indolently stroking my cock, straining my eyes to see any glimpse of another person, another set of feet. I turn my head to get a better ear shot. Silence.

I shimmy out of my boxers and use them to wipe myself clean. If there is someone else in the room with her, I don't wish to know.

Those sounds were meant for her and me alone. Whether or not she was aware of my presence before, I'm certain she is now. I crawl off the bed, ball up my boxers, and toss them into the hamper in the corner of the room. I don't bother getting a fresh pair out of my suitcase for fear of making any more noise than I already have. On my way back to bed, I slowly close my door to the washroom, leaving the room in utter darkness.

If she wants to play, I'm game.

4

ENZO

I run through the hospital lobby toward a lavish round desk and ask for Katia Cifuentes in labor and delivery. Bombarded with a slew of questions, I answer as politely as I can, given my lack of patience at this particular moment. The woman behind the desk hands me a badge that reads *Visitante* before directing me to the elevator bay.

On the ride up, I'm buzzing with the lingering feeling of the woman's hands on me. Her fingers in my hair and the feel of her hips against mine, undulating under my body. The look in her eye before she was torn away. That look has been haunting me for the past twelve hours, trying to solve the equation written on her stunning face.

Enthralled by beauty and intrigue, I found her face irresistible, despite the one waiting for me back home. Does that make me a scoundrel? Have I cheated on Ana? The thought roils a wave of nausea in the back of my throat and I tamp it down with a deep breath.

I didn't exactly cheat, but I wasn't entirely faithful either. I danced with a beautiful woman in my home country. And who knows what would have happened if she had stayed in my arms? My impudence sours the taste in my mouth.

Ana didn't even want to join me on this trip, despite the celebratory nature of my visit. Does that not show a lack of support in her character? Unwilling to be by my side for these moments that make up a meaningful life?

The birth of my first nephew. Cyrus always joked I'd be the first to have children. That my romantic nature would make me a young father. And here I am, thirty-three years old, unmarried, and childless. I feel like a young maiden in Victorian England equating herself to an old hag.

The happiness held for my brother is not altogether devoid of bitterness. He found Katia in Portofino while promoting a new chain of restaurants. Her olive oil exports brought them together for countless negotiations. Encounters, I imagine, that had been chaste in the beginning, devolving into some sort of forbidden workplace romance. A story that does not yet have an ending but is on its way to becoming a happy one.

While contemplating Ana, I'm uncertain if my feelings for her match the depth of Cyrus's unwavering devotion to Katia. We both prioritize locality and convenience. No honest effort is required on either side for things to work. The ease of it is part of the appeal—her unwillingness to fight or challenge my thoughts; she simply agrees for the sake of saving time. And though we share a field and she is far more intelligent than I, there is something fundamental missing from her intelligence. Something that may require an alternative perspective. As with most things, her beauty caught my eye first. The soft sweep of her hair and the sharp point of her nose. Yet, past the surface, there lacks a depth of anything other than her work. She is passionate about one thing, and it was never me.

Now, as I reflect on the stranger from last night, still feeling the fire that ignited my palm the moment she took my hand, I can no longer overlook the gaps in my fiancé's affections. The quiet hesitations or dismissals that always left me questioning if I may be too much, or not enough.

I need to find this stranger, find out who she is. Because if one ephemeral dance with her could make me want to throw my life away, I deserve to know my dance partner's name.

I make a mental declaration to go back to that speakeasy and ask around about my mystery dance partner. Her demeanor suggested that of a resident rather than a tourist.

The elevator dings and a soft feminine voice announces the third floor. The doors open into a system of arrows leading me through a maze of beige walls. Another circular desk stands in the middle of the room with a sign that reads *"Estación de Enfermeras."*

I ask for Katia's room, flashing my visitor's pass for good measure.

"Lorencito!" an excited whispered voice calls from behind. My brother wears the brightest smile I've ever seen across his tired face, a small bundle in his careful arms.

Splendid effort is required from me to avoid overwhelming giddiness upon first seeing my nephew.

"This is Marco." Cyrus hands me his son, taking care to show me how to support his head. Swollen slits, his eyes blink at the new world around him. His tiny feet kick, struggling to break free of his swaddle, and the enormity of this tiny body hits me.

A *baby*. My *brother's* baby. My nephew.

A small fist raises toward me and I instinctively lower myself so he may reach. He explores my face, his fingers finally opening to examine the shape of my nose. A tear drops to the blanket he's wrapped in. One, then another, then more. I weep tears of absolute euphoria as I hold the kin of my kin for the first time. Cyrus squeezes my shoulder.

From the corner of my eye, I see him smiling at the picture his son and I make. We stand in the waiting room, oblivious to the rest of the world spinning by. Brothers sharing a moment of triumph over a newborn of their own blood. I take a breath and hold it in my lungs for a few moments, attempting to commit this moment to memory. Marco yawns, his toothless mouth making the smallest "O" accompanied by a tune of coos. His eyes flutter closed, then open, then closed.

"Come," Cyrus says, "let's put him down for a nap. He should sleep while mama sleeps." I follow him down yet another set of beige hallways into a double room, never once shifting my attention from the child in my arms. I put one foot in front of the other, following Cyrus's silhouette.

Katia is propped up in bed asleep, her hair sweat slicked to her forehead. She looks beautifully at peace, a blanket tucked loosely under her arms. In a chair to her left is a woman, her body twisted in a way that cannot be comfortable. She's asleep, her cheek pressed against the back of the chair. Her dress...

Emerald green. Almost black.

A green more prominent in the sharp light of morning, and a face even more beautiful than I remember. Before, I saw her face in flashes of shadow, muddied with the sensation of her body against mine. But here, in the clear unbroken rays of light, she's the most beautiful woman I've ever seen... again, for the first time. Her chest lifts with shallow breaths, and I try to make sense of why the stranger I danced with last night, the woman who has me questioning my entire relationship with Ana, is sleeping next to Katia in her recovery room.

Cyrus hovers over Katia as he wipes the dampness from her brow, and I lower Marco into his crib, careful not to wake him. Awkwardly, I wait for Cyrus to finish attending to his family. The woman stirs in her chair and my first instinct is to flee. I step out of the room and wait beyond sight of the door.

A few moments later, I hear Cyrus telling Katia to go back to sleep. He steps out of the room, searching for me, and I wave him down the hall, out of earshot. Before he can ask why I've felt the need to run, I ask him the only question I've been wondering since last night.

"Who is the woman sleeping by Katia?"

Cyrus smiles familiarly. I find it unsettling. "Oh, that's Mia. Katia's daughter."

The linoleum floor beneath my feet fails to hold solid. The walls spin and my mouth is painfully dry. It's not possible. It's too cruel. Too cruel to fall under the spell of a woman who will make me my brother's antagonist.

I knew Katia had a daughter. Cyrus would boast of her ambitions to take over the family business, her high marks while at university. Having no face to put to the name, I could have never imagined the woman I saw last night. Cyrus grabs my shoulder in that big-brother way of his and steers us toward the elevator bay. We ride the car down and make our way through the lobby to the exit. Cyrus takes out a metal cigarette holder and offers me one. If I were back in New York, I would have declined. I promised Ana I'd quit on our first date. Yes, the occasional drag calls to me every now and then, and I feel compelled to answer. An occasion such as this, when I have an anvil placed against my chest. My every decision hangs in the balance between two women and the effigy of a "good brother."

We smoke in silence for a moment, the breeze carrying the evidence away. The smile on my brother's face never fades.

"How'd she do?" I ask.

"How do you think?" He nods his head approvingly. "She did beautifully. I knew she would."

"Are you scared?"

He scoffs. "Not at all, *hermanito*. Did you forget who raised you? You were practically my firstborn." Pride softens his smile. "I worry about you all alone in a foreign country, Enzo."

"I'm hardly alone."

Cyrus fights the urge to roll his eyes. "How are things with you and Ana? Last time we spoke, you had plans for a proposal."

"I did."

He takes another drag and gestures for me to continue.

"She said yes, but I'm not so sure anymore, brother."

Cyrus lets out a heavy sigh. "Okay. I'm going to forgive you for not telling me right away. I know I've had my hands full with getting ready for Marco's arrival. But the real question is why hesitate now when you were so ready to move to New York for her last year? She said yes. You should look happier. What, were you expecting her to say no?" he asks, catching me off guard.

I had considered no other outcome. In my mind, a positive response was a given, although not for the reasons one might assume. Most men expect an enthusiastic reaction when they decide to ask the question they've been waiting their whole lives to ask. However, Ana and I had approached our engagement night differently. We treated it like a business transaction, discussing plans for our future over dinner. Making love that night was like any other night we had shared before—mutual, transactional, yet undeniably pleasurable.

I shake my head. Doubt sitting heavily upon my shoulders. "There's something missing," I think aloud. Cyrus leans back as he takes another drag and repeats the same gesture for me to keep speaking. I look up at the towering glass building. There are two remarkable women in one of those hospital rooms, and a child that binds us all together. And here we stand, two brothers on the outside. Fixated on the facade of the building, I remember her flushed face as she gazed up at me through hooded eyes, the fabric of her dress running like oil through my fingers as we swayed to music that will play over and over in my mind for years.

"Ana doesn't dance."

5

Mia

Four Days Before the Wedding

My phone pings every few seconds, and I open bleary eyes to find my room drenched in sunlight. My cheek sticks to the pillowcase as I peel myself away, a one-eyed glance at my phone telling me Simone is on her way over for breakfast.

Breakfast?

I feel disgusting.

Not only because of my performance last night, but for what I failed to do afterward. Shower, wash my face, properly get ready for bed so this future-present version of myself doesn't feel like complete shit. Once I opened the washroom door in the small hours of the night and saw Enzo's door open, the teasing need overtook me.

He was lying in bed, completely at peace, his chest moving evenly in a deep sleep. I didn't watch him. Not exactly. But I saw the serenity on his face and couldn't think of anything else as I tiptoed back to my room.

My body was still warm and nimble from a night of dancing after my obligations, and I considered climbing on top of Enzo. I thought of straddling him, feeling the hardness of his body between my thighs and riding him awake. I wanted to. *God, I wanted to.* Since Marco's baptism, I've tried to think of others when bringing myself pleasure. Yet, in the moment, every moment, it's his face I see. It's his name I call out silently, secretly. And so, I thought, why not show him what I've been up to? How I've lasted this long with him an ocean away.

I left the bathroom door open just enough to elicit his corrupt curiosity and crawled on my bed. I hiked up my long skirt and spread my legs to find myself already wet with the knowledge of his presence.

Spreading my wetness from my opening up to my clit, circling first my middle, then forefinger, my hips came up to meet my touch. All reservations softened as I thought of Enzo's face, so still in the moonlight. His eyes would flutter open, hearing me play with myself, and he would come to me. He would crawl on top of me and sink so deep I would know nothing but the fullness of him inside, his weight pressed against me, pinning me to the bed as I stretched around him. His mouth on mine as he worked his pleasure out on my body. He'd be rough with me, punishing. I wanted all of it, and I nearly begged.

Please. Please. Please.

I was so close. *So close.* I thought of him spilling onto my thighs, my stomach, my chest.

Please. Please. Please.

Then I heard him. He was there with me. He heard my plea, and he was giving me what I wanted as best he could. I heard the telltale bang of the headboard in the other room as he finished with a stifled groan, and I followed with a wail of contentment of my own. It is beyond me how I managed not to scream his name, but I didn't. Thank God. That would have been another level of embarrassment.

Sitting in silence, the high abating, I waited for him to walk through the narrow washroom doors and see me sprawled out on the bed in my post orgasm sheen.

But he never came.

The door on his side latched closed with a click, and I remained frozen in place, rejected. Shut out.

I must have fallen asleep soon after because here I lay, in a mess of my own making.

His door remains closed, likely still asleep. Seizing the opportunity, I rise from bed and strip the sheets, taking extra care to be as quiet as possible, then step out of my own clothes and throw them on the same mound. In the washroom, I turn the shower knob to full heat. No time to run a bath this morning. I go to lock his door from the inside, then think better of it. Might as well keep up this little tease. If we are to play this game, I'd rather be the cat than the mouse.

Scalding water hits my shoulders, and I bring the knob back to level out the temperature. Once it's just right, I take my time. I groan as the full weight of my actions last night dawns on me, and I'm overrun with a rush of humiliation. My skin grows hot, not just from the water. What made me think he would wake in the middle of the night and come to me after not seeing one another in years? Did I expect him to cheat on the woman he has back home just because I naively attempted to serve myself to him? I know I wouldn't want him like that. The compunction is short lived as I remember the sound of the headboard. His stifled grunt as we came together—separately.

After discovering he would not only be attending the wedding alone but staying in the room next door, I finally gave myself permission to peruse through his social media. A private person, his posts exclusively consisted of special occasions. But his last post from six months ago sat like a stone in my chest. Him and Ana in a dimly lit restaurant booth, smiling up at the camera with a generic anniversary caption. They might as well be siblings the way they sit next to one another, barely touching.

I didn't recognize the man I met three years ago in that photo. I saw a reserved man starving for adventure. *Settled,* I thought hatefully. I tapped the photo, careful not to double-tap for fear of utter humiliation. Her profile was a collection of sunsets, meals, the view from famous New York hiking trails, and one selfie from her birthday last year.

No Enzo.

I don't buy it. What my mother and Cyrus have—I buy that without pause.

Refusal bubbles through me. If this game is so childish, why is he also playing? If he sees me as callow, then why join me? These conflicting thoughts and feelings confuse the hell out of me and my moral compass. If I knew *for sure* Ana was still in his life, would I be so willing to tempt him? My answer should be "no," without question. And yet I hesitate. I'm not sure if her presence or lack thereof in his life makes much of a difference regarding my want for him. Would I risk turning into "the other woman?" Becoming a cliché? God, I hope not. But there it is again, that doubt hovering in the back of my mind, making bargains and negotiating deals around the concept of honor. It takes two to dance this number, and I've been dancing with shit partners for far too long.

I finish showering and step out. Wrapped in a towel, I grab my things and get ready in my room, locking my side of the door, suppressing the impulse to play for the time being.

My phone pings with an email from the new vendor.

I have a surprise when I see you again; it reads.

I blink at my phone, reading it over to make sure I haven't misread the words. What could he mean by this vague message?

Another ping sounds with a text from Simone asking if I'm even awake yet. Disregarding the previous message, I reply to Simone with a sleeping emoji, just to vex her. She quickly responds with a photo of her and Marco in the courtyard. A man's shoe in the corner of the frame. I stamp down the urge to peek over my balcony and see to whom the shoe belongs.

I type out a quick response.

Get off your ass and help my mother.

Send.

Ping.

Ta gueule. Come down here and help her yourself!

With my mother in mind, I make haste, running curl cream through damp hair and giving it a few gentle scrunches, letting it air dry while applying a bit of makeup. I step out of the towel and pull on a black maxi skirt and a backless, sage-green top that knots behind my neck and grazes just above my navel, while the skirt sits right below, revealing a glimpse of my midriff.

I slip on my sandals and make my way downstairs, banishing the flutter in my stomach, knowing I'm about to see him. In the kitchen, my mother and Cyrus are cooking back to back. One whisking eggs while the other fries peppers in a skillet.

"*Ciao, mi hija,*" they both chime at me.

"*Ciao*. Need any help?" I ask.

"No, no, go be with everyone outside. We'll be out soon."

My heart thrums in my chest. Simone is posing for Marco as he draws her in chalk on the courtyard floor. Matteo sits across from her, his legs extended and crossed as if lounging in his own home. He's wearing the same shoes as in Simone's photo.

"What are you two doing here?" I ask.

Marco jumps up and runs to me with chalk covered hands. I grab him before he can mark me and spin him around, pinning him in a bear hug. With a gentle nudge forward, I pat his bottom and he runs back to keep working on his chalk masterpiece.

No sign of my neighbor.

"Did you not read any of my messages?" Simone asks. I take out my phone and scroll through the endless feed of messages from my cousin. The word "beach" repeats, and I let out a whiney groan.

"We are to enjoy a breakfast cooked by your lovely parents, and then we're off to the shore. We need to network with local tourists if we intend to gain popularity at the club this summer."

She's right. With Simone as the face of the speakeasy, her exposure to tourists is paramount in creating the type of sleepy island vibes we're going for.

"Plus, you get to wear that dark little number," Matteo says, eyebrows raised.

"All of my numbers are dark and little," I deadpan.

My mother and Cyrus emerge from the kitchen behind me, plates of food in hand. I reach to grab a plate from my mother when another set of hands beat me to it.

I hear him before I see him.

"*Buenos dias*, Mia," Enzo says with a friendly smirk on his stupid, gorgeous face.

"*Buenos dias*." I pull my hand back, faking an itch on my shoulder. He takes the plate of fresh fruit and places it on the table without casting a second glance in my direction.

Oh, he is definitely playing.

"When did you get in last night?" I ask innocently. Let him squirm. Let him think my performance was a heedless mistake and not entirely meant for his ears alone.

"Cyrus picked me up around five p.m.?" Enzo's voice lilts at the end. "I didn't get a chance to say hello." He holds both of my shoulders and kisses first my right cheek, then my left. His stubble leaves tiny bites across my face, and I imagine that same sensation up my legs, on the inside of my thighs. He lingers for the faintest second before brushing the shell of my ear with his lower lip. Goosebumps trickle down my arms. He pulls away and gives me a knowing smile.

I stand, gaping.

Matteo coughs obnoxiously and saunters over to the table to take a seat, while Simone picks up Marco, unafraid of his chalky hands smudging her sundress. She places him in his usual highchair next to my mother's designated seat at the head of the table, Simone taking her own seat on the other side of Marco. Cyrus then follows, popping open a bottle of champagne to add to the orange juice and sits by my mother. That leaves two empty chairs, side by side. Enzo pulls one out and gestures for me to sit. I do.

"So, you're running the grove now? Congratulations." He continues the conversation as if he didn't just half seduce me in front of my entire family with a simple brush of skin.

"Yes."

"She's in charge of everything behind the scenes at the club as well, while Simone and I handle the on-stage stuff," Matteo interjects.

"The bar is hardly a stage, Matteo," Simone says.

"They come for your music, but stay for my drinks, *mon cur*." Matteo's patronizing tone breaks through.

I face Enzo before answering. "That's right, I help these two with the speakeasy." I gesture to Matteo and Simone as though they were my very own bickering siblings. "Besides helping Mama run the business with the olive groves."

Enzo blinks at me and smiles, his face warm and welcoming. "That's impressive, Mia. I'll have to pick your brain on budget reports for my next research project." He places a hand over mine. There's no ring on his finger, no tan line, no indent of the skin, no indication of him belonging to anyone other than himself. Just a strong, undecorated, calloused hand. He mindlessly rubs his thumb across the back of my knuckles. Once, twice, then gone.

"What do you do?" Matteo's tone could sound less offensive, but I don't blame him for his false territorial pretense.

"I'm sorry, I don't believe we've officially met," Enzo says, full charm. "I'm Enzo, Cyrus's brother. I'm an agricultural engineering professor at NYU."

"I know who you are." Matteo doesn't acknowledge the second part of his statement.

Enzo waits for him to make his own introduction. He doesn't.

"Matteo, *sois gentil*." *Be nice,* Simone scolds in French. "I'm sorry about him. He's just the bartender at the club. He *thinks* he's part of the family."

Matteo curses in Spanish under his breath, but does nothing to defend himself. "I'm Simone, Mia's cousin."

"My late sister's daughter," Mama adds.

"I sing," Simone says plainly. Reducing her nightly performances at the speakeasy to a simple karaoke session. In reality, Simone sings in four languages and covers decades of genres with a voice that spans five octaves. She speaks humbly, but on stage, she abandons all humility. From her outfits to her voice and presence, she is an elegant, timeless package wrapped up in a woman who stands no more than five foot seven in five-inch heels.

"Yes, we've met," Enzo says.

Simone tilts her head in confusion.

"At the baptism." He gestures toward Marco, and the table breaks out into sounds of familiar remembrance.

Enzo is taking all of this new information well. I realize everyone had indirectly met even before the church, and I may be the only person to know such a trivial fact. The night a stranger took me away from Matteo's always-possessive watch and we danced to the beat of underground drums accompanied by Simone's voice. Until I was whisked away in an embarrassingly Cinderella-like manner. The stroke of midnight being the birth of my baby brother. Though I was able to keep track of both shoes.

The conversation continues with bursts of laughter and a flow of orange juice and champagne. Enzo picks up two slices of mango from the tray and hands one to me without breaking focus.

Is this a power play or is he just being nice?

Don't think about it too much.

I take the slice and put it in my mouth. Our drinks delightfully complemented the tartness mixed with the texture, and I finally relax in the moment. Being around family.

My mother breaks into a round of stories from our past. Our adventures in Greece, accounts of miscommunication with taxi drivers that led us to new and unfamiliar cities. She is careful not to mention my father, storytelling around an absent character, penitence hidden behind her words, but the smile remains on her face as she recounts our former life.

Enzo continues to avoid looking my way, though I sneak quick glances, watching his mouth move as he listens to my mother with intent. He's disregarding me while I sit just inches away, and it's unbearable.

So, I ask, "How's Ana?"

He rears his head as though he just now realized my presence at the table, a flicker of suspicion passing over his face before settling into a wary stillness.

He blinks. "Fine." I don't believe him. He clears his throat. "She's fine," he repeats, this time a bit more convincing, with a smile to his words.

Marco grows restless at the other end of the table. "We both need a nap, *Marcito*. But there's work to be done," Simone says.

Cyrus's chair screeches across the stone floor as he stands. "Before you go, I just want to toast to this week. It's a rare thing for all of us to be here together. To my family. *Mi mundo.*" Cyrus raises his glass and the rest of us follow suit before taking our final sips. He gives Katia a quick kiss on the forehead before sitting back down.

"Shall we go?" Simone asks, directing her question toward Matteo and me.

"You should join us, Enzo," Matteo says. I see right through him. He's just itching for an opportunity to put his *machismo* on display. "Have you seen the beaches here? Almost as beautiful as the women."

"Highly unlikely," Enzo says. "I would love to join you. Cyrus, are my best man duties needed for today, or can I go play with my new friends?"

"Have him home by midnight," is all Cyrus says before we rise from the table and clear the plates.

Matteo and Simone take Marco through the glass doors on the opposite end of the courtyard and upstairs for his midmorning nap, while Enzo carries the bulk of the heavier trays and discarded bottles of champagne into the kitchen. He gets to work on the dishes without being asked. My mother fights him for the sponge, but his massive stature requires no contest. She secedes with a trail of familiar Spanish words I've heard directed at me over the years and makes her way back outside.

Now alone, I grab a clean dish rag from a nearby drawer and dry the dishes Enzo washed and placed on the rack. "Are you upset with me?" I ask.

"Why would I be upset with you, Mia?" His focus remains on the running water.

"I apologize if I woke you while coming in late last night." His hands work like two trained mechanical arms, lathering each dish precisely before running each item under the water and placing it on the rack for me to dry. "You don't have to come with us to the beach today if you're tired."

To this, he laughs. A deep sound that resounds in the middle of his chest.

"How else will I see you in your 'dark little number'?" His head drops and hooded eyes start from my legs and travel north, devouring the sight of me like a predator. He reaches my midriff and stays there a moment, his jaw tense. Heat builds in my belly where his molten brown eyes pierce me through, holding me stock still in place. He hands me a glass and I take it without breaking away.

"*Dépêchez-vous*, Mia," Simone calls for me to hurry from the courtyard.

He blinks, forfeiting his hold on me for the moment. I dry the last dish and lay the rag flat on the counter before starting for the stairs, practically running away, taking each step with alacrity, as though I'm being chased.

In my room, I gather a few items into a large tote bag and put my bathing suit on underneath my current outfit. Rushing out the door, I'm met with Enzo coming up the stairs. His hands are in the pockets of his billowy, loose-fit trousers, a nonchalance about his gait that drives me mad with frustration. "Wait for me," he says, again not meeting my gaze. I can't take it anymore.

Look at me. See me. Look at me.

"Have I done something?" I ask, failing to hide the hurt in my voice. He stops, his breathing prominent in the rise of his shoulders. "Why won't you *look* at me?"

Half facing in my direction, his gaze lands yet again on my midriff, not daring to venture higher. And yet his focus is thorough. Studying the sliver of skin between my skirt and top as though it's a problem that needs solving.

"I can't bear it. I thought I could, but I can't."

I shake my head. "What?" I hear the palpable anger in my voice despite my constant need to appear in control. "Please." It's almost a whisper. The break in my plea allows no room for false confidence. His head swivels up to meet my eyes, and there is pain written there. Tired and wounded, with furrowed brows and a twisted mouth.

I stand, seized, legs wide, my thumb wrapped tight around my fingers. He removes his hands from his pockets and takes three long strides toward me. My chin tilts up in some fictitious resolve.

"Please?" His breath blows a curl away from my face. He's close enough to taste. "Are you begging?" The accusation in his voice whips me across the face, and God help me, as much as I want to slap him right back, part of me *is* begging. Part of me wants to continue to beg until I am sated with the fullness of him. "Do you want something from me, *little* Mia?" He's provoking me. Using these words that so clearly vex me, and yet all I can do is stand, petrified by the hunger in his stare.

"I..."

His arms wrap around me, holding me to him. One wide hand across my shoulders, the other cradling the back of my head, fingers in my hair. He holds me to the crook of his neck, and I can smell his earthy scent. My arms lift around his narrow waist, taking in the sturdiness of his back and shoulders.

His breath tickles my temple as he drips secrets into my ear. "I can't look at you the way I want to, Mia. Not in front of them." I close my eyes, poised in the covetous growl of his voice. "If I look, I'll want to touch. I'll want to taste. I'll want to run my tongue down your spine and find the spot that makes you shiver." His pinky plays with the hem of my skirt as he pushes slightly against me, and I can feel him hard against my belly. "I'll want to hide under this tease of a skirt and find what you have waiting for me between those dancer's legs. I'll want you to ease this ache I've been living with for years, Mia. And we both know I can't do that."

"Why not?" A question I already know the answer to. I ask another I'm not sure I *want* to know the answer to. "Are you ashamed to want me?" His warm skin and the sheer headiness of his words muffle my voice. His throat works before giving me an answer.

"No." A pause. "Yes." A breath.

"Do you regret it? Asking me to dance?" He pulls me in closer to his chest. Our legs entwined while standing, the press of his length a searing dagger held to my core. The heat of him so profound against my bare arms. A slight tremble in the way he holds me conveys a wordless apology. "Because of Ana?" I ask. I want to challenge him freely, without the remorse of another woman's heart hanging in the balance.

"I regret nothing when it comes to you."

"Is this because of Ana?" I press again.

He pulls away, breaking our embrace, and I grow cold at his absence. "Wait for me downstairs."

"No. Enzo."

He holds my arms as though consoling a frightened child.

"Tell me the truth." Surprised at the amount of power in my voice, I don't hesitate, I don't break. I keep his gaze, intent on having my questions met with ample answers. I fight against his grip and lift my hands to his chest, forcing his attention.

"Ana left me."

The words hang suspended in the air between us. My mouth parts in a speechless, dumbfounded visage.

"Be careful next time you call out begging in the night. I might just answer." He grabs my wrists and removes my hands from his chest before turning on his heel. His insinuation crashes over me in an ice-cold wave, the purr in his voice strumming across my spine, and I am flooded with a primal thirst.

"Wait for me downstairs." He calls with his back to me, hands in his pockets again. I watch as he disappears through his open door, left in the blinding light of the corridor, trying to blink his promise into reason.

6

Mia

We arrive at the church just in time to witness the conclusion of the previous party's vows. Taking our seats in the back, we patiently await our turn at the altar, the priest's words booming across the pews as though the voice of God is indeed present. Intricately carved statues of saints stand upon individual columns, ever watchful over the devoted souls who seek solace in their prayers. Candle chandeliers embellish the vast archways, casting an orange glow upon us parishioners. Stained glass windows perch high between alternate pews, daylight dances upon the polished hardwood floor in a myriad of vibrant hues. For a faith practiced on the basis of humility, there is nothing meek in the grandeur displayed in this sacred house of God.

The triumphant melody of the organ fills the air as the couple stands united, marking their first moment as husband and wife. Prompted by the choir, we rise from our seats, the angelic voices of children in white robes offering their melodic devotion. With the newlyweds leading the way down the aisle, their guests follow suit, creating a bustling procession toward the exit. We scheduled our service for half an hour later, giving the congregation ample time to prepare.

Soon, members of our own party trickle in, fighting against the current of people exiting the church. My mother hands Marco to me so she may greet our guests, and I gaze over a sea of familiar faces. Simone lingers beyond the church doors, puffing at the end of a cigarette. Aunts and cousins, old and young, all recite the same expectant pleasantries and cooing over the baby in my arms. A single unmoving silhouette at the back of the church catches my eye. A face, once unfamiliar just days ago, but has now taken center stage in my every waking fantasy. And a confirmation of what I feared may be the truth. My stranger was never really a stranger after all.

Lorenzo.

He appears mesmerized by the glow of the stained glass windows, their biblical scenes frozen in the mosaic. Cyrus approaches his brother with an affectionate pat on the back, breaking his reverie. They share a smile and hug while my mother is busy engaging in phrases of gratuity directed at our attending family and friends.

The church bells sound, reverberating through the building, and Marco fusses from the mounting noise. Cyrus and Lorenzo start in our direction, and I feel just as distraught as the child in my arms. My heart races in a confusing blend of dread and excitement.

Though I would never blame a child for my own adversities, Marco's delivery pulled me away from the most beguiling evening of my life. This child, who we are all here for today, ripped me from the arms of a stranger. And it is now the same child who has brought him back for me to meet here in this sacred place.

The crowd slowly dwindles, giving Lorenzo and Cyrus the opportunity to join our party, which has now made its way toward the front of the church. The figure of Jesus's crucified body hangs over the altar, watching as the lives of his followers unfold.

Lorenzo is wearing a navy blue suit that almost matches the color of my dress, perhaps some sort of celestial joke. I thought him magnetic and attractive in the billowy shirt he wore that night on the dance floor, but here, I can see the ripples of muscles beneath his white button-down dress shirt, the way the suit's fabric stretches to fit his arms and thighs. His tie is a matching navy blue and knotted expertly around the thickness of his neck. Where the other night his hair hung loose to frame his face, it is now slicked back, leaving no inch of him masked by brown locks, his beard trimmed close, the stubble dusted lighter at the edges.

My mother greets Lorenzo with a warm familiarity reserved for family. *They have met before.* She holds his head with both hands in classic Katia fashion and kisses his cheeks, rounding off Spanish greetings and thanking him for a gift they'd received prior. He responds in kind, his face creased in a genuine smile, apologizing for not saying hello at the hospital, he explains he didn't wish to disturb us. *He was at the hospital?* As he speaks, he steals a glance in my direction, a secret winking in his eye. My mother claps her palms together and turns to present me to my stranger. He regards me as though I am exactly who he expected.

"Enzo, this is my daughter, Mia," she says. "*Mi hija*, this is Cyrus's brother, Lorenzo."

In the dim light of the club, I didn't make the immediate connection. I have seen his face before. Perhaps younger, thinner, and clean shaven. Whether in a dream or within the faded pages of an old family album. Now older and much more distinguished, with delicate lines etched around his eyes. It wasn't until Simone pulled me out of his arms that a spark of recognition ignited.

Lorenzo takes my fingers in his hand.

"*Encantado*," he says.

His deep voice takes me back to the dance floor when he spoke only a simple request. I lean in to kiss him on both cheeks and he lets me, returning the gesture. The hair on his face grazes my cheek, and he smells as he did that night, citrus and spice. Clean and unpretentious. We step away and I take in the sight of him.

"*Encantado*, Lorenzo," I say. "It is nice to finally meet Cyrus's brother. He speaks of you constantly." I cringe at my attempt at small talk.

"Likewise, Mia. Please, call me Enzo. My brother tells me you're a dancer. You'll have to show me around, take me to a few clubs in the city," he says with a smirk.

Someone calls my mother over, leaving the two of us alone. Seizing the opportunity, he moves closer, his face now a breath away from mine. He still has not released my fingers. "I happen to be quite a dancer myself." His words strum across a cello's lowest string. Having traveled across the better half of Europe, I'm attuned to men's advancements. A shift in the cadence of their voice to lure me in, posing to appear irresistible. Although his words allude to the idea of a predator, I know I'm in no real danger.

"It'd be my pleasure," I say.

My mother breaks off from another conversation to ask Enzo where he is staying. His hand falls from mine. "I'm renting an apartment at the Violet House by the beach," he says.

Katia scoffs. "That won't do at all. Why did you not invite him to stay with us, *querido*?" my mother asks.

Cyrus shrugs, bouncing Marco to keep him entertained. "He insisted on being by the beach."

"We are plenty close to the beach. Next time you stay with us, *si*?"

"I leave for the airport in a few hours. But next time I will be sure to impose," Enzo teases.

Simone approaches us with outstretched arms, Matteo following close behind her. She takes Marco from Cyrus's hands as they are both introduced to my stranger.

The organ sounds again, marking the start of our ceremony. Marco's wails harmonize with the grand instrument, and Simone's bouncing intensifies, desperate to calm her baby cousin. Our guests make their way down the aisle, filing out between the pews to take their seats. Enzo and Cyrus take the front row to the left as my mother and I take the right. The priest approaches the altar in an ornate white chasuble. He crosses himself and our guests follow suit, tilting their heads down in silent prayer. Father Andrés gestures for us to be seated as he begins. His voice resounds within the church, filling every corner with a divine presence as he leads us through prayer and the choir fills the room in sacred harmony.

Simone hands the baby off to Cyrus and my mother before they approach a table at the head of the aisle. They gently undress Marco from his day clothes, and my brother cries out, naked and new.

Father Andrés requests the child's godparents and I rise to stand by my mother. Enzo joins me, removing his suit jacket and rolling up his white shirt sleeves. He takes his place by my side, and I notice the veins that run along his forearms. Dark skin dusted with a layer of hair.

The scene etches into my mind at this moment. Standing at an altar, celebrating new life beside my once-upon-a-dream. I do my best to favor logic over romance and accredit the identity of my stranger to mere coincidence. Every thought I have had of him until now was unsullied by the prospect of yet another chance encounter. The promise of returning to the club with the hope of a second dance. That dream is now inconceivable. My stepfather's brother is not someone I would do well to get involved with. I know this; he knows this—he must.

Father Andrés directs us to bring Marco forward, and Enzo takes him from Cyrus, then we ascend the few steps toward the baptismal font. Together, we cradle my young brother. Enzo supports his body and I his head. The priest's chanting continues as we lower Marco into the water. He stirs at the swift change in temperature, but soon settles. Father Andrés cups a palmful of blessed water and hovers it over Marco's forehead, allowing droplets to trickle down. Water splashes against my arms and a smile breaks across my face as Marco calms. Enzo's shirt sleeves darken from the water, yet he remains unwavering, holding Marco with steady arms, disregarding the likelihood of discomfort. I meet Enzo's gaze, hidden beneath furrowed brows. Only I can discern the intensity of his stare, a secret for us alone. Father Andrés continues his blessing with each palmful of sacred water. Enzo looks at me now as he had when my head rested against his shoulder. He licks his top lip, then his bottom. I stare, mesmerized at the movement of his tongue. He chuckles and lowers his gaze back to Marco.

"*En el nombre del Padre, y del Hijo, y del Espíritu Santo. Amén.*"

The church echoes the priest's acknowledgment of the Holy Trinity, and the organ sounds again. We lift Marco from the water, causing him to stress his tiny lungs. He screams, his wails only breaking for air. My mother and Cyrus crowd us with a white towel and take Marco from our dripping hands. We receive towels to dry off and resume our places at the altar.

Father Andrés's voice is melodic in prayer as he takes a vial of anointed oils and crosses first my forehead, then Enzo's. We receive his blessing and return to our seats.

The rest of mass proceeds as it does every other Sunday. Repeated phrases and songs recited in the name of ritual. Regardless of my belief in the words I speak, I cannot deny the placebo effect on my peace of mind. I accept this form of pseudo-faith and try not to poke around doubt for the sake of normalcy.

Once Father Andrés concludes and the music quiets, the roar of chatter envelops the echoing chamber. My family and I stand at the altar with Marco, now dressed in his white christening outfit. His gold crucifix hangs around his neck like a promise he does not yet know he's made. We take turns holding him, and Enzo is reluctant to give him up. He holds Marco in the bend of his elbow, the relaxed muscle of his bicep supporting his head. Marco smiles up at his uncle, his fist wrapped around one finger, and instead of glee at the view of them together, I am perturbed. Enzo is not my uncle. He's not my anything—other than my stranger. He's as much my uncle as Cyrus is my father.

Never has Cyrus made me feel like a child in my own home. When he and my mother began dating four years ago, I was off in college, traveling and enjoying my freedom. It wasn't until I came home, graduated, that I found an older man insistent on my opinion over a property overlooking my mother's olive groves. I loved him instantly for Mama. He was kind above all else and never reminded me of my father. He didn't intrude on my relationship with my mother, and always gave us our space when it was apparent we needed it. When the house was finalized, he insisted I take a wing to myself, allowing me the privacy and independence I longed for, despite being under the same roof. Was this so he may have my mother all to himself without interruption? Possibly. Probably. Though I'd rather not think of that now. This is all to say that Cyrus was never my father, nor will he ever be. He is my mother's fiancé, the father of her youngest, but love of her life? I suppose we both have to share that title with Marco now.

Our guests crowd the large doors of the church's entrance, women in lavish dresses and heels waiting for men in Sunday suits to pull their cars around. The priest and choir have all departed to the corners of the church, all services concluded for the day. Simone and Matteo find me at the altar and ask if they can hitch a ride with us. I tell them to find Cyrus, and they leave me to my silent non-praying. The baptism font is cool to the touch, a stone bowl now filled with tepid blessed water. I brush my fingertips along the water's surface and watch the ripples dance.

"So, you're the godmother?" Enzo's voice echoes in the empty church.

"And you're the godfather," I turn to face my stranger. His white shirt-sleeves still folded under the elbows. His tie swings forward as he reaches for his forgotten suit jacket.

"Cyrus told me to wear blue," he explains. "Though it clearly looks better on you, Mia." My name spoken in his voice is like a finger pressed against the base of my spine. He gestures to my dress. "Or do you prefer green?"

I descend one step from the altar to meet his height. "You came to the hospital." It's not a question.

He nods. "I did."

"Did you—"

"Did I know before?" A pause. "No. I knew you as much as you knew me that night. Strangers." Enzo brushes a curl away from my face. "But, I do remember—you said you did know me." His fingers linger behind my ear, brushing against a freckle I know raises slightly from the cuff. His thumb rolls over the small blemish as if examining it. "Who did you think I was?"

"I didn't know at first. I didn't know when you asked me to dance," I explain.

He nods his head in understanding and his hand lowers to his side, sliding into his pocket.

"I saw a photo of you. Before. You were standing by your brother, both of you shirtless on a beach in Italy."

He smiles in remembrance. "Yes. I was much younger then. Still a boy." He pauses, allowing me time to respond. I don't. "I suppose I lied, then."

I tilt my head at his words.

"I knew you less than you knew me. I had never seen a picture of Katia's daughter. Only heard words of pride."

It is now my turn to nod. I take the last step down from the altar, and even in my heels I am forced to look up to meet his gaze.

"I never got to thank you for the dance," I say.

His face goes stern. "There's no need. Now that we're family."

"We are not family." The words burst from me before I have a chance to think them through.

"No?" He steps even closer, the toe of his dress shoes between the point of my heels.

"No," I say in defiance. Heat emanates off him. My breath picks up as if in the first minute of a mild jog. "You're a stranger, Enzo."

He hums low in his chest at the sound of his own name. His cello, singing for me. He runs his tongue along his lips and I am entranced yet again.

"I'd like to dance with you again." Enzo bows his head and I am frozen. Absolutely frozen in place. This man takes all semblance of rebellion away from me. Under the gentle light of his gaze, I yearn to obey. To please him. To entertain until a smile graces his lips once more. I'm beside myself with resentment and anger for these feelings, but have them I do. His mouth agape, stare fixed upon my lips, I am unable to stir a single inch. The mingling scent of his breath, infused with subtle notes of citrus from the cologne he chose this morning, permeates the air.

Our hands remain still, and I fight the urge to close my eyes, my body threatening to melt into his. The tip of his nose brushes mine, and I no longer care who I am or who he is. I no longer care where we are, consequences be damned. All I care about is this requited, magnetic pull. His scent, his nearness, the plaguing image of my hands pressed against his bare chest as he grips my undulating hips. All I can think of is what he tastes like, what he sounds like. The wonder of his face as I make him feel better and better with every passing moment.

"Mia." My name is a whisper on his so-close lips. A question, asking for permission for something we both crave.

Yes. I open my mouth to say *yes*. I scream it over and over in my head.

"No," I say instead. "We can't."

He nods once in understanding and removes himself entirely from the moment. "Of course," he says. He rubs the back of his neck and regards me again with a sad smile. "It was lovely to meet you, Mia. Truly." He turns on his heel and walks down the aisle toward the church doors.

I take a moment to steady my pounding heart and wipe the damp from my palms along the sides of my dress. My gaze lifts, instinctively drawn to the grand crucifix, as if it beckons me. *Happy?* My silent questioning reverberates in the hallowed space. *I stopped it.* I severed the taut string that threatened to sound another note. Once again, I held my mother's happiness and pride above my own true desires.

The truth remains. This connection, his and mine, could never come to fruition. It would cause unbearable pain upon too many lives we hold too dear. And after witnessing his relationship with Cyrus, I couldn't bear it if I were the catalyst to tear that bond asunder. It would be reckless to pursue such an ill-conceived relationship based on the fleeting passion of a single dance.

I straighten my shoulders and walk out of the church to join my family.

The sun is bright and blinding, and I shield my eyes for a moment as they adjust, finding my mother and Cyrus saying goodbye to a few dwindling guests. I take Marco from Cyrus's arms and hold him close to my chest, hungry for physical touch.

A taxi pulls up to the curb, and Enzo opens the door. He waves at my family and gives me a pointed look before stepping into the back seat. I return his gaze, my face as unmoving as the stained glass saints'.

"Why does he insist on living in that dirty city?" my mother says with disgust.

"He loves his job, *querida*," Cyrus says.

"Men don't love jobs. They love women. What's her name?"

My head spins so hard I pinch a nerve.

"Who?" I ask, hoping there's an appropriate amount of curiosity in my voice.

"Ana," Cyrus says, "I'm told there's to be a wedding."

"*No,*" my mother whines.

I repeat the word in my head. *No. No, no, no.* He's engaged? He was engaged to a woman in a different country when he first asked me to dance. He had promised himself to another, and yet, moments ago, he uttered my name with a yearning that could buckle the strongest resolve. It can't be. I stopped him. *I* made him wait a moment and *think*. Was he thinking of her? Of Ana? My emotions swell from hurt to rage and back again. Disgust roils in my belly at the thought of her disappointment. A feeling of betrayal for a faceless woman. I look up into the bright sunlight to pinch back the stinging threat of tears. "She's wrong for him, Cyrus," my mother says.

"He must make his own mistakes." Cyrus's words are not directed toward me, yet they fit all the same. This whole thing was a mistake. Meeting him, taking his hand, dancing the way we did, what just happened at the altar—it was all a mistake. Yet, I'm called back to the tender touch with which he traced the freckle on my ear. The warmth of his hand holding mine. His darkened sleeve by the baptismal waters as he cradled Marco. And that lingering fragrance of citrus and sunlight.

For years after, these plagued thoughts of desire bring ephemeral moments of bliss in my solitude. When the house is asleep and the hours are small, when I'm alone, in my wing of our villa, I think of him, and I touch every inch of myself. I taste my fingers and press my face into my pillow and ride the memory until all I see is white, and his face.

I don't see him again until three years later, for my mother's wedding.

7

Enzo

Four Days Before the Wedding

*F*uck. Three years and a failed engagement later and she still has a hold on me. Still commands my thoughts, my body, as though I were a puppet and she the master. Delicate fingers pulling my strings to watch me dance. I hoped seeing her again would break the spell she's had on me for years. That touching her in person would revoke the fantasy conjured in her absence. Yet I evaded the probable truth—that this infatuation would worsen if indulged.

It wasn't supposed to happen like this. She was never supposed to know about Ana leaving me. I intended to keep up this facade, to divert the spotlight to where it should be. At least until the wedding excitement subsides. Once I return to New York, I can evade their judgmental gazes upon finding out about my failure. Revealing the truth was a devious move, borderline malevolent.

Hard as stone, my trousers are too tight, all from a few exchanged words with Mia. This complicates things beyond my ingenuous belief that I could merely ignore her. After my blatant misleading three years ago, it was wrong of me to drop such a bomb of information on Mia like this. After the baptism, I left her to interpret our encounter however she pleased. I omitted crucial details about my relationship with another woman, from the instant I invited her to dance to the moment I stepped into that taxi. Leaving her to wonder whether I was a mere tease wasting her time or perhaps a man with true intentions of courtship. In a way, I was both. In a way, I still am. Despicable. It's impossible not to toy with her when she makes it so easy. However, my conscience raises its brows, reminding me of my manipulative actions, as I'm left feeling like an old man playing with the naiveté of a young woman.

When she came down for breakfast in that little two-piece outfit, the first thing I saw was her back on display as it was that night in the club in her green-not-black dress. Her hair, longer now, falling just above the small of her back, tickling a narrow slit of exposed skin above her full hips. I could still feel the roundness of her pressed up against the hardness of me.

Her head whipped back and forth. *Was she looking for me?* I wanted to reach out, to touch her shoulder, but hesitated the moment before contact, reaching for the tray of food Katia held instead. The wind of her hair brushed my nose in a delicate clean scent, her eyes wide as she smiled, like seeing an old friend rather than a scoundrel who left her half seduced with no follow through.

She scratched her shoulder nervously, calling my attention to yet another part of her to obsess over. It was all I could do to not look back, to not mentally undress her in the middle of that courtyard and drag her back upstairs. Nevertheless, I could never be so rude as to not give her a proper hello. I finally held her shoulders and kissed both cheeks in greeting. Pulling her in half an inch to feign a kiss to her ear. Payback for last night. Disgrace be damned, I smiled.

Being near Mia is like trying to stand still on a ship in the middle of a storm. My equilibrium shot to pieces. The small talk at the breakfast table was tortuous. I was practically squirming in my seat with the need to touch her. When I finally did lay my palm across her knuckles, unexpected vulnerability surged through me. Exposed, I felt the judgment of those at the same table as though they could read every depraved thought in my depraved mind. Every starving fantasy around this younger woman who practically came for me last night while the rest of the house slept. The thought jolted my cock, and I removed my hand from hers, determined to keep my longing looks to a minimum.

I nearly lost all control in the hallway. As futile as my efforts were, I could no longer avoid her. The insistent nature of her gaze. I could no longer resist the urge to hold her in my arms and breathe her in deep, letting her weight soften into mine. Her echo of a plea brought me back to the keen jolt of pleasure we shared separately in the night, and I needed her to know. She had to know that if she asked, I would serve. I would deliver her from the depths of her own sorrow and carry her to the highest peaks of happiness if she allowed me. With one word, one look, I would be irrevocably hers.

Eyes like daggers pin me in place, golden brown and hooded under thick, dark lashes. Her stare binds me by some higher being to obey, to oblige, to please. Am I the one manipulating her, or is she holding the reins in this game of we-really-shouldn't? Any attempts to establish a paradigm in maintaining distance while keeping control of my erections in her presence prove futile the moment her gaze meets mine.

Whether I'm sweating from the heat or my train of thought—or a combination of both—I can no longer stand the feeling of my shirt on my back. I remove it and toss it into the hamper across the room. The damp air does little to relieve this fever brewing within. In the washroom, I splash my face with cold water and run wet hands down my arms and behind my neck. This soothes my nerves and I stand with my eyes closed, breathing for what feels like more than enough time.

I change into my swim trunks and pull on an opened button-down shirt, the thin cotton fabric billowing wonderfully cool around my bare chest and stomach as I move. I grab a pair of sunglasses, a Yankees baseball cap, and a towel before heading downstairs.

Cyrus is on the floor of the living room with Marco, playing with an array of colorful toys. Katia is at the kitchen table with her laptop open, tapping a pen to her temple.

"*Ciao,*" I say.

"*Ciao,*" they reply in unison without looking away from their current occupations.

The courtyard fountain sprays a delightful mist on my bare chest as I head for the front drive, where Matteo, Simone, and Mia are all sitting in Cyrus's old convertible. Simone is in the driver's seat, wearing a sun hat large enough to shade the group of us and stylish sunglasses. Hints of Marco's chalk dust her sundress, but she wears it well. Matteo rises from the passenger seat as I approach and pulls the chair forward for me to climb into the back, next to Mia.

On the brief car ride to the beach, Simone and Matteo discuss marketing strategies. Matteo makes an argument for strengthening social media presence, while Simone insists these networking field trips are far more valuable. Mia and I are silent in the back seat. She watches the coast whip by from her window as if she could see what lay past the horizon. She fidgets with the fringe of a towel sitting on her lap, and I resist the urge to reach for her hand, remembering the bomb I just dropped on her. Is she upset with me?

We unload our things from the car and Simone hands me a stack of flyers promoting the speakeasy. The front has a glossy picture of Simone on stage, mic in hand, with a live band behind her. On the back is the address, phone number, club hours, and social media handles, plus a free drink if you bring it to "the hot bartender." It actually says that. I don't need to guess who designed these.

"Hand these to interesting people. We want to maintain a vibe," Simone says, emphasizing the word "interesting," as if I am supposed to understand what she means by such an insinuation.

The sun is relentless, eased only by the occasional sea breeze, and the sand is warm between my toes as we walk down the beach. We cross countless half naked men and women of all adult ages, and further down the beach, a pair of topless women pass us. They nod and we nod back, unbothered. I try to stifle my shock. Living in New York has definitely shamed my ideas of sex and modesty. My little apartment suddenly feels a million miles away. I wait for a pang of homesickness, but it never comes.

We find a spot far enough from the water to avoid the tide, and Mia fans out her towel onto the sand. I do the same, mindful of her space. Simone sets up her towel by Mia with no such intention.

Matteo has acquired a football from somewhere and is already kicking it along the sand toward a group of boys. He removes his shirt and throws it at Simone with a wink. She rolls her eyes and folds the shirt neatly at the foot of her towel while Matteo runs off with the rest of the shirtless young men in a huddle of testosterone I no longer feel the need to join. A younger me would have had a fear of missing out and play just as rowdy as the rest of my peers for the sake of camaraderie. Now, the thought makes my bones ache.

Simone removes her sun-dress, exposing a blush pink two-piece that does wonders for her figure. Mia unknots the bow behind her neck and works her top off over her head before stepping out of her skirt, revealing a "dark little number" indeed. A midnight blue two-piece with a high waist bottom that accentuates the under curve of her supple ass as well as the narrowness of her waist. A delicate clasp buckles the top in the back, like a bra. How much force would it take to break it? I watch her every move, yearning for this innocent display to be exclusively for me rather than everyone else on the beach. She sits by her cousin without a word.

"Well, if you're here, you'll be put to work, Enzo," Simone says. "Go walk around and hand those out."

"You two won't join me?" I ask.

She shakes her head as if I don't know a thing in the world.

"Boys come to *us*," Simone explains, gesturing to the both of them lounging on their towels. "You—boy—go mingle. Use that cute face of yours to bring us more drinking patrons."

Mia shoots her cousin a look before shielding her eyes from the sun and giving me a concurring nod.

I readjust my hat before offering a polite bow and take my leave. With my shirt unbuttoned, I approach several strangers with an air of pseudo-confidence, conjuring up my most charming smile before handing them a flyer. Some dismiss me while others stop and ask for details. Striving to appear knowledgeable, I share the minimal amount of information possible without sounding foolish. Successful, I engage in several flirtatious encounters before running out of flyers to pass around. I return to our spot in the sand to see Simone and Mia speaking with a pair of shirtless men. Simone places her hand on one of the men's shoulders, and he seems pleased with her candor. Mia smiles up at the other man, holding a cigarette between two fingers with her arms crossed. She bends down to pick up a flyer and hands it to him.

"Back already?" Simone asks.

"I ran out of propaganda," I tease.

Simone introduces me to the two men and I forget their names as they're spoken. The four conclude their small talk and the men leave with promises to be at the club later that night.

Mia lets out an exasperated sigh and retrieves three beer bottles from her bag. She hands one to me, then to Simone. I put the cap between my teeth and bite down to crack it open.

"Don't do that!" Mia says. I look at her like a scolded puppy.

"That's terrible for your teeth."

Her blend of a Spanish and French accent is adorable. I chuckle and take a sip. It doesn't taste like piss for a change.

She cracks her own open with a bottle opener and hands it to Simone, who repeats the motion. We stand in the sand, sipping on our not-bad beers, watching the waves.

Matteo runs by, expertly weaving a ball between his feet while four men chase him down the beach. One man guards a makeshift goal made out of a large towel held down by two beach bags. Matteo runs at full force, flicking the ball into the air with his foot before delivering a blow. The goalkeeper shuffles back and forth in anticipation before missing completely. Matteo yells triumphantly as the ball flies through the goal. The other men embrace him and he is lost in a sea of skin and sweat. Matteo breaks free and runs toward us, grabs Simone, and kisses her forcefully on the mouth. She lets him, holding her hat atop her head, dipping back in acceptance.

Matteo releases her and grabs Mia in the same motion. He kisses her with even more force, his hands on her waist, her back. Her face twists, her palm pressed against his chest, the other pinned to the side. The men hoot like a pack of animals.

Matteo breaks the kiss with a loud smack of his lips and looks right at me with a smirk before running back to his group of monkeys.

Mia looks at me, mortified. I take a sip of my beer and continue to watch the waves, trying not to shatter the bottle in my hand.

8

Mia

S imone laughs at my annoyed expression. Matteo's blatant display of peacock behavior has painted me an ingénue. And he did it on purpose, with a wordless challenge in Enzo's direction. He might as well have pissed all over me to prove his point. I have half a mind to pull Matteo all the way back to the house by the ear and chastise him. Though, seeing me perturbed would only further suspicion since the kiss wasn't particularly uncharacteristic of him. He's always been open with his affection for my cousin and me. Whether or not I was involved with someone, surreptitiously or not.

"Is this a smoking beach?" Enzo asks.

Simone produces a gold case and passes me a crisp cigarette to hand him. He takes it from my fingers, careful not to make contact before pulling a lighter from his pocket. He cups his palm around the tip to shield against the breeze. Simone pops one between her lips, hands me another, and Enzo passes his lighter to us. We all smoke in silence. By the time we reach the last few drags, Simone gathers another stack of flyers to hand to Enzo.

"We haven't gotten any potential prospects since you returned. The day is dying," she says.

Enzo pulls one last drag and takes the stack from her before walking off.

Simone lays forward on her towel and pulls at the ends of her bikini top, allowing her back to bathe in uninterrupted sunlight. She props her chin up on a fist and looks up at me. I click my tongue and shake my head at her.

"What?" she says, palms up in innocence.

Vexed, I grab a stack of flyers as an excuse and follow in Enzo's direction. I don't know what to say to him, if I should say anything at all. When we left for the beach, I was the one upset over his delusive pretense. Now it's his turn. This game is infuriating, and I'm not sure I'd like playing anymore. Not if it brings us both such strife.

I spot him walking in the distance along the damp sand line, placing one bare foot in front of the other, letting the tide flow through his legs as he stalks across the beach. He doesn't stop to speak with anyone or even raise his head as a few topless women turn to watch him walk by. He holds himself tall with a straight posture, as though he's walking with a destination in mind rather than idly stomping toward the horizon. I think to call his name but don't, picking up my pace instead, a few flyers escaping my grip. Behind me, Simone is a distant mirage as she lies on her stomach, a man crouched down in front of her. Matteo is still off somewhere playing his boy's game.

I finally catch up to Enzo and grab the back of his arm. He spins, his face twisted in confusion and anger. I take a breath and consider offering an apology, though I'm not sure why I'd be sorry. Before I have a chance to decide, his lips crush onto mine. His hand slips behind my waist, and my arms naturally glide up his bare chest, around his neck.

I have spent years dreaming of what it would be like to kiss this man. Torturing myself with our moment in the church, wondering what would have happened if I hadn't stopped him.

The cool waves shock my unsuspecting feet, the sensation euphoric, and I pull him in closer as he deepens the kiss. His tongue slips through the slit of my lips and flicks at the sky of my mouth. He tastes like sea breeze and sweet smoke. An unbidden sound escapes me, and he holds me tighter, my heels lifting from the damp sand. The flyers scatter around us, spinning in the wind. I tease at his bottom lip, holding his neck for support, and he lets out a low hum, vibrating the skin between us. Heat pools and the muscles between my thighs tighten. My barely covered breasts press greedily against the hardness of his chest. I'm so small in his arms. Safe, with a hint of danger. Anyone could see us. Anyone who knows me from the groves or from the club could walk by and relay the gossip of such an encounter with my mother, his brother, our family.

We break apart, stares locked and searching, the edifice of our reserve, fallen to pieces. Our paths now inexorably entwined.

"I had to get him off you," he says.

I don't know whether to be offended or swept away. His kiss had everything to do with Matteo's false claim. He felt the need to remove another man from my lips by replacing my last kiss with his own. This territorial testosterone driven act had little to do with me and all to do with him. I shove his chest, forcing him to remove his hands from my waist.

"I am not yours," I say. Heads turn in our direction at the rise in my voice. "You made me out to be a fool after that dance. You would have made me an accomplice to your cheating if I hadn't stopped you. And now you ignore me. You refuse to look at me. You insist on playing this game for three years, off in a different country, and *this* is how you make your first proper move? Not because of me, not because you want me now that you're free, not even over some lascivious itch we both need scratched. No. Because you saw another man kiss me, and you can't stand it. All this time you could live your false life with your fiancé, pretending to be someone you're not. A fiancé you deliberately did not mention out of indignity or contrition or whatever the fuck. As long as you could imagine me alone, pining over you."

He opens his mouth to retort but I don't let him.

"I am not a fantasy. I am not some taboo, off limits, wet dream built for your fucking pleasure."

"Of course I can't stand it," he seethes, "I can't bear it. Any of it. That one dance made me question every decision I have ever made in my life up until that point. And I'm sorry for the part I made you play then. I'm grateful you stopped me from kissing you in that church. It ate me up inside, and I had to tell Ana. Her forgiveness shocked me. But I never told her it was you. If I had, I'm not so sure we would have continued for as long as we did. The memory of that dance—of you—still plagues me. It's the reason I didn't go through with the engagement. You're the reason, Mia."

I step back.

"You're my brother's stepdaughter," he continues. "Do you realize how distasteful that makes me? To want you as I do? To sneak around like a schoolboy with a crush, wanting you, dreaming of you, thinking of you as I do? You can't imagine the shame I carry for what those thoughts bring me to do. I hear the music of your voice in my head and your body is there, against mine when I'm alone. You think I *wanted* to picture you every time I'd fuck Ana, every time

I'd kiss her goodbye? You think it felt good imagining you instead of the woman I was supposed to marry?" He takes a few breaths, his voice now even. "Of course I loathe myself. Of course I can't bear the thought of you with anyone else. I had to run away from you. To another country, to another life, because you make me dream too big. And that scares me."

Curious heads have now turned away, and I stand speechless. He's trembling as he takes my hand in his, an innocent enough gesture.

"Why not come clean about Ana? Tell Cyrus," I say.

He shakes his head. "This week is about them. Not me. Not us."

I nod in understanding. He's not selfish when it comes to family; an attribute we share.

"I'm sorry about the kiss. You're right. You don't belong to me. But you don't belong to *him* either," he continues.

I want to belong to you, I almost say. I want to fight until we are both heaving with anger at one another for harboring what we feel. But I'm tired. A sigh slips out in surrender. "Could we just try to get through this week without ripping into one another? For our family's sake?"

He nods and lets go of my hand. My heart falls at the loss of contact and we walk back the way we came, side by side.

The sun hangs low across the sea line, casting an orange glow that bounces off the sand. The breeze billows Enzo's shirt like curtains in an open window. He notices me noticing and takes my hand with a smirk. I turn away, attempting to hide a smirk of my own. We walk without a word, his thumb languorously running up and down the length of one of my fingers. A small enough gesture that would raise questioning brows of those who might know us personally. The strangers on the beach don't seem to mind, and we relish in this moment of public isolation and anonymity. For a brief moment, we're not hiding. From the world, or from each other. He holds my hand as though it's an everyday thing we do. As though he knows he'll hold it again later today and the rest of our tomorrows. He holds my hand with no sense of force or claim or territory.

Simone, now in clear view, is laying on her back with her top still untied and draped precariously over her chest. She holds it in place as she sits up, and Enzo drops my hand, innocently stepping to the side.

"Where'd you two go?" Simone asks.

"Recruiting," I say. "Where's Matteo? We should head back."

Simone ties her top in place and stands to search the beach.

"There." She points a long finger toward a group of nudists. "Figures," she says. "So predictable. Look for tits, you'll find Matteo."

We dress and gather our things. Enzo offers to tie my top and I let him.

"You looked lovely in your little dark number by the way," he whispers for me alone. I reach back to touch the tips of his fingers as they linger down my spine. Goose flesh ripples my skin, and I hand him my bag to carry. He takes it.

We catch up with Matteo, and he breaks free from his group. "Nice company," he comments. Simone makes a show of rolling her eyes. "Why don't you dress like that, Simone? I'm sure we'd sell out the house every night if you did."

Simone curses him in French and shoves her bag into his chest. Matteo laughs at her miffed response and plants a messy kiss on her cheek. She waves him away like the mosquito he is, wiping at her face.

We discuss the success of the day as we make our way back to the car. Several people apparently approached Simone in our absence. Though she assures me she would have gotten much more attention had I stuck around and been her wing woman. I half apologize and climb in the back seat of the car. Enzo sits by me, his hand splayed across the seat between us. I'm unsure if this is an invitation. He makes a point of watching the shoreline pass by, the sun casting a golden glow, reflected on the ocean's surface. Sea things breach the waves, and his lips tilt up at the edges in amusement. "You don't see this in New York," he says, almost to himself.

"What *do* you see?" I ask.

Matteo's profile breaks my periphery, subtly eavesdropping.

"Rats," Enzo says. A disgusted demeanor betrays me. "Hungry, fearless rats."

Simone listens as well, her gaze meeting mine in the rearview mirror.

"And not small, cute ones that cook under your hat, like in that little film. As big as my foot, and ugly." He feasts on the view of the ocean, as though his words were someone else's. "The entire city is ugly, actually. Yes, the architecture is impressive, the industry is incomparable, the people are mostly kind, and the history is rich, but..." he trails off, searching for the words in the horizon. "Look at this," he breathes, "It's nothing like this. I've forgotten. How could I have forgotten?" He shakes his head and finally tears his gaze away as the rippling sun brushes the edge of the earth and turns toward me. "How beautiful my country is."

We drop Simone and Matteo off at the speakeasy, where Matteo's scooter is waiting by the entrance. He collects their bags and escorts my cousin upstairs, thanking us for the ride. Enzo thanks us in turn for including him in today's assignment. We climb up to the front and I take the driver's seat. An ocean breeze chills my bare skin in the most delightful way. Enzo is quiet the rest of the way home, focused on the road ahead as though he were the one behind the wheel, alone in his thoughts. We pull into the driveway and I put the car in park before cutting the engine.

He's touching me before I'm aware of it. His fingertips brush my knuckles, still poised on the keys in the ignition. He trails his touch up my arm, over my collarbone, and across the line of my jaw. "Enzo," I breathe, readying myself to argue.

"Wait."

He holds the side of my face, the flesh of his thumb pressed against my lower lip. All sense of debate vanishes at the way he's touching me. He is too achingly close to *think*. I lean into his hand and kiss his palm. He purrs a low rumble in the depths of his throat and I open my mouth and trace his thumb with the tip of my tongue. Eyes fixed on my lips, he grips my jaw with his fingers. The scent of sand and sweat and lust fills the car, and I rub my thighs together to quell the ache that lies between them. His gaze travels down, drinking in my discomfort. His other hand flexes against his thigh, rippled muscles along his chest and abdomen constricting through his open shirt. I taste the skin of his thumb and imagine what the rest of him might taste like. What the salt of him would do to me. The thought births an ache even deeper as wetness begins to pool and absorb into the fabric of my "little dark number."

An indignant click of his tongue and all too quickly, his touch is absent. The car dings to alert an open door, and there's the distinct sound of shoes on gravel. I pull the parking brake, remove the keys, and climb out of the driver's seat. Enzo is already halfway down the drive with my bag slung across his back. We walk through the abandoned courtyard, the only sound the trickling fountain and the echo of our footsteps. I look up to the oncoming evening sky and inhale the summer air, the scent of our olive groves carried on the breeze.

Enzo opens the kitchen doors and plops my bag onto one of the stools. He retrieves two crystal glasses from a cupboard and fills them both with water, handing me one without a word. We both drink. He refills his glass and stalks upstairs. I leave mine in the sink and continue this poor attempt at follow-the-leader.

Once in our respective bedrooms, I hear him rustling about through the washroom doors as I slip off my shoes and grab the pack of Marlboros and a lighter from my bedside table. The balcony doors open with a swift breeze, and I take my place in the terrace's corner, one leg tucked under the other. Light pours from the window above the bathtub, accompanied by the clanging sound of water running through pipes.

Across the courtyard, the curtains to my mother and Cyrus's bedroom are half shut. A sliver of light casts a comforting glow across their tiled floor. The string lights over the courtyard below turn on with the setting sun and dance in the whistling breeze that chills the back of my damp neck, and I take another long drag of my cigarette, enjoying the small respite.

A few minutes pass and the pipes silence. A soft bloom from Enzo's bedroom spills across the terrace floor before he emerges from his set of glass doors in a towel.

My breath hitches.

His hair is wet and dripping. His bare chest was on display all day, but here, in the gleam of night without even an opened button-down to hide behind, I witness the true beauty of him. The roundness of his shoulders, the straight lines of his collarbones, the tight V that wraps around his waist and guides my attention to what l beyond the towel hung loosely on his narrow hips. I can still sense the wetness within my swimsuit bottoms and feel filthy in front of his freshly showered self. Here I am, covered in sand and sea and lotion, while he smells of my jasmine soap and coconut shampoo.

I offer him a cigarette and he shakes his head, beads of water falling to the floor around him. He runs a hand through his damp hair and whips the moisture away with a flick before approaching my corner of the terrace. His bare feet slap wet against the tile, reminding me of an obscene sound.

"I lied," is all he says before his mouth is on mine again. Where his kiss on the beach felt desperate and needing, this is possessive, demanding. His hands are on my waist, my back, my neck, my ass, taking what he needs. Droplets of water fall from his hair onto my face, the illusion of rain. His hands slide behind my neck to the knot of fabric holding up my top, and he pulls at the strings, revealing my swimsuit covered breasts. He holds me in place, his tongue exploring the inside of my mouth, tasting every inch of me, and I can't get enough. I can't get close enough. My palms are cool against his warm chest, the rocky hills of his back. My cigarette, now damp, falls to the floor, and my fingers brush against his towel.

Our breath is hot, our tongues fighting for dominance, teeth clashing. I grab onto the edge of his towel, ready to rip it away. But he grabs my wrist and puts a step between us. His lips are swollen, as I'm sure mine are just as plump, our chests heaving. I need another cigarette.

"I'll never be sorry for kissing you," he says, letting go of my wrist. "Goodnight, Mia."

He strides back into his bedroom, leaving the glass doors ajar. The breeze rustles the curtains, and I glimpse the skin of his leg as he pulls on a pair of boxers. My chest heaves as I try to regain control of my breathing, the ringing in my ears growing louder before it quiets. I knew this wedding week would be challenging enough, though I had not expected the conflict now clashing in my mind. There's no use denying the truth. We both want the other, and we're too afraid of our families to want openly. I'm his dirty little secret, and he is mine.

But I've kept secrets before. And so has he.

I pop another Marlboro between my lips and light it, taking my time to smoke it thoroughly before going inside to take a shower. I crawl into bed smelling of jasmine soap and coconut shampoo.

9

Enzo

Three Days Before the Wedding

The smell of fresh coffee wakes me. I fell asleep with the taste of her on my lips and could think of no better way to end every night for the rest of my life. It's been less than forty-eight hours since my return to Spain, and the allure of my homeland has come full circle, prompting me to question why I left in the first place.

The sight of topless women on the beach startled my Americanized sensibilities, triggering an unexpected sense of indignity, and I could have interpreted Matteo's possessive affection toward Mia as a simple gesture between friends, as I did with Simone. As such behavior is so common here, no one would question it.

In New York, in America, the kiss of the woman you love is territorial. Something to fight another man over in the alley behind a bar for some archaic idea of honor and loyalty. Bullshit. We are familiar with the idea that women reflect men's honor, but we still frown upon intimacy outside of a monogamous relationship. At least for some men. Others find it quite arousing to see their woman in the arms of another man, to watch her brought to pleasure by someone she doesn't care for while looking into your eyes.

I am not one of those men.

It was the look Matteo gave me after. That smug demeanor, as if he suspected something between Mia and I, and he couldn't stand the thought of her choosing me over him. In truth, I don't consider Matteo a threat. Of course, her choice is paramount. From an outside perspective, it would make sense for her to choose him. A young woman deserves a young man who can keep up with her, grow old with her, experience life at the pace she finds comfortable.

Though, another part of me knows with utmost certainty that I could make her happy. I would continue to choose her above all else, every day, without question or condition. If given the chance. But these are evanescent morning fantasies brought on by the memory of her kiss and the stubborn stiffness tightening my boxers at the moment.

With a few deep breaths, I inhale the strong, bitter scent that eventually coaxes me from the sheets. I wash my face, brush my teeth, and pull on a shirt and trousers.

Mia's door is closed, with not a sound through the walls. Not a sound at all, now that I think of it. The normal morning buzz of conversation and sizzling breakfast things, of orange juice being poured into crystal glasses, Marco's small feet stomping on the courtyard floor—nothing.

Downstairs, the kitchen is clean, with a few dishes drying on the rack. Two mugs sit on the countertop by the large espresso machine, steam trickling from the milk frother. The only other indication that someone was recently bopping about the kitchen is the open fridge door. I survey the living room, dining room, and family room. No one.

I take a small sip from one of the mugs and an unexpected sourness hits my tongue. These must be test shots. I grab the crystal pitcher of milk from the fridge and close the door before pulling two more double shots of espresso. Velvet liquid drips into the waiting cups as I steam a small jug of milk. "Hello?" I call out, pouring hot milk into the cups and failing at both attempts to make a tulip out of milk foam.

A grunt sounds from beyond the pantry door propped open by a step stool. Mia wobbles up the steps with an oversized bag of whole coffee beans. I grab the child-sized bag and bring it to the counter.

"Bit much for your morning coffee, don't you think?" I tease.

"We were running low," she says, and slides the nearly empty coffee container across the counter for me to fill.

I pour the beans to the brim and close up the bag. There's a simple domestic pleasure in the task we've just accomplished together. These intrusive thoughts of happy endings and wild possibilities are inexorable.

Mia grabs a spoon from a nearby drawer and feeds two servings of sugar into both cups. I wince at the overpowering sweetness I know they now possess, but say nothing to allude to my dislike. She stirs each cup in her little routine, a wan smile across her clean face, curls pulled back on top of her head, and tiny gold hoop earrings dangling from her ears. An oversized crewneck university sweater envelopes her small body, the sleeves longer than her arms. Her bare legs are on display in loose lounge shorts that cut off at her upper thigh. They do nothing to hide the crease where the back of her strong thighs meet the curve of her ass when she turns to rinse the spoon in the basin. Her straight spine and nimble bare feet navigate the kitchen with grace, greeting mundane tasks with a dancer's expertise. A dangerous, punishable thought crosses my mind, and I grab my cup, desperate for a distraction. Looking away from her tempting form and out the window, I see someone has turned off the courtyard fountain. *That doesn't help this eerie silence.*

"Mama and Cyrus are down by the groves. They have some business to take care of before the wedding. And Simone took Marco for the morning. She does that. Says he helps to attract new patrons, but I don't believe that. I think she's just a mom without a kid of her own yet." She's almost speaking to herself, her thoughts merely dictated from an internal transcript.

Mia gathers her mug in her sweater covered hands and brings it up to her face. She sniffs the coffee, but doesn't bring her lips to the brim. I suggest we sit in the living room and she nods without a word, wearing a tranquil expression as if she's awoken from a delightful yet forgotten dream.

She nuzzles herself into the L corner of the sectional, her feet tucked underneath, while I take the edge of the sofa. We sip our coffee and I prepare myself for the unduly sweet taste, but it doesn't come. The coffee itself is strong enough to cut through the sugar and milk, playing its own notes with accompaniment. Delighted at the surprise, I take another sip. Mia enjoys her cup as well, holding it close to inhale the scent with every breath. Steam swirls around her face and I'm tempted to say something, though I'm not sure what.

"I don't want to talk about last night," she says. Her gaze meets mine, and for a moment I fear she's expecting me to steer the conversation. "I want to talk about my mother," she says instead.

"Okay," I agree.

"How much do you know about her?"

"Only what Cyrus has told me, which isn't much from before he came into your life." I take a sip of my decidedly delicious coffee and relax against the sofa.

"My mother doesn't speak much of our life before your brother. His debut marked a change I will always be grateful for. Though I am reluctant to give him all the credit. It was my mother who changed our lives. Cyrus was only a catalyst. His love for her the fuel, so she may drive us all 'into the sunset,' as it were." She takes a contemplative sip from her mug and stares into the swirling liquid.

"It was not always like that, though. There was a time when I felt like we were more sisters than mother and daughter. We were partners, navigating life together. It's why I chose business as my major. I wanted to know how things worked, how to run a machine of individuals, how money played both parts of cause and effect depending on what side you were on in the dichotomy of supplier and consumer. I always wanted to be the supplier, believing they held all the power. But then, during my courses, I learned how consumers dictate the demand. All supply comes from the demand, and back again. Chicken—egg." She balances the mug in her lap to mime a scale between both palms. "Of course, I don't need to ramble on to you about topics learned on one's first day in business school. You run your own research programs. Grant funded or otherwise; I'm sure you understand just fine."

I remain silent. My presence in the room inconsequential to the conversation.

"I mention this primitive concept because I don't quite understand where it lies within family. In theory, on paper, if one were to draw out the brackets of our relation to one another, both our names would be on the page, but our brackets would never touch. The only person both our brackets touch directly is Marco. He is the only living being who shares our blood yet."

My throat hitches on her last word. My hopeful mind envisions another possible way Mia and I could touch brackets on this page of which she speaks. But she is clearly alluding to the possibility of future siblings for Marco. Imaginary children between Katia and Cyrus that have nothing to do with my near-midlife wanderings. If she sees the twists my mind is taking, she doesn't comment on them, enveloped in her lament.

She goes on to tell me of her understanding of family always being singular. One person. Katia. That home was an abstract of the different hotels and communes, mostly in France. The two would bounce between places over the years before finally settling back here on the island where Katia grew up.

Mia was already making her own reckless mistakes by this time. Believing she no longer required the stability of home and family. But don't we all? No matter how old or young, being surrounded by those we love in the comforts of home, those are the constituents of a good life. And good food, though that goes without saying.

"What I mean to say with all of this is that, as the child of the family, I was the consumer. I was in demand for all the things children need to grow and be happy. And I had a limited supply." She shifts her weight, unfolding her legs, then crossing them. "I remember the day my father left. I was Marco's age now. We lived in a flat in Nice. I remember the windows were tall and dirty and the floors had certain hotspots where the pipes ran through. I would sit on these spots like a cat finding rays of sun. They say early memory is a sign of trauma, but that is for a hypothetical therapist to unpack. It was the only time I can recall my mother crying over a man. She cried for one day. It was the entire day, but I remember it was just that one day after he left. Of course, she would cry all the time over silly things like my primary school graduation or when I left for university. But according to her, tears were too precious to waste over a man. That was, until she met your brother." Her smile returns, a degree brighter now.

"The day after the crying stopped, we packed up the few things we owned and drove along the coast of France. We hopped towns, and my mother worked odd jobs, mostly waitressing. She always loved being around food. And fashion. The thrift stores in Paris are like high end boutiques anywhere else, but I digress.

"This is where she noticed the differences in the taste based on the type of oil the restaurant used. Olive oil, she found, was best when it came to taste, no matter what it was the restaurant specialized in. On bread, in pasta, preparing fish, chicken, steak, it all needed olive oil as much as it needed heat. We traveled all over France. We'd reconnect with my aunt and Simone here and there before making our way to the next town, giving me a small glimpse as to what a family of more than two could look like.

"The older I got, the fancier the restaurants we would work. That also meant the more money the restaurant's patrons had to spend. And where there's money, there are men willing to spend it. Men made their way through our lives like phases of the moon, though thankfully not that frequent. But never again was that demand satisfied. It took me a long time to realize my mother was enough for both ends of that scale to balance." She releases a deep sigh and continues, "Paris was the best of the worst. The people were haughty, the restaurants were tiny, but the food was superlative. I can't remember the name of the pretentious little bistro on the *Champs-Élysées,* but guess how much they would pay for each bottle of olive oil?"

"One thousand per bottle," I deadpan. She laughs at my overestimation, running a feather down my chest.

"Close enough. Seven hundred euros." She nods at my gawking expression. "I'm sure there are more expensive bottles sold to more expensive restaurants, but that one in particular I always remember because the sous chef was my first."

I stiffen. The smile slips from my face.

She shakes her head. "You are jealous?" She laughs again as I shift in my seat.

"He was twenty-four, I was two weeks away from my nineteenth birthday. My mother worked her way up to management. Climbing the service ladder with every new restaurant in every new city. At this bistro, she made the orders for select ingredients through trusted vendors. The owner only cared about the food and let my mother have free rein on basically everything else. Including the staff. She wanted me to get to know the food service industry and got me a job waitressing, after completing my coursework, of course. She saw how the sous chef would watch me carry trays in and out of the kitchen. How he'd wipe the sweat from my brow on particularly busy evenings. The special attention he would give me when the wait staff would gather to memorize the specials for the night. I came into my mother's office to read one afternoon after school before my evening shift. Only the cooks were there, preparing ingredients and cleaning up their stations. My mother wasn't even in yet, she must have been off at the docks ordering some expensive fish or something."

She pauses, tilting her head up to the glass ceiling, the coffee forgotten in her hands. "Would you like to know his name, or shall I spare you?"

I shake my head slowly.

"Very well. He came into the office, took the book from my hands, and kissed me. I had never been kissed before. I read about what it was supposed to feel like—to be kissed, to be fucked. But none of my books back then ever mentioned the *first* time. How it can hurt in the beginning. He was attentive and soft when I needed it and rough when I wanted it.

"We snuck around for a handful of months after that. I learned not to get too close to anyone growing up. Don't make close friends, only acquaintances to help get through the school year. And so, like every other person during that time of my life, he passed. My mother got a better paying job in Portofino, and we were off to another country, just like that. I never cried, never felt anything more than lost. Sleeping with a man I did not love never bothered me until I got older. I don't regret it. Looking back, it was presumably for the better. No large emotional strings snapped. It was a mutual infatuation and quite satisfying, as I remember." Her cheeks flush as she remembers another man in front of me.

"I watched my parents love each other the best they could at the time, which was not good enough. They were too young to navigate the world around a child. Well, he was. My mother did not have the luxury of leaving as he did. Which brings us back to demand." She shifts positions to place both feet on the floor. "You know what happened after we moved to Portofino. My mother met your brother, and we are currently side characters in their happily ever after. Something we must not interrupt. It is best if we end this..." Her forefinger moves between us, lost for words. "Whatever this is that is happening between us. We are not in control of the situation.

We continue to put each other in questionable circumstances, and it's not..." She shakes her head, searching for the words.

"It's not proper," I finish for her.

"Yes," she agrees.

"All right." The sweat on my palms loosens the grip of my now empty mug. "I won't apologize, if that's what you want."

She shakes her head. "No, I don't want you to apologize. That would cheapen those moments, and that is certainly not how I feel. It's just, we are too close. Us. This. It would devastate the foundation of what Cyrus and my mother have spent so long building. We cannot do that to them."

"What about what we want? What about what *you* want?" I ask, not knowing the answer for myself either.

A sad smile breaks across her tired face. "I've spent the majority of my life doing everything I can so I won't ever see my mother unhappy again. It doesn't matter what I want. I have the rest of my life to decide what that might or might not be. But for her, now, I can give her a wedding day. I can give her a family of more than just me."

"You know she never felt like you weren't enough family for her. Even *I* am sure of that."

"That might be true, but it doesn't mean she's not happier now than she would be if it were still just us two. I was with her when that blue cross appeared. When she discovered she was going to have another child twenty-three years after her first—and what she thought would be her only. Marco was as much an impossible dream come to life for both of them. And his existence is exactly why we cannot continue this dance. There is something here. Surely, I am not imagining it. If I were, last night wouldn't have happened. Or the night before. I can feel it rising, and if we act beyond last night, I'm afraid everything will fall apart. Perhaps we could consider it — *this* — if Cyrus and my mother's relationship were only casual. But they're getting married, Enzo. Here, behind this house, a few short days from now. They have a child together. We are too close."

"I am so tempted to let you destroy me," are the only words I have to offer.

She's being rational, a voice of reason I've been able to hear this entire time, and I can't stand it. I can't bear hearing these words from her lips. The denial of something she clearly wants as much as I do. But I understand wholeheartedly why she sees this sacrifice is necessary. I can also see she is not being wholly honest with me, or with herself.

"It was one dance, Enzo. One dance three years ago." *And two kisses and one mutual auditory masturbation incident.* She sees the ineffable words on my face and lowers her gaze. "We're even," she says.

"Not even close." I rest my elbows on my knees and lean forward. "What are you saying exactly, Mia? You've told your life story as an oblique way of actually telling me you are in high demand for one thing that's been missing since your father left."

Her left hand twists at her right wrist as she waits for me to continue.

"Stability. Perhaps male stability, to be exact. But my science deals with resilience, growth, genetic predispositions rather than the development of daddy issues."

"Fuck you," she whispers through her teeth, a warning in the back of her throat.

"You're saying you wish for us to control our selfish urges to rip each other's clothes off and fuck as well as we dance? You're telling me you want to be the good little daughter, devoted and pure, while still crawling into bed and touching yourself loud enough for me to hear? Begging me to come relieve the ache between your thighs?"

Her breath thickens, nostrils flared—adorable. It's euphoric, doing this to her, eliciting this sort of reaction from her in so few words. I rise to my feet and stand before her. Her back presses against the sofa in anticipation. I place one finger under her chin and tilt her face to regard me with wicked eyes. She's furious, and my skin pricks with the sharpness of her gaze. At this moment, she hates me for exposing our truth. And I love it.

"Tell me to stop, Mia. Use your words. You've told me a lovely story, but don't sit there and act like that wasn't also an act of seduction. You say we're too close, but you're not telling me to stop. You're screaming for me to fuck you and whispering caution all at once. Which one will it be?" She blinks, the accuracy of my observation realized across her face. "What was his name? On second thought, I would like to know." Her throat works as she rubs her thighs together diminutively. "Say his name."

She licks her lips. "Luke."

White hot envy lashes across my face, a burning that climbs up from stomach to chest. My ears ring at the sound of another man's name on her lips, making me feel quite violent. A man who had her. Who fucked her in whichever way she wanted. Soft. Rough. Her words disrupt some primordial nature deep in the pit of my mind that has otherwise lain dormant. That was until a dance nudged it awake. I have never felt this kind of fury, like poison running through my veins. A lie that takes my very sanity away with every passing thought of her face as it is now, on the tip of my finger. I am terrified. Is this love? It can't be. It shouldn't be. This is lust, possession, dominance. This is sex, and it must be sated.

I force the heat to quell with one deep inhale before asking, "Did he ever make you come?" in a voice that is unlike my own.

Her face twists, she wants to be offended. And yet, she doesn't shy away from my touch. She nods her head instead, pressing against the tip of my finger. "How?" I ask.

"Fingers."

"Mmm," I hum with trivial understanding. "Tongue?" She shakes her head. "Ever?" Another shake. And then, she makes one move that might as well condemn us both on the spot. One slight shift of her weight that tells me she never meant it. Every logical word spoken in defiance of the idea of us... has been a ruse. A lie she has been telling herself to feel less like the selfish little creature she wants so badly to be.

She spreads her legs.

An invitation. Her honey dark stare holds all the stipulations of her speech. I imagine this very same expression, this same angle, with her lips wrapped around my cock.

"Close your legs, Mia."

She shakes her head again. Ever defiant. My voice drops, "If you don't close your legs like a good girl, I will be too tempted to banish every word of reason you've just expressed and rip those little sleep shorts off you." Alone in this vast house with not even the sound of the fountain to interrupt my thoughts, yet I whisper anyway, "I'd be too induced by the sight of you bare to not lick every inch of what I see and truly taste your forbidden cunt. Tell me to stop now, or I may never find the strength to again."

Taken aback at my promise, her brows still stitched together with a guise of hatred, she pushes her legs apart further, her weight poised on the balls of her feet. Her sleep shorts ride higher along her thighs, almost bearing herself to me.

She's calling my bluff. But I am not bluffing.

I flick her chin away with a swish of my fingers and drop to my knees, the coffee table digging into the middle of my spine. "Show me."

Her hands grip the bare flesh of her legs, skin stretched across her knuckles. One hand twitches at my command but doesn't move.

"Your statements of controlling our urges are evidently fictitious. Either show me how wet that cunt of yours is right now, or we go upstairs in our separate rooms and not speak again for the duration of this holiday. Because I can't stand it anymore. I can't stand not knowing what you look like, what you taste like, what you feel like." Her face carries a subtle vulnerability, a crack in her carefully crafted facade. "So I ask you again, Mia, show me."

And to my disbelief, she does. A trembling hand moves across her thigh to the inseam of her shorts. She hooks a finger around the flimsy fabric and pulls it to one side, revealing wet lips. I rock back on the heels of my palms and let out a sigh I've been holding for years. She watches me with the same hateful countenance.

"Touch yourself, Mia. Show me what you wanted me to see my first night here."

Not an ounce of chagrin hints across her face. Only obstinate obedience. She circles the bud at the top of her pussy, and a small jolt makes its way through her body at her own touch. I'm impossibly hard. A second finger slides up her folds and teases the edge of her entrance. Her shoulders, legs, chest, all shudder with every pass of her fingers, and I can no longer contain the need to touch her. Focus still on me, she brings her finger, wet with her own arousal, up to her mouth... and sucks.

I grab her wrist. "Filthy girl," I say.

She smirks. Her eyes flare with surprise as I bring her same finger to my mouth and drag my tongue from palm to tip. Hints of her arousal remain, but not nearly enough. I make to remove her shorts, and she brings her legs together and lifts her hips in compliance. I knead her calves, digging my fingers into the flesh of her muscular dancer's legs just enough to make her squirm. My hands glide up the length of her lithe legs toward the roundness of her ass. She shifts her weight for me, allowing the right amount of her to hang off the edge of the sofa. Her head slides down the back cushion, her chin still dipped, watching my every move. I stroke her knees with my cheek and coax her legs wider until she is fully displayed, bare, wet, and absolutely gorgeous.

I kiss her knees first. One, then the other. She quivers as I nip and lick and kiss up her inner thighs, giving every inch of her the fastidious attention I've yearned to give. I make my way up to the beautiful V at the top of her thighs, the oversized sweater bunched up at her waist. I plant a line of kisses along her midriff, something I wanted to do all day yesterday as she walked around in that little outfit, skimming my tongue from navel down to the top of her pussy. She jolts, and I kiss her mound, breathing the scent of her deep into my lungs, forming a redolent memory I know I will never forget.

"Beautiful, Mia." A whispering hum, telling her a secret she already knows. She pants as my hands trail up her thighs, tickling the edges with my nails, and her demeanor slips from hate to curiosity.

I work one finger down her glistening folds and spread her lips with both thumbs. She bucks at first, then relaxes back into the cushions. Her skin is soft, smooth, decadent.

Wet, pink ripples of flesh open for me, and I become exceptionally aware of our surroundings. When are the others expected home? Are there any appointments or assistants of whom we don't know? Coming to drop off items for the wedding? The thought excites me further.

I shift myself in my shorts, my cock begging to be let free, then dip my head and lay one introductory kiss on her pussy. She lifts with acceptance, and I smile against her skin. My tongue finally glides up her middle, and her back arches in response. She gasps, a sound that has me spreading her wider still. She tastes like every goal of my life not yet met. She tastes like the air in the morning before the sun rises. She tastes like the salt of my country, a home I didn't know I needed to return to. I take my time, kissing every corner of her.

"*Que rico, cariño.*"

She gives a light giggle at my praise. She is painfully delicious. Speaking my mother tongue against her silk flesh fills me with a sense of ancient longing. I circle the swollen bead of her clit with the tip of my tongue before running it down to her opening and back again. Sounds of ardent satisfaction emerge from the back of my throat as I devour her. At this moment, she is irrefutably mine. She writhes beneath me as I command her body to respond without the repentance of where, when, or whom. Her lashes flit closed, hands gripping the head of the sofa cushion. Her calf muscles strain into hard balls as she tries to balance on the tips of her toes. I hook my thumbs behind both knees and relieve that pressure, opening her even more obscenely for my mouth. She squirms in protest, and I glare up at her in warning, stilling her. Gazes locked, I continue my meal, tasting and sucking and nipping at her, before breaching her entrance with my tongue.

"Fuck," she breathes.

I rest her heels on my back and cup her ass in my hands, holding her for my mouth like a beast eating from a chalice of divine sustenance. Her feet rub against the fabric of my shirt, needy twitches and kicks as I fuck her with my tongue. Her breathing grows louder, moans now escaping with every thrust in a mumble of *yes*es and *fuck*s and *oh god*s. My cock begs for the slightest bit of friction, the sound of her voice almost toppling me over the edge. I chase her moans, willing them to morph into screams.

I settle her back down on the sofa and skim both hands up her torso, feeling every curve of her slight frame under my palms. I work my touch under her oversized sweatshirt and find her breasts, no cumbersome bra to unclasp, no mechanism in the way. Just two round, warm, soft breasts waiting for my touch. The buds of her nipples are already hard as I roll them both between thumb and forefinger. This elicits an even deeper moan as I suck on her clit. Her hips undulate underneath me, and I bob my head to keep my mouth on her. I knead her breasts, rolling and pinching and flicking, deliberately giving every bit of her uninterrupted consideration.

Mia's head falls back, her legs shaking as her heels dig into my shoulder blades. She's close. Her hands in my hair, gripping me from the root as she grinds into my mouth, and I suck on one lip, then the other, before removing my touch from her breasts. I enter my tongue once again and hold her by the waist as I move her entire body up and down onto my face. Her wetness drips down the sides of my mouth, down my chin. Nuzzled into her folds, I massage the tip of my nose against her clit. Rolling on my face, her movements are now frantic, her whimpers now wails. She is on the edge, and the sadist in me is tempted to remove my touch entirely until she begs me to make her come. I want to hear her say that word again as she did the other night, but all she gives me are sweet sounds of blessed pleasure. Heady gasps and sighs only interrupted by the occasional curse of affirmation.

She brings one hand down to mine and holds my fingers in her tight grip. I comply, holding her hand as though I were a gentleman helping her up. She cries a sinful sound as her body convulses before fully seizing, trapping my head between her thighs. She squeezes my hand, my head, her other hand gripped tight against my scalp, and a shameful sense of pride washes over me. An undeniable satisfaction of triumph.

I want more.

Her body trembles beneath me, shaking legs draped across my shoulders, and with her hand still gripped in mine, I pull her in to meet my face. She wipes my chin with her thumb and kisses me, savagely. Her tongue explores my mouth, tasting herself on me, in me. Her arms wrap around my neck, pulling me closer to her, and I kiss down her neck to the loose collar of her sweatshirt, my hands running back up her stomach to feel her breasts again. She grabs my wrists and pulls away, hysteria in her stare.

"What are we doing?"

"We're not done."

10

MIA

Three Days Before the Wedding

Enzo stands on steady legs while mine are rendered useless. Tremors ripple through my every muscle from that orgasm. He helps me up with a kiss. Tender this time, tentative. "I need more," he whispers against my lips.

"We shouldn't," I protest.

He shakes his head. "No. I gave you your chance. This is happening. If you're saying no now because you didn't enjoy every moment of my mouth on your pussy, I'll gladly apologize and never touch you again. But, Mia," he brushes a curl behind one ear and holds my face in his hands, unable to avert my gaze from his as he searches my features for the truth, "if you're saying no now because of guilt, because of everything you've told me, because you don't want anyone to get hurt, we can work around that. We can both get what we want and no one will have to suffer."

"How? How could you possibly believe that? I'm half naked in my living room with the best man's face drenched in *me*. How could this work?"

"Deadlines." The word tugs at my intrigue. "We give ourselves a deadline. We satisfy our appetites for one another in every way we can imagine, every way we can think to relieve ourselves of this abstinence."

"You really think that will be enough? That we'll fuck and the act will fulfill the both of us enough to never touch again?"

"No. Not at all. If anything, this is worse. To have tasted you now and know, come Sunday, I'll never taste you again—it pains me beyond description. But all the pain in the world, the inevitable heartbreak, would be worth it. None of this is fair. But what choice do we have now?"

"We could stop?" I whisper. Not believing it myself as my voice lilts at the end in question.

"No, we can't." He laughs a golden, deep laugh, which brings a hazy smile to my face.

"Okay," I agree. His brows pinch with skepticism, waiting for me to change my mind.

"You're saying yes?"

"I'm saying *please.*"

His mouth is on mine again, and I am defeated. My efforts irrelevant before my most basic desire. He tastes of sweat and salt and a tangy sweetness that reminds me of peaches.

Me. He tastes like me.

I'm all over him, he smells of me, his beard damp with my arousal. It's painfully intoxicating, seeing this man so ready, so eager, so needy for me. I tug at the edge of his shirt, needing to feel him bare. He takes the hint and swoops it off in one motion. My thighs are slick from his previous assault, and I rub them together now, pressing myself against him, yearning for more. He's right, we aren't done. Will we ever be done with one another? He stirs self-contempt within me, creating a tantalizing blend of seduction and empowerment. Every command he utters, every piercing glare he bestows, ignites in me a simultaneous desire to rebel and please. A walking paradox, I preach about family honor and "should nots" when I can't go more than a few days without offering myself to him.

Shame. I should feel ashamed. Instead, there is only burning, liquid hunger.

We fall back down to the sofa, our mouths dancing as our bodies have before, and he settles between my thighs, his bare chest against my sweatshirt. My breasts ache to be pressed up against him as I roll my hips underneath his and feel his erection. I glide a palm down and am delighted at his size. With his mouth still exploring my jaw, my neck, nipping at my ear, my collarbone, I unbutton his shorts and slide my hand inside. I don't have to search. He is there. Warm and ready and waiting. While I'm no virgin, his mouth on me a few moments ago was uncharted ground. I have seen and felt a small number of men, and they have all treated me well. Satisfying me in ways expected of their age and capabilities. But Enzo, by the feel of him, is stunning. My fist wrapped around his width, I brush my thumb against the swollen tip. He jerks, elbows buckling. I smirk into the side of his neck at the power I hold in my hand.

"Easy, Mia," he purrs low in my ear. He glides a hand up to palm one breast before wrapping his fingers around my throat. Not hard, not threatening, but firm. And all at once, the power dynamic has shifted. We both have one another in an indefinite death grip, relentless to let the other gain full control. I stroke him, testing his waters. He nips at my collarbone before sinking his teeth into the flesh of my shoulder, making me cry out in a blend of pain and utter rapture. I envision the thin straps of my green dress, bruised skin exposed on the day of my mother's wedding, and realize I must stop him before he marks me as his.

"Careful, Enzo," I warn. "If you brand me, it will be that much more difficult to feign innocence." I brush my finger over his tip again and find a bead of moisture there, spreading it across the head. One finger now slick, gliding over painfully taut skin. He deepens his bite a moment more before releasing me.

"You wicked little thing," he snarls. "Up."

He spins us into a new position, his cock abruptly absent from my grasp as I face the living room. The indignity of our surroundings is overwhelming, and I fight against him to change positions. I want to look at him and only him, undistracted by my own humiliation. But he has me pinned across his stomach, my ass in his lap, my back to his chest. He's digging into the small of my back, grinding against me in earnest. He brings one hand to my legs and coaxes them open to resume his touch, sliding his other hand back up to my throat. Gentle this time, guiding my chin up.

"Look," he whispers in my ear. Reflected in the glass of the conservatory ceiling, we make a sinful image. Me, spread open, his hands emerging from behind me like some sort of four-armed goddess pleasing herself. His thumb glides in inexorable circles around my clit while two fingers nudge at my entrance, not yet breaching. I buck at the savage sensation setting off lovely alarms within me. He entraps my legs with his, wrapping his calves around my ankles, spreading me wider, the pain of the stretch subdued by the pleasure of his touch.

"Are you watching?" he asks.

I nod.

"Good girl."

I let out a whimper at his words. His praise pulls the heat from me, and I have an insatiable urge to hear him say it again.

Enzo kisses my neck and shoulders, pulling a taut line deep inside me with expert sways of his fingers back and forth across my swollen clit. His hand releases my throat and cups one breast, squeezing and pinching his way around the soft skin. He rolls my nipple as he did before and electricity courses through me in a wild frenzy. My back is so arched, it almost leaves his chest entirely, my body feeding itself to him.

Then, so slowly, he sinks one finger inside, letting each knuckle settle before pushing in deeper. My walls clamp down around his single finger and he hisses in my ear, his voice low, iniquitous, "I can't wait to see you stretch for me."

He hooks his finger to press against the walnut sized spot on my inner wall, and I have the sudden urge to relieve myself. After that first orgasm on his mouth, the pressure reaches an almost uncomfortable degree. His other hand palms my breasts, my waist, my hips, before coming down to join his right. With one hand working a finger in and out of me, his other uses two fingers in a V to massage my pussy. The crook of his fingers hit my clit with every pass. He uses both hands to work and pull and coax another orgasm out of me, and it's working oh so well.

Caution rises in my chest with the need to relieve the ever growing pressure in my abdomen.

"Relax, love," he instructs, his fingers working masterfully around and inside my sex. "I think you can take another." He pushes a second finger into me, and I'm so full, the sensation on the brink of pain but not quite.

My hips move of their own volition, my body demanding more as I ride his fingers. All the while, he's grinding into my ass, his cock a reminder of how much more I have to look forward to.

"Come for me, Mia." His words are like hot wax dripped on rope bound skin. A devilish command.

Sweat beads between my breasts, behind my neck. I ride and writhe on his fingers as the pressure builds and builds. My chest grows hot, my heart pounding as I finally split in two, my orgasm ripping me apart in a convulsion of pulsating muscles. He doesn't stop.

God help me.

His fingers move faster, dragging my orgasm out longer and longer until his touch is electric. Live wires ignite along my skin, contracting the muscles of my stomach, my legs, as another sensation has panic rising.

I have to pee. I am going to pee. I have felt this before, though never this intense and never to completion. I like to think I know my body well enough to know what it is capable of. But here, I'm not so certain. I attempt to clench my thighs together; the pressure increasing in my lower belly, but his grip on my ankles is too strong. He fights me, his fingers unceasing.

"*Enzo,*" I beg. "Not here. You'll make a mess of me."

He kisses along my neck, sending a twitching sensation to the small of my back.

He gives a low capitulating growl and releases my ankles, his touch losing speed as he finally relents but doesn't back off completely. I crane my neck and he finds my lips with his, a soft kiss of gratitude. His two fingers drag in and out of my channel, in no hurry now yet still ever effective. I lift my legs and the pressure subsides.

Indolent strokes bring me back to that rising hill, and I can see my next orgasm on the horizon. He notes my breathing, my body giving away all my secrets as it moves with him. A dance we've been waiting years for. His kisses are long and deep and drugged. Where I came before in wild, bucking, mind-shattering bliss, I am now in a different kind of ecstasy. Where every movement is deliberate as I climb the ladder rung by rung—one small step at a time... until I'm on the very edge.

My hips row against the waves of his touch. Teetering on the brink of here and him. And then, I'm falling. I'm falling and screaming and his mouth is still on me, his tongue tangled with mine. He holds me close as I ride my orgasm out into the depths. My body convulses again as he strokes my thighs, my stomach. Where he was half cruel a few moments earlier, he is now gentle and soft.

I squeeze my eyes shut and the room spins, my head too heavy to lift from Enzo's shoulder. We stay like this, held in the aftermath of my mess with our reflection looking back at us. He moves a damp lock of hair from my neck and kisses the hollow of my shoulder. His quick breath tickles my skin as his lips linger.

My breathing levels as the high from my third orgasm abates. I reach for the hardness digging into my back as I turn to face him and lower myself between his legs.

"Mia," he says, almost panicked.

I unbutton the clasp on his shorts.

His hands are around my wrists before I can set him free. "Not here." There is no playful inflection in his tone.

"Why not?"

He gives an exasperated look. "For the same reason you just stopped me from making you squirt all over this lovely living room. You'll make a mess of me."

Part of me wants to suggest we go upstairs. There's no way we're finished here without him being just as satisfied as he's made me.

"No, I won't." I move to unbutton his shorts again, but his grip is ever tight. I raise up off my heels and brush my lips against his. "Trust me," I whisper. His grip loosens at my words and I don't dare hesitate for fear he'll change his mind.

I work the clasp open and pull the zipper down. He springs free in front of my face and my mouth goes hot, salivating. My initial estimate of his size was conservative. Enzo is large and long and mouthwateringly hard. My pussy flutters at the thought of taking him, feeling him hit the top just to drag back out and do it again. A fullness I can't.

I wrap one hand around him, my long fingers appearing even more slender in comparison. I stroke him once, and again. His lashes flutter open, then closed while his hands grip the sofa's edge. I'm not sure I've ever been so turned on. The sight of this—of *him*—at my whim. The dominance and authority I wield with a simple motion.

Another bead of moisture appears at the small hole on his tip and I lick it away with a flick. He tastes intoxicating. I lay the flat of my tongue at the base of his cock, right above his balls, and drag up slow, slow, slow, until I flick the tip again.

"*Fuck, Mia.*" Enzo's stomach muscles contract, his whole body going rigid. I repeat the motion, moistening him from base to tip with my tongue. His breathing goes short, like he's jogged a mile. On the third stride, I wrap my lips around the tip and suck. His head rolls back, the cords in his throat working. I swirl my tongue along the mushroom head of his cock and watch him twitch in submission.

With the tip of him on my lips, I do my best to relax my throat and brace both hands on his thighs as I swallow him down. He's trying so hard to be silent, to not make a noise. Challenge accepted.

I breathe through my nose and flatten my tongue to suction the inside of my cheeks, churning my tongue at the tip on my way up before taking all of him again. His hips buck underneath me, and I repeat, determined, bobbing my head as I fuck him with my mouth. His quiet attempts dither as he vibrates with a guttural growl deep in his chest. My cheeks burn from the suction and I smirk around his cock as he hits the back of my throat. My body fights me, threatening to gag and end it all now. I relax my shoulders and wiggle my toes as a distraction as I ease him down my throat.

My eyes water, tears streaming down my face, and I glance up to see him watching me with a visage of loathing and lust, half glazed.

He brings one hand toward my cheek and softly brushes away a tear. "I love seeing you like this." I rumble the back of my throat, adding to the sucking sensation. His eyes roll back at the vibration and he chuckles into the open air. "You like this, don't you, *filthy girl*."

I run both hands up his chest in answer and use my nails to drag down his stomach to his thighs.

He grits his teeth, a laugh escaping through a worried throat. "Easy, Mia," he says. A few curls tumble loose from my bun as I work my head up and down his shaft, and he tucks one behind my ear then holds the sides of my head. "Slap my thigh if it's too much," he instructs.

Then, it's him fucking my mouth instead of the other way around. He thrusts up into me slow and deep at first, then fast and hard and thrilling. My heart races, sweat dripping down my back. Fighting the urge to gag, tears cloud my sight as I dig my nails into his thighs, but I don't slap. I want this. I want him. Every drop.

"Fuck, Mia, I'm—*fuck,* wait—," His hands grip my head, in my hair, his head thrown back. Every muscle in his stomach, chest, neck, arms, all contract with the building tension as he's about to release down my throat. Wetness drips between my thighs, a pooling heat. "Mia, I'm gonna—" I moan permission around him. "Are you sure?" he asks. Even on the edge of his release, he asks.

I nod my head and brace my hands on the back of his knees.

He picks up his pace, heat rising in his cock, before my name tumbles from his mouth and he's spilling down my throat. I swallow, keep swallowing, keep swallowing, as his hips cease their violent motion.

One last suck, and I release him, making sure I haven't wasted a single drop. I lick the salt from my top lip, then the bottom, savoring every bit of him. "I told you I wouldn't make a mess," I say.

I want to remember his face at this moment. Regarding me with adoration, brows pinched in wonder, mouth agape. His hands are on my face, wiping the tears and sweat away. "We're in trouble." He pulls me up by the face and kisses me. One long kiss before cradling me in his arms and shaking his head. I'm straddling him now, our bare sexes so close, it's all I can think of. He holds me to his chest. "What the fuck are we going to do now?"

"More," I answer.

He bellows into my hair, our bodies one tangled, sticky mess. I close my eyes and breathe him in, redolent of sex and sweat and each other. I smile against his neck, perfectly content to stay here as long as the earth spins. Our heartbeats find a rhythm, our breath slowing back down to a normal rate, and we remain entangled in one another without words, both speechless, with so many questions we are afraid to learn the answers to.

He's right — we are in trouble. The fact he sees it as clear as I do tells me everything I need to know.

My heart will break by the end of the week.

II

Enzo

Three Days Before the Wedding

Something vibrates against my leg and I fish my phone from my pocket.

"It's a student," I say. Mia climbs off of me but I grab her by the chin, stopping her with a kiss before letting go.

"Someone's hot for teacher?" She gathers her shorts from the floor and shimmies them back on, her plump ass jiggling itself into the garment. I stand and answer the call, kneading the back of my neck. Lily is mid-sentence, determined to have this conversation whether or not I answer the phone. I let her finish and try my best to get a word in.

"Look, Lily, I'm sorry, but I am on vacation. Your dissertation is on my desk, I will have my notes ready for you by next week. The deadline isn't for another month. Please try to refrain from calling me again. Goodbye." I hang up before she argues against my choice to leave the country during one of the most important times of her academic career. Annoyed though I am, I smile. Amused by her tenacity, though still upset that such a clinical obligation interrupted what was one of the greatest experiences of my adult life, I silence my phone and mute Lily's contact for good measure before making a quick call to my TA.

Mia hands me my shirt with a small smile. She's cleaning up our mess, and I've abandoned our moment.

I'm being an ass.

I grab her arm just below the elbow as soon as my TA answers the phone.

"*Hello? Professor Alarcon?*" his tinny voice says on the other end as I give Mia an apologetic look. She tucks my cock back into my shorts and gives my balls a gentle squeeze.

"You'll make it up to me," she whispers. I stand, thunderstruck at the silky confidence in her tone.

Yes, I absolutely will.

I bring the phone up to my ear and ask the junior engineer to draft up a recommendation letter for Lily despite the headache she's continuously provided.

Mia gathers our mugs and takes them to the kitchen. I end the call and pull my shirt back on before following her over to the sink and kiss the back of her neck.

"Stop." The word isn't harsh but stings anyway. "Everyone will be home soon. We should get cleaned up for this afternoon."

"This afternoon?"

"Cyrus really tells you nothing, huh?"

I shrug.

"We're having an outing on his boat."

"My brother has a boat?"

She laughs at the genuine surprise in my voice.

"Yes, he has a boat. Named it after my mother and everything." She dries her hands on the towel hanging off the basin and turns to face me. Her cheeks are flushed, bare legs crossed at the ankles, a mess of dark curls atop her head. The smile on my face widens as I drink in the sight of her post-orgasm loveliness. A satisfaction emanating from the way I regard her. She likes to be looked at, to be admired and called beautiful.

As I rest my hand on her hip, the unambiguous creak of the iron gate followed by Marco's laughter pierce the air. My hand instinctively retreats, and I shift my weight, distancing myself from the woman whose throat I just fucked.

Tiny human footsteps sound across the tiles of the courtyard, followed by the clicks of high heels. Simone trails behind Marco, a scarf around her dark hair and glasses shielding her eyes. Mia licks her lips then wipes her mouth with the back of her hand.

I rush back to the sofa, making sure we have left nothing contentious behind. I trusted Mia not to make a mess and she fulfilled her promise. The sofa is spotless, though a bit disheveled. I straighten the cushions and fluff out the pillows. An otherwise immaculate living room to the ignorant. I glance up to the windows of the glass conservatory ceiling and smirk at the memory of our image.

Marco runs straight for Mia's arms, and she picks him up, holding him in the corner of her elbow. Simone removes her sunglasses and sighs as she enters the kitchen as though she's just gotten off an eighteen-hour shift. "You're a tourist, Enzo, where do you people find the audacity?"

I try not to let her words cut too deep. "Not a tourist," I correct. "But I understand your concern. Some people act rather entitled, whether at home or abroad."

She nods, agreeing with my every word, then continues in a slew of Spanish and French as she recounts a presumptuous group of

American men. They asked why she didn't partake in the nudist activities of others on the beach. She invited them to the speakeasy, saying they could come see her show if they were interested in seeing more of her. Naturally, they assumed she meant an entirely different kind of show. She was rightfully offended.

Simone's words fly faster than her mouth can keep up. At this point, I'm not sure it would matter if anyone were in the room at all. I slip away, reluctantly removing myself from Mia's presence, and leave her at the mercy of her cousin's enraged venting.

Upstairs, I place my phone to charge on the bedside table and quickly send an email confirming my attendance at the next environmental conference. My skin glows with a sheen of sweat, my face and chest flushed. There's a bustle downstairs, a low billow of laughter that must be my brother's. I brush my teeth and wash Mia's sweet scent from my face and beard, jumping in the shower for good measure without bothering to wait for the water to grow warm. After I'm cleaned up, I throw on what I think is an appropriate boating outfit, grab the guitar Cyrus gifted me, and head back downstairs.

Katia looks lovely in a blush pink sundress that compliments her olive skin, distracted by some sort of complicated math problem residing in the fridge. She gathers some contents and dumps them into a basket before noticing me at the bottom of the stairs.

"Ah! Enzo, there you are. You're ready? Where's Mia?" Her frenzied words remind me of Simone's commentary earlier, though not as hostile. She's wearing an enormous hat, not unlike Simone's style. The similarities between the three Cifuentes women go beyond the physical. The curve of their noses, their high cheekbones, the curl in their hair, though Mia's is more coiled than Simone's waves. It's their personalities that stand out in the crowd. Wildly different, though steeped in the same flavors. Where these two women are verbal and present in the way of their dominance, Mia is subtle and clever, almost catlike. Pronounced in the way she moves. Everything is a dance.

I approach Katia and kiss both cheeks. "Mia must be getting ready, though I'm not sure where she is now," I say.

Simone sits on the floor of the living room playing with Marco.

"*Lorencito*," Cyrus says as he ascends the cellar stairs with four bottles of wine. I grab two and place them on the counter.

"Why didn't you tell me you got a boat?" I ask.

Cyrus's brows pinch. "I told you. I didn't tell you? I thought I told you. See, this is why you need to come home. How am I supposed to keep up with what you do and don't know? Life is better here. You can't have a boat in New York."

"No, Cyrus. *You* can't have a boat in New York. Plenty of people have boats."

He waves my words away.

"You know what I mean. Fine, you could *own* a boat there, but you can't *have* it. No time. Always work. No way to live."

My phone buzzes in my pocket—the universe laughing at me.

I let out a defeated sigh. "How can I help?"

Katia hands me the basket full of food and ushers me out to the car. The trunk is small yet wide. Matteo walks up the drive as I finish packing everything in and close the boot. A sleeveless white shirt puts his tattooed arms on full display, and he removes his sunglasses, greeting me with a sneer. "Looks like you're the help today," he says.

"I didn't know you'd be joining us," I say, shielding the sun from my eyes.

"If it's a family event, I wouldn't miss it."

We walk back up the drive and through the courtyard. A ghost of cigarette smoke rises from Mia's balcony. I blink and remember her knelt between my legs, her hands digging into my thighs, the preeminence of her focused stare. I banish the image for now, not wanting to grow hard at such an inopportune moment.

Matteo and I enter through the kitchen doors and ask what else needs to be loaded into the car. "Just us, now," Cyrus says. "Where's Mia?"

"I'll go get her," Simone volunteers.

Matteo kisses Simone on both cheeks as she passes him and takes her place by Marco. My chest tenses with a sense of familial jealousy. This *boy* is more comfortable in this house than I am. He takes his liberties with Simone and Mia, and they either don't mind or don't wish to upset him. Anger and hatred take over logic, but before I can protest, I see him with Marco, gently playing and cooing at my nephew, and I realize he might see me in the same light as I see him. An outsider. He lives here. I don't. We both made our choices, and I'm starting to believe I've made the wrong one.

The universe laughs at me once again as Mia and Simone make their way down the stone steps. Mia is breathtaking in a wine-colored dress that flows just above her knees, her back—of course—exposed. A signature prerequisite in all her outfits and something for which I am quite thankful.

Matteo is on his feet and kissing Mia's cheeks before she makes it down the last step. He whisks her up in an embrace, her feet brushing the ground, puts her down, and gives her a spin. "*Ay dios, Mia.*"

She rolls her eyes and pushes him away with a smirk.

"You didn't spin me. Why didn't you spin me?" Simone says, her arms crossed over her chest.

"You're not wearing that," Matteo says dryly.

During Simone and Matteo's banter, while Cyrus and Katia gather Marco up from the floor and get him ready, Mia is trying her damnedest not to look at me. Her cheeks and neck are flushed as she holds her hand against her shoulder as though she's hiding something.

Oh... The bite.

I want her to remove her hand, to wear my mark proudly. To show Matteo and any other boy who dares to approach her that she requires no one else. She has me, at least for now.

She asks her mother how she can help.

"Of course, you ask now, when everything is done."

Cyrus carries a fussy Marco out toward the courtyard and we all follow as Katia locks up the glass doors and we walk down to the car.

"Enzo, why don't you ride with me?" Matteo offers.

I face our little group. My skin is crawling to be near Mia and far away from Matteo at the same time.

"Sure," I say, meeting Mia's eyes for a moment. She gives a half shrug and my inner voice screams at me in protest, but I follow him, looking for a car. He approaches a Vespa scooter and hands me a pink helmet.

"Here," he says.

I chuckle.

"What?"

"Nothing, nothing," I say, strapping the feminine thing atop my head. "I was expecting a car."

Matteo shakes his head at me. "Have you ridden one before?"

I nod.

"Then you know this is more fun."

I nod again, amused by the absurdity of this day. He swings a leg over the seat as though he's mounting a steed, and I climb on behind him. "Hold on."

I place my hands on his waist and scoot forward, his back touching my chest. If it were anyone else, any other man, I wouldn't mind so much. But because it's him, I feel like I'm being made a fool, as though he's putting me in this uncomfortable position on purpose just for the sake of humiliation. He wants Mia to see me strapped to him in a pink helmet. Little does he know, she doesn't care about such appearances, and nor do I.

As long as I can dance, I have nothing to be embarrassed about when it comes to her.

I wrap my arms around him tighter and slide closer, calling his bluff. He stiffens for a moment and turns to look back at me. "Ready?" I nod and give his stomach one forceful slap. If he wants to act like an ass, I'll treat him like one.

He revs the Vespa's tiny engine and the wind takes us down the Alcúdian coast. I'm grateful for the roaring air as it whips past, no room for conversation.

The sun is high and bright, glittering on the water, and I will never grow tired of this view. The air smells sweet and crisp, the breeze making my eyes water as we ride.

Matteo pulls into a small car park, and Cyrus's convertible follows shortly after.

We dismount the scooter as they all climb out of the car, and Matteo and I help carry everything toward the docks. Simone takes Marco in her arms, putting her sunglasses on him. He holds her around the neck, speaking gibberish as we walk with full arms toward a small yacht. "Here she is!" Cyrus says proudly.

"Cyrus, this isn't a boat," I say. "This is a small floating house."

He nods, teeth flashing in a mischievous grin.

I clap him on the back. "*Felicidades, hermano,*" I say.

He gives my chest two affectionate pats.

We climb onto the deck of the two-story yacht that must be sixty feet long from bow to stern. "Welcome aboard *The Katia,*" Cyrus says.

"You'd think that'd be more flattering, but it's not," Katia says to no one in particular.

Cyrus passes his wife-to-be, kissing her on the cheek before giving me an insistent tour. The interior is pristine, with a living and dining area complete with a television and mini wet bar. The controls are an impressive complication of levers and buttons, the chamber narrowing toward the front where a few steps lead down to a small bedroom, a bathroom, and a storage closet. Out on the deck of the stern, there's a spiral staircase that leads to the second story with an open lounge area. At the top, there's a second steering wheel and a set of controls blocked by a windscreen. Unprompted, Cyrus explains the superior visibility from the second story at night and that he prefers to drive with the wind in his hair and Katia on his lap. She gives him a playful slap on the arm.

We settle into the space before departing, and I help Katia fit the food into the small fridge. Then we open a bottle of wine to let it breathe. Mia is out on the deck with Matteo, and I find myself glancing in their direction now and then, ensuring his hands maintain a respectable distance. Simone emerges from the captain's chamber, where she's put Marco down for a nap. "I've forgotten how disgusting boats make me feel. And we're not even moving yet. I might join him for a siesta later."

I give her a friendly smile and sneak another glance toward the deck.

Matteo's hand is on Mia's shoulder, above the mark I've left. She politely removes him and makes for the spiral staircase toward the top deck. Matteo looks out onto the water, his shoulders slumped. I can't decipher if her politeness is for his benefit or hers. She shouldn't have to be polite. She should demand the space she deserves. Even if it's space away from me.

Simone slips past me and tucks herself under Matteo's arm. He holds her close and rests his cheek to the top of her head. My shoulders relax as my hate for the boy lessens. He is an ass, but he is also young and in need of family.

Cyrus hangs off the edge of the top deck and shouts a warning in Spanish that we should all strap in for takeoff. I climb the spiral staircase to find Mia sitting in the captain's chair. She peers at me over her shoulder, her lips pulled up at the corners. Her hair is down and long, brushing against her postured, freckled back. Cyrus is at the head of the deck, cracking open a few bottles of beer. He hands one to me, then to Mia. We take them and clink necks. "Katia, get up here, *cariño*!" he yells.

Matteo and Simone appear from the top of the stairs. "Katia's watching over Marco during departure. Want me to switch with her?"

"No, no, Simone, come sit, enjoy the ride."

Mia turns the key and the floating tiny-house roars to life. Jets from the back deck heave in a violent roll of foaming water. The boat sways from side to side, and Mia turns the wheel ninety degrees to the right before pulling a lever. We're moving before I recognize the sensation, my legs adjusting to the lack of equilibrium.

"*Mon dieu*, I'm going to be sick," Simone says, holding onto Matteo's arm.

He laughs and rubs her back. "Breathe, *mon cur*."

"Sit down," Mia yells over the sound of the water and wind. "Standing makes it worse."

"You know how to make it out of the marina, yes?" Cyrus asks.

"*Claro*, Cyrus," Mia says with a laugh at the edge of her words. As though Cyrus was asking her if she knew how to walk across the courtyard back home.

My stomach drops as the boat jerks to life, and I steady myself on the railing, trying to take deep breaths through my nose. This is definitely better than flying. Though not entirely.

"Not you too, Enzo," Mia teases. In my periphery, Matteo's smirk tells me he's enjoying the impression of my discomfort.

I take another steadying breath and a sip of beer. "I was born for life at sea."

My brother's guffaw of laughter thwarts my attempt at nonchalance.

"*Mentiroso*," Cyrus says.

I shrug and sit back, focusing on my breathing as I try to rest my face into an expression that resembles comfort. The water is vicious as we exit the marina, and the boat slices through the current, creating its own ripple of waves in its wake. Wind tangles itself through Mia's hair, a look of utter calm on her face. After a moment, Cyrus climbs down the spiral stairs to check on Katia and Marco, leaving her to captain.

"Someone please put a cigarette in my mouth," Simone says with a whine. Matteo fumbles through his pockets and pulls out a crumpled packet of Marlboros and a lighter. Simone lights one and takes a long drag, audibly exhaling with delight. "*Trés bien.*"

Mia raises two fingers in a silent request, and Matteo hands me the crumpled pack. I pop one in my mouth, light it, and take one drag before handing it from my lips to Mia's waiting fingers. I light another and keep it for myself before handing the pack back to Matteo. He takes it with a stiff lip.

It's so easy to push his buttons.

We ride the waves for another ten minutes, heading toward the middle of the sea, the breeze refreshing, the sea spraying us generously. I taste the salt in the air and memories of my childhood with Cyrus flood my mind. Mia brings the boat to a steady rhythm and turns off the engine, letting us bob in the undulating water as she climbs out of the captain's chair and adjusts her dress. The damp fabric clings to her body, revealing two perked tips across her chest. She drags on the cigarette and passes me with a deliberate brush of her hand against my ass.

Simone raises her arm for Mia to help her up, and she does. "Please tell me the wine is ready." They climb down, and I move to follow, but Matteo blocks my path, a cigarette hanging between his lips as music sounds from the speakers built into the boat's side panels. He pats my shoulder and gestures for us to stand by the railing. I play along.

He kneads my shoulder, meaning to inflict pain, and I hide a wince.

"This wedding is not the only one we'll be celebrating, huh?" His words fall flat. "Ana, yes?" Realization dawns across my features and I school myself.

"Right," I say with a smile, giving him nothing more.

He nods, unbelieving. "Where is your Ana? She did not want a free trip to *España*?"

I open my mouth to lie.

"Or does she even know you're here?"

I step back, his hand falling away from my shoulder to rake through his sea damp hair.

"The others may be blind, but I can see when another man has his mark on a woman. Mia is like my sister," he says.

"You kiss your sister? Mark your territory?"

"Do you? Mia's practically your sister by association, soon to be by marriage. I'm no scientist like you, what is the word for your brother's stepdaughter? Step-niece? That seems a bit cumbersome."

"I've never kissed Mia." The lie tastes sour on my tongue.

"Your brother's word, not mine," he says, half under his breath.

I look at him with genuine confusion.

"*Mentiroso.*"

Where once violence would have been my immediate answer, I have now calmed—or so I'd like to believe. I choose to feign ignorance, forming a lighthearted chuckle as I suck on the tip of my cigarette.

"Mia is my family, as she is yours. More, actually, come the end of this week. I understand you wanting to protect her, but I assure you, she is in no *real* harm in my presence," I say.

He postures at my emphasis. "She has a hickey on her shoulder. A bite mark. Something that was not there yesterday."

I shake my head, my mouth twisting into what I hope portrays innocence. "Mia is a grown woman. If she wants to go out and get a love bite, she has every right to."

He shakes his head and turns to face me fully. "Yes, she is a grown woman. She is also young. *My* age." He stabs, twists. "This will only end badly for both of you. Think of Ana. Don't be a stereotype, Enzo."

I laugh. I laugh and laugh and laugh. "That is quite rich, coming from you."

He takes a hurt step back. "What's that supposed to mean?"

I gesture to his frame, his tattooed arms, his libertine fuck-boy outfit, the *hair*. "I'm sorry Matteo, I don't wish to fight, or to insult you," I say, taking another hit. "To be honest, I am thinking of Ana. I'm thinking of all the ways I've failed her and how I intend to better myself as a partner in the future. And I assure you, my mistakes will not be repeated."

He steps back at my words, his posture subsiding.

I pat his shoulder. "Now, let's join the others, yes? *Buena*?"

He nods once, taking me at my word, though I still sense a hint of skepticism. Part of me is glad he's here for Mia while I've been off living a different life. Infinitesimal as it might be.

We join the rest of our little party on the lower deck. Marco is now awake and in Cyrus's arms, his head lying lazily on my brother's shoulder. The speakers bump out some cross between classic French rock and modern hip-hop.

"Turn that trash off, please," Katia says.

Cyrus suggests I play the guitar he's brought on board, and the women hoot in concurrence. My cheeks turn crimson, but I oblige. As I did the first night on the island, I tune each string one by one before stroking all six at once, a soft melodic tune hanging in the misty air. Then I play an old French song.

"*Compagnon disparu!*" Simone bursts in recognition. I nod with a smile.

She sings with the melody, her voice silky in the afternoon breeze. Cyrus puts Marco down and spins Katia into his arms. They sway back and forth with the music. Marco fusses at being put down, and Mia picks him up, avoiding a full-on meltdown.

Matteo offers his hand to Mia, and she takes it. One hand in Matteo's, one around Marco, surrounded by boys who love her. My fingers continue without my having to think about their next move, my muscles remembering the pattern and melody of the song. Simone sings with little effort, and Matteo holds Mia close to him, Marco bouncing on her hip between their swaying bodies. They frame a lovely image, Mia in the arms of a young man, someone her own age, someone not so *close,* as she worded it. She seems comfortable, though still keeping enough distance to remain unconvincing.

The sea breeze ruffles my hair, pulling up skirts and rapping the tarp above against the boat's frame. Simone hits high notes with ease, moving through the music with her tantalizing, soft voice, and I strum my fingers across the final chord, my family applauding and demanding another. I oblige, keeping with my old repertoire.

I tickle the strings, playing the first few bars of "*La Femme de Mon Ami.*" Simone falls into the flow of the song as if we've spent weeks rehearsing as she finds the proper octave and cadence to match my melody. She is no amateur, her vibrato hitting in the best possible places. She sings with closed eyes, the music moving her body as the waves move *The Katia.* Matteo sways back and forth, Mia holding Marco's tiny hand in her small one as they dance.

A gnawing feeling hits my chest, a sharp, pulling pain straight down my center. A pain I can only describe as heartache. I see Mia spread out in front of me, her muscular legs wrapped around my shoulders as I torture her with my tongue. The other-worldly delight it brought as she writhed at my mercy. What started as a dance, a game, an intrigue of lust, has grown too close to the sun. And now I'm burning.

Matteo's words repeat in my mind, my promise of loyalty. No one is hurt yet. No one but myself, as this pain seeps through my veins. Mia's body moves to my music, and a pang of alarm hits me. Memories of the first night I confessed my love to Ana flood back, bringing with them the nervousness that came with such vulnerability, the possibility of rejection, of never hearing those words returned by the one person you long to hear them from the most. That night, she did say it back. Yet I couldn't shake the feeling that habit, not genuine intent, motivated her words. At first, I was an exciting retreat from her real life. But once I became part of her routine, I faded into the background, losing the allure of the chase. We never danced.

Telling Ana I loved her was the beginning of our downfall. Her reaction a red flag I should have recognized then.

Simone and I finish our song, everyone in a fit of sweat and smiles. My fingers tremble as I stand and place the guitar on the cushioned bench, wiping the sweat from my palms across my trousers. Preoccupied, the others don't seem to notice as I slip back into the cabin toward the captain's quarters. Inside, a king-sized bed touches the walls on both sides. I sit at the edge and hang my head between my knees, taking a few more deep breaths, trying to steady my racing heart. Panic on the horizon, I close my eyes and see Mia's face. Her gorgeous, soft face, laced with hatred, with confusion, with *love*.

I stand, my body a shell too small for its matter. This morning, a deadline seemed like the perfect excuse to go forward with our appetites. Even though I knew this sort of realization would be inevitable, though I didn't realize it would be so soon. Only a few scant hours too soon. I laugh, a strangled sound escaping my throat at the audacity of my naivety.

I don't hear the knock at the door or the narrow wood creak open. There are hands on my back. Small hands with long fingers and short nails. I turn and see Mia's face. The one I see every time I close my eyes. Her brows pinch in worry, and I know I want to see all of her faces. Every possible expression she can make, I want to witness the beauty in every single one.

We kiss, and she greets me with equal measure. The deep red of her dress clings to her chest, and I hold her close. She's warm underneath damp clothes, her breasts pushed up against me. My hands grope and grab and knead until they find her pliant ass. The feeling is as exquisite as I remember, holding her in my palms as I devoured the most intimate parts of her. She tastes like the ocean and sweet smoke. I break away, our chests heaving. There's molten honey in her gaze.

Something moves from the corner of my eye and we both whip our heads to see Simone standing in the open doorway. She rushes out of view, and Mia looks up at me in alarm, her swollen lips agape. I let her go, and all at once, I'm alone in a small room that grows smaller and smaller.

12

<u>Mia</u>

Three Days Before the Wedding

I catch Simone's wrist, and she spins on me in a rage. "*C'est quoi ce bordel*, Mia," she seethes between her teeth. "What are you doing?"

I hold her shoulders and shush her as best I can. "*Rien*. It was nothing."

"That didn't look like nothing. That looked like a very passionate something. Something you should not have with *him* of all men," she whisper-yells.

I run my hands down her arms in an attempt to calm her. The judgment in her tone pierces right through me, and I grow hot with the need to defend myself. "It's only until after the wedding. When he leaves for New York."

She shakes her head in disbelief.

"It's just sex," I say with high shoulders.

"No. No, Mia. *Petit cousine*. This is *wrong*. And that was not 'just sex.' I've seen you do 'just sex' with men who you wouldn't bring home. That kiss was different. That was *passionné*."

I shake my head, doubt bubbling up my throat. "Please, either way, just say nothing. Don't make this a big thing. *Je t'en supplie,* Simone, I'm begging you."

Simone's gaze flits behind me, and I hear Enzo close the bedroom door. She gives him a shrewd look. "Why? Why not celebrate your incestuous endeavors," she spits.

Enzo's chest hovers behind me, his hands on my shoulders. "It's not like that, and you know it," he says.

"I know nothing, apparently." She turns to leave, and I squeeze her arm, forcing her attention again. "I won't say anything. For *Tante Katia's* sake. I promise."

My ears grow hot, anticipating her sentencing words.

"But you two cannot do this. He's old, Mia."

"Hey," Enzo responds in a hurt voice.

This makes all three of us laugh. My cousin pulls me into a hug. She strokes the top of my head, the action not unlike my mother's.

"I'll explain later, I promise," I say.

"No need. I think I get it," she says, letting me go. She looks behind me and eyes Enzo up and down before joining the others out on the deck.

Enzo leans in from behind and whispers in my ear, "Did Simone just check me out?"

"I can't tell. I'm still in shock."

His hands tremble at my waist, and we stand for a moment, my back not yet touching his chest. His heat radiates on my bare skin, and I fight the urge to melt into his hold, giving his hands a tentative squeeze before they fall to his sides and we both head through the sliding door. I'm not sure what caused him to run away, but there is no time now to unpack whatever it is he's going through.

"*Qué sucedió*?" Cyrus asks. The silence is incriminating.

Simone leans against the railing of the deck, giving me a critical look. I slowly shake my head at her when she opens her mouth to speak.

"Ana left me." The words come from behind me. Enzo brushes past and plops down dramatically on one of the deck's lounge chairs, his head in his hands. "That's why she didn't come."

Cyrus's face is a picture of pity for his baby brother. He shakes his head. "I told you, *Lorencito*, I told you not to uproot your whole life. There are plenty of universities here."

"I uprooted nothing. I chased a life, a career."

Cyrus throws his hands up in the air. "So easily influenced. *Career.* Who ever told you to become an engineer, huh? And why didn't you tell me about this breakup? I could have been there for you."

"Because you would have told me to come home." Enzo's voice raises half an octave.

Cyrus nods exaggeratedly, his hands wide, gesturing it was an obvious statement.

"And I was trying to avoid this, what's happening now. This week isn't about me. It's about you and Katia. So, please, brother, let it go. I'm fine. I just got..." Enzo runs a hand through his hair. "Overwhelmed, for a moment. I'm fine. Please." His words are so convincing I half believe them to be sincere. If he were indeed heartbroken over another woman, how can he look at me the way he does, kiss me the way he does?

Flooded by doubt, my nose stings.

Matteo shakes his head and mutters under his breath, "*Mentiroso.*"

Cyrus sits by his brother and hugs him. Their frames are so similar, though Cyrus has settled more into a bread-and-wine body type.

"I cannot say this is a surprise," Cyrus says. "She was, how you say, *mousy*?"

Enzo's eyebrows raise.

"Yes, yes, you know, not adventurous, diffident? Not for you," Cyrus explains.

"Cy," Enzo groans, "don't be unkind."

"You need a good Spanish girl," my mother interjects.

"Or French," Simone says with a pointed look at me.

"Or both," I say, countering her goad with a challenge.

This makes Matteo scoff. "Are we done with the pity circle? I'll grab the food." He crosses the deck back into the cabin, and my mother follows to help.

Cyrus leans back in his seat and squints up into the sky. "Do you remember why you learned to play the guitar?"

"A girl," Enzo says as I sit across from them, intrigued.

"Not just a girl. A girl Mama did not approve of. And by association, she did not approve of your music, either."

Enzo nods, seeming to recall the far away memory.

"You have always been reckless with women. Always running after the wrong ones, despite your best interest."

Enzo's gaze flits up to meet mine. "I can't help it."

A swift breeze mists my back, and a shiver runs down my spine.

Cyrus continues to lecture his brother, trying to convince him to stay after the wedding, to move back to his home country. Matteo and my mother approach with trays of expertly cut fruit. They place the trays on the table between the lounge chairs and we all dig in. Watermelon, grapes, apples, pears, an eclectic spread of cheeses and bread sliced into small cubes. Matteo runs back inside and grabs wine glasses, then pours a generous amount into each glass and passes them around. We raise our glasses and toast to the soon-to-be-married couple. Marco claps his tiny hands and squeals in approval as they kiss.

We eat, we drink, we smoke. The sun grows heavy in the sky as it brushes against the horizon, dipping its toe into the sea. The clear turquoise turns a deep blue and glitters on the surface, the salty air chilling as the evening drags on, and I head into the small storage closet to look for an abandoned coat. I find a thick, cream cashmere sweater and wrap it around my shoulders. The soft fabric is heavenly against my cold skin and smells of dust and a faint hint of lilies.

Back on the deck, I climb the side of the railing to shimmy myself toward the front of the boat, everyone gathered to watch the sunset. The bow is flat with a large cushion in the middle surrounded by a protective railing. The boat's nose tilts up to display the flag of Portofino flapping proudly atop a long pole. Cyrus has my mother trapped between his arms under the flag, a picture I wish I could frame and remind myself that such love is possible. Even after a lifetime of disappointment.

I wrap the soft cashmere around myself and gaze out toward the vastness of the water.

"Where'd you get that?" Enzo startles me after such a long stretch of silence.

"The storage closet below deck."

"It's my mother's," he says with such confusion.

I examine the fabric, worn at the edges but still in wearable condition.

"Should I—" I shrug the fabric off, but he protests, placing it back over my shoulders.

"No, no. It's cold. You should wear it, it's just, I never expected to see that sweater again." Heads turn at the slight commotion we've caused. "There's a hole just here." He touches a finger to the back of my neck and pulls the fabric to the side for me to see. "I hung it on a hook rather than a hanger. She was terribly upset."

"She was more than upset, eh? She yelled at me for letting you around her things," Cyrus says. "But that was my job, to protect you, even from her."

"I needed little protection. She wasn't cruel, she was..." Enzo searches the water for words, "particular."

Cyrus waves a hand at his brother, dismissing his words of defense.

Enzo drops his voice for my ears alone and says, "It looks better on you, anyway."

I curl into the warm fabric and wonder what the woman who last wore this was like. What she would say if she saw me wearing it now. The garment is suddenly heavier with the weight of the past, and I itch to remove it, but the bite of the air is too crisp. Enzo rubs my arms to warm them.

The sun takes a final bow on the horizon, the shimmering water now dulled and the breeze properly chilled. Matteo climbs around the side rail with a bottle of champagne and a handful of flutes, passing them around, and we toast to the tangled couple perched on the tip of the boat.

Marco is fighting to hang off the edge of the port, but Simone holds him by the waist, finishing her drink with a long sigh. "Take us home, Mia. We have a show to put on and a monkey to put to bed."

Marco shrieks around Simone's tickling fingers, "No bed!" His laugh a pulling cry of innocence and wonder.

I down the rest of my flute and shimmy through the port side, the rest following, knowing the bow is about to be drenched in sea water. I climb through the cabin, into the captain's seat, and start up the engine. The roar vibrates the floor, water boiling from the back deck, and I tell everyone to find their seats and stay put before running *The Katia* back down the coast toward our dock. The ride back is harsher than before, the waves now gaining height as the moon rises in the sky. I maneuver around them, taking some in stride as we ride for home.

The cashmere slides down my shoulders, the cabin providing a much needed respite from the cold. Enzo comes through the sliding door and joins me in the passenger seat. The rest are still outside, either on the top or back deck. The cabin is the worst place to be for those without sea legs, but Enzo doesn't seem as bothered as before. He makes himself comfortable beside me and we share a pleasant silence, the hum of the boat our only company. He presses a knee against my thigh and leans his head back with closed eyes. I place my hand on his point of contact and squeeze lightly. His eyes crease but remain closed.

We stay like this for the rest of the way home. Enjoying the fraction of a touch between our legs and yearning for so much more.

"Simone, why don't you ride with me? We'll go straight to the club and get things ready while they take Marco home," Matteo suggests once we arrive at port.

"Marco can come with." Simone has my little brother on her shoulders. "He slept enough on the boat. You'll be good, eh, *Marcito*?" She bounces him twice and he giggles a half-gibberish "*sì*." The two look to my mother for permission.

"How can I say no to the both of you?"

Simone gives an exaggerated gasp, pulling Marco off her shoulders to stand on his own. He does, running circles around all of us in the dock's car park.

"Well, ride with me anyway," Matteo says.

She complies, strapping on his spare pink helmet and mounting the scooter behind him. They wave and agree to meet us at the club.

The rest of us climb into the convertible, Marco sitting between Enzo and I as a well-placed barrier. My dress has dried, the fabric no longer clinging to my skin, the night air warming as we drive away from the water. I left the cashmere sweater on board *The Katia* for fear of removing the sacred garment from its resting place.

The rocking car relaxes my muscles as I savor this moment of peace. Marco lays his tiny legs across my lap, and I hold them, warming him with my touch. I keep my eyes closed, breathing in the crisp air as it whips past, leaving my hair in a tangled, salty mess.

I dream of the bath I'll run when we get home and groan internally at the delayed gratification. Enzo would hear the water running as I take my time getting the temperature exactly right, sprinkling salts and gel into the tub. Would he join me? Would we continue what we started this morning, or was that all we'd allow ourselves? If his behavior on the boat was any indication of his resignation, I'm not sure how we could share the same space going forward. I wonder if the kiss in the cabin was a goodbye or a glimpse of what's to come.

Simone finding out changes nothing of our agreement. While she promised to keep our secret, I have reservations about the extent to which she'd uphold it if questioned. Would I even want her to lie? Do I want to hide this so well?

Matteo has his suspicions, though I've always known as much. From that first dance, if he remembers Enzo or not, he's always tried to scare men away from me. Guarding me like a prized toy. He is the annoyingly flirty guardian I never asked for. Never needed, always meddling and insinuating himself into my life.

If he does it out of wanting me for himself or not, I've never been sure. He's never given that possibility an honest chance, not that I'd entertain the idea if presented. Though there was a time I saw myself with him. His charm and devotion near blinding. Then, he reverts to his barbaric nature, acting as he did on the beach yesterday, and I am slapped in the face with the realization that his affection for Simone and I and this entire family has been based on loneliness. He needs somewhere to belong, and I know it's not with me.

We turn into the speakeasy's car park and take our reserved spot. Applause spills from the cracked door, and the bouncer lets us through with a nod and a fist bump to Marco. If he belonged to anyone else, our entire party would be turned away.

We descend the stairs to the underground space. Red velvet curtains lace the walls, allowing the music to hang in the air without echo. Muted conversations trace from booth to booth, giving patrons a sense of public privacy. Our servers and dancers make their rounds while the band plays on stage. Matteo is already behind the bar, teaching the other bartenders how to charm themselves into earning extra tips. Tourists and regulars mingle on the dance floor and among the seating areas, while private lounges host intimate parties, blocked off by sheer curtains pulled back in invitation. Cyrus and my mother take Marco and claim an empty lounge, leaving the curtain open to watch the night. The room is warm and humid, charged with the expectation of excitement and romance shared among the clientèle.

Enzo takes my hand in the dark and brushes his lips against my ear. "This is where we met," he reminds me with a whisper. Champagne lingers on his breath, and I crave one more sip.

I squeeze his hand in mine and extend my neck in mock encouragement. "Dance with me, Enzo," I say.

He looks around to the bar, the private lounge, and up toward the stage where Simone stands in the wings, directing things behind the scenes.

"Here, now?" he asks.

"Here. Now."

"I thought you preferred dancing with strangers?" He places a hand on my waist, keeping me at arm's length as he guides my steps toward the dance floor.

I lay an arm around his neck and he brushes my forearm with a light kiss. We melt into the crowd, seen and unseen among the familiar and unfamiliar. His hands are on me again, and the memory of this morning floats on calm waters in my mind. His fingertips on my thighs, his lips against my knees as he pushed them apart with delicious slowness.

We dance, reserved, leashing ourselves at the possibility of being noticed. I want to run my fingers down his chest, across his back. I want to feel him tremble beneath me as I felt this morning as he touched the back of my throat. But I keep my hands where they are. One across his shoulder, my fingers playing with the curled hair on the nape of his neck, the other in his hand as he steers us through the music. His vast hand on my waist is warm and safe. His touch does not linger too high or too low. Our bodies leave enough space between them for prying eyes to make little assumption.

It's maddening being this close and not within the other. He spins me one way and back, the wind of our twirl springing vivid ocean scents. He leans his temple against mine, and in need of a distraction, I ask him, "Why did she leave you?"

We sway in silence, our hands and temples the only points of contact.

"I think you know why."

"I can't imagine."

His grip tightens around my fingers just on this side of too tight. "I don't want to talk about her." His tone is low, a warning.

Part of me wants to push, to know why a woman like her would leave a man like him. I open my mouth several times just to close it again, the question escaping me every time.

"It was me. That's all you need to know," he says.

"Did you cheat?"

"I told her about our dance, if that's what you mean."

"But she forgave you."

"Drop it, Mia."

Obey. Defy. The two battle in my mind.

"She didn't just leave. She ran. And she was right to." He leans in to brush his lower lip against the shell of my ear. "I'm having enough trouble as it is having you this close without being inside you." His words ignite, my skin too hot. "I don't want to think of another woman right now."

I want to believe him, but there's a small voice in the back of my mind whispering, *nice save.* His warning doesn't go unnoticed. What could he have done to make her run? Why didn't he chase after her?

I will not run so easily. And if I do, it will be for the thrill of the hunt.

"You wish to continue this, then?" I ask.

"Have you changed your mind?" His breath tickles the small hairs around my neck.

I don't answer. His steps dither at my silence.

I dip my head into his neck and glide my tongue from collarbone to jaw line. He tastes like salted air and citrus. "What do you think?"

His fingers span the width of my lower back, digging into my waist as he fights the urge to crush my body to his.

He growls my name into my ear. An oath. "Don't," he says.

I flick his lobe with the tip of my tongue.

"*Wicked little thing.*" His hand skates up my spine to cup the back of my neck as he pulls me away, his grip irrefutable. "You want me to break?" He holds me steady, his thumb pressing against the soft flesh beneath my ear. The rest of our bodies move at the mercy of the music.

"Hurt me," I say with a sigh.

He blinks, a line creasing the space between his brows.

"I won't run." I bring one leg between his and swish my hips to the beat of the drums. A simple step that could alter the trajectory of the dance.

He pushes me away into a spin, holding my weight on the down-stroke.

"Unless you want me to," I breathe. "You want me to run? Knowing you'll catch me?"

He twists my wrist into another spin, and I follow his lead, my hair whipping past as the crowd circles my vision. Enzo comes back into focus, pulling my body flush to his.

His chin dips, studying my face. "You want me to chase you." It's not a question, but a discovery. He chuckles, his breath blowing damp hair away from my face. "Run, Mia, run."

I blink at the tonal shift in his voice.

His shoulders shake with a hearty laugh. Fear peaks, ever curious in the back of my mind. "If you're a good girl, I'll chase you for as long as it takes. I'll run after you all across this island until you're begging me to stay."

I scoff at the racing certainty of his words. "We'll see who begs."

As long as no one knows.

The thought stings. The harshness in its truth. Simone will keep our secret, I'm sure of it. I've kept plenty of hers, though none as malignant as this.

As though summoning her with my thoughts, the music ceases and my cousin takes the stage, thanking the band. She can't see us from her vantage point. I know this from being blinded by the stage lights while watching countless rehearsals.

Simone thanks the crowd and announces her next performance date before retiring the band. Drinks will continue to be served; the bar will remain open until the small hours of the morning. She saunters off stage with lively applause. My mother and Cyrus remain behind the sheer curtain, laid back in the same roped-off lounge, their gazes on each other, Marco sipping on an elaborate fruity drink between them. A quiet celebration.

My shoulders relax in a moment of relief. We didn't get caught. But what a thrill, nonetheless.

The heat of eyes on the back of my head has me turning to see Matteo looking straight at us. His chin tilts up in prejudice. In truth, I care least about his perception. I'd even relish in the fun it would be to see him squirm at my refusal.

I cup Enzo behind the neck and lower his face to mine. My eyes trained on Matteo, I kiss him. Matteo's mouth opens in disbelief. I'm confirming every one of his suspicions over the past few days. Little does he know, we've been playing this game for far longer. A brief moment of hesitation sways into submission as I slip my tongue between Enzo's lips and taste the need he holds. My gaze breaks, lashes fluttering closed in pure enjoyment. Enzo seems to find himself, pushing me away at the waist.

"What are you doing?" He looks around and finds Matteo's stiff jaw.

"Let's go home. I need a bath." I grab Enzo's hand in mine and lead us both off the dance floor.

13

ENZO

N egative associations had long tainted my memory of my mother's sweater until tonight. Until I saw Mia wearing it. How can the same sweater, with its timeless elegance, convey such disparate meanings when draped over different shoulders? Mia brings new meaning to things I've marked as lost. She confuses and captivates me at once. And, though I'm loath to admit it—I'm scared.

"Enzo," Mia calls from our shared washroom.

I'm on my feet, following her voice without question. Smoke and steam waft from under the cracked door, beckoning me closer. The door creaks open to reveal Mia soaking in the tub, a discarded book and empty wineglass on the floor. A cigarette sits between two of her fingers. She extends a foot toward me, and I reach out to take it. I can't think when she's near. I can't seem to do anything but reach out to touch and taste.

Her skin is wet and slick, and I sit on the edge of the tub, rubbing my thumb into the arch of her foot. A twitch at first, then she settles into my touch with a low groan of satisfaction.

"Sleep with me tonight," she says, switching feet.

I press a knuckle into her other foot, gliding a hand up her calf to hold her steady from behind the knee. She sinks deeper into the water, bubbles shifting to expose a glimpse of pink.

"Are you sure?" I ask.

Mia removes her legs from my touch and stands, soap and suds cascading down her body. She extends a hand toward her towel and I oblige, taking it from the hook and handing it to her.

"Please."

It's all she will ever need to say.

I follow her back into her room and strip the clean clothes from my freshly showered self.

Mia dries off and hangs her towel on the back of her vanity chair. She shakes out her curls with the tips of her fingers and gathers them within a silk scarf on top of her head. She extends a hand toward me, and I take it as she leads us toward her bed.

The room is dark, the air is thick, and her scent is strong. I lay my head on her pillow, the smell of her coconut shampoo filling my lungs. Her back is almost too hot to touch from the bath as it presses against my chest, scooting herself closer, forming her body to mine. My hardness sits above the curve of her ass, no doubt digging into her, though she doesn't seem to mind. She grabs my hand and folds her fingers between mine as she pulls me in. My palm rests between the valley of her breasts, moving with the rise and fall of her breathing. Our legs naturally entwine, and I finally let myself relax into the position.

I brush my lips across the freckle on her ear. "Goodnight, Mia."

She mutters between even breaths before sleep takes us both.

I wake to an empty bed. Cramps and spasms caused a night of intermittent sleep. A note sits waiting on the pillow by my head. The handwriting is feminine and fluid. The letters crowd one another as though the sentence is one long word.

Gone to work. Didn't want to wake you.

The ache from gaining sea legs yesterday caused muscles I didn't know I had to pull and cry as I crawl myself out of Mia's bed and wash the sleep from my face. I get dressed in my room and find three missed calls, four texts, and a voice message from Ana. Guilt and panic cloud my next move. Though I know I have nothing to feel remorseful about. Right?

I scroll through the missed texts.

Are you available for a call?

I know it's late, but this is urgent.

Enzo.

Please call me when you get this.

Her businesslike candor is reminiscent of her straightforward nature, leaving me annoyed at her disregard for the time difference. She knew months ahead I would be here for my brother's wedding. I even invited her after our separation, hoping to extend the inevitability of our failed relationship. Deceiving myself has always been a skill few would find practical. What's more, it would have allowed me an excuse to remain within proper company, not wiping tears off the face of another woman as she swallowed me down.

I love seeing you like this.

I run a hand through my hair, remembering my filthy words. Words I wish to say again, in many contexts. I loved seeing Mia in my arms last night. The fullness in my chest as I held her in sleep. In truth, I love seeing her in a variety of ways. In every way, really. I could simplify the statement further, but I won't explore that idea now.

I ignore the messages and missed calls and delete the unheard message from Ana. We said everything that needed to be said months ago. The rest should remain as is — an ocean away.

My thighs whine with every step down the stairs and into the busy kitchen, where rich scents of coffee and toast rumble my stomach in greeting. Cyrus and Katia say their good mornings and give me a rundown of the day. Cyrus apologizes for not disclosing any form of itinerary for the week and thanks me for my ability to flow with the nature of his lifestyle. I've always been a dinghy in his waters, idly riding the waves of his life without a single grievance. Was his influence in my decision to leave Spain due to a lack of my presence in his life or a lack of him in mine? Either way, I've missed him. And I know he's missed me.

We drink our coffee and eat our toast. Simple food that tastes heavenly in the morning sunlight. Marco is bathed and dressed, asking for his older sister. Katia soothes him, explaining how we will see her soon when we visit the groves.

I run upstairs and change while the car is packed. The ride to Cifuentes Olive Grove is shorter than one song, the length of a pleasant walk. We turn onto a dirt road, and Cyrus parks close to a side entrance marked for employees.

The air is humid, the smell of greenery and life potent as rows upon rows of trees sway in the summer breeze. We enter the building with a welcoming blow of a nearby ceiling fan. A receptionist nods at our arrival and waves a familiar hello, then we climb a set of stone steps that lead to a vast room full of free-standing desks. Employees in light summer clothes sit at their open laptops. Boisterous voices discuss a football match that was allegedly rigged. The men and women nod and smile in our direction as we pass before resuming their prominent deliberations.

Open windows flow along the far wall, framing a parade of trees in full majestic rows. The vastness of their presence is breathtaking. Profound. My chest swells with pride for Katia, for what she's built and maintained. The trees mirroring the endeavor she's so far lived.

Three ceiling fans spin at full speed across the long room, causing a delightful current. We walk across the length of the room toward a set of double doors.

I hear Mia before I see her. Her bright voice is commanding and sure. She speaks in a language I haven't heard in ages. "*Molto bene, rinnoveró il tuo ordine.*"

She speaks in crisp, melodic Italian. Curls fall across her face as her attention shifts, and I have to will my legs to maintain their cadence. Her usual summer clothes are missing, replaced by a sleeveless white blouse tucked into black pleated trousers. No flowing maxi skirt, no crop top to tease at her midriff, no open back. She smiles at her family and looks at me for one vivid moment before her gaze falls back to the notepad in front of her. She scribbles a number down and shows it to her mother. Katia nods approvingly.

Cyrus and I sit on a long leather sofa across from Mia's desk, and Katia hovers over her shoulder as she continues the conversation with an Italian restaurant on the mainland. She ends the call and kisses her mother on both cheeks. "I have a few more calls to make, don't wait for me," she says.

"Have you renewed the *Café de Flore* account yet?" Katia asks.

"Yes. This morning."

"*Bueno*. And our meeting?"

"Expected any minute."

Brilliant, beautiful. The phone rings again, and she answers, "Mia Cifuentes."

I look over at my brother, who is wearing a face I seldom saw growing up. One I am happy to know now frequents his features. It resembles that of contentedness, happiness, and love. We sit, admiring the women in the room.

Cyrus gives my knee a quick pat as he stands. "*Vamos.*"

The muscles in my legs protest as I join him. I give Mia a backward glance before exiting the opposite side of the office. She doesn't see me, as she's wrapped up in another call. This time in French.

We head down a set of private stairs that lead straight outside. The sun stings my eyes, and I bring a hand up to shield them from the intrusive light. Cicadas chirp all around, singing their mid-morning tune. If I flex my ears enough, I can hear the ocean under them, a steady hello and goodbye along the shore. Cyrus and I walk around the building, and the first row of trees comes into view beyond a short wooden gate. There's a distinct scent of horses nearby, but I see none.

Our shoes crunch the loose dirt and gravel underneath, Cyrus unhooks the flimsy gate, and we walk through, the trees swaying at their tips, branches rocking in their suspended perches. The leaves are more yellow and orange this time of year, with some green toward the root of each branch. Vines crawl up their trunks in intricate patterns, binding them to the spot. Undertones of grass and olives hit my nose in a delightful breeze, and I breathe in deep, my lungs expanding my chest.

We walk down the first row of trees, each neatly ordered in a straight line, disappearing behind a hill. They seem to go on forever from this angle. The rows spread out enough for two cars to drive through. Even American cars.

The canopy provides a lovely expanse of shade, with light only breaking through as we pass from uniform row to uniform row. A tractor drives by on the far side of the gate, and the driver waves to Cyrus, he waves back, then his phone blares in his pocket and he apologizes before looking at the screen with a twisted face and answering. He excuses himself as I continue my walk, sweat beading at the nape of my neck, sliding down between my shoulder blades. The humidity reminds me of being a boy, running through thick, unkempt fields chasing a ball while other boys chased me. I smile at the hint of nostalgia and wipe the moisture from my upper lip.

Footsteps sound from behind me and I turn to see my brother studying his phone in confusion.

"Something wrong?" I ask.

He opens his mouth to answer.

"Good, you're here." Katia approaches behind him wearing the same large sun hat as before. Mia is in deep conversation with a man by her side. He wears a pale blue suit, his blond beard and hair disheveled in an effortlessly charming way. He smiles down at Mia with large white teeth and brushes a lock of curls away from her shoulder. I stop myself from stepping forward.

"*Cariño*, this is Luke, our Parisian liaison," Katia says.

My heart hardens in my chest at the name. It can't be the same Luke, can it? Based on her story, his age doesn't line up. He's far too old. Though, if I'm any example of Mia's type when it comes to men, it wouldn't be much of a surprise. I try to calm my racing heart with reason. Mia wouldn't be so cruel as to have me meet the man she told me about yesterday morning. Not after everything. Would she?

Katia introduces Cyrus, and they shake hands before exchanging kisses across both cheeks. Mia's smile is small and polite, her hands coolly tucked into her trouser pockets. Katia introduces me as well, and we exchange the same welcoming gestures.

"Luke," I say, "you're a chef in Paris?"

Luke gives a bashful laugh.

"Oh, he wishes," Katia answers for him.

"Just a connoisseur of French cuisine. The oil made here sets the stage for the best courses you'll ever taste, *vraiment.*" His accent is thick, the words rounding around themselves before making their way out.

I smile at his overindulgent compliment and wipe the drops of sweat collecting at the back of my neck.

Luke continues, "My company has sent me to take a tour of the grounds, get an idea of how our largest vendor operates."

Mia places a hand on his arm and guides him toward the gate. "The best way to see everything is on horseback, if you're up for it. Two hundred acres is far more than you could possibly see on foot in one afternoon. The stables are this way."

They walk with a sense of familiarity. With the four coupled up in front of me, I follow behind, feeling like an outcast child once again.

We walk through the gate toward the stables, and the smell of hay and manure becomes more prevalent. An older gentleman in coveralls and tall boots prepares the horses, and we all take turns mounting them one by one. I hesitate for half a breath before securing my left foot into the stirrup and swinging my right over the horse's rump and into place. A decade old muscle memory takes over as my hips and knees carry my weight over the horse's back.

We ride at a polite trot for some time, making our way over hills and through the wide expanse of pristine trees. Mia's black horse is massive, leading the way on muscular legs. I can see why she chose such a horse for herself.

Luke's stance and balance suggest he may have ridden before, though he perhaps does not know full well how to control the beast. He will likely find bruises in uncomfortable places come morning. His elbows protrude out at odd angles as he tries to keep his balance, his knees splayed to allow the mare to steer herself if not prompted.

Katia and Cyrus appear natural upon their own individual steeds. Their strides are close enough to reach out and touch one another while keeping their knees at a safe distance.

I ride in silence behind everyone, allowing my family to impress their client. He might be comfortable enough on two legs to look at Mia as he did, to touch her hair in a way that makes my skin crawl, but seeing him on his gray mare, the confidence lost in his face as his suit fades in the morning light, I'm unbothered.

The sun travels higher in the sky, and we've made a considerable circle around the land. We come to where the rows of trees end and turn back again. The wooden gate meets a large plot of grass that hosts a neighboring dairy farm, and we wave at the cows as they pass, chewing and chewing.

In our turn about the property, I've found myself in the middle of our brigade rather than behind it. I trot behind Mia and Luke, unintentionally hearing their conversation but thankful for it, nonetheless.

"It's a shame only this island gets to see your talents, Mia. You should be in France again, a force amongst the culinary jungle. Won't you consider?"

Mia's legs flex through her thin trousers as we climb back up yet another hill. She turns her head and smiles at Luke, unequivocally meeting his stare. "Though I am flattered by your offer, Luke, I am quite happy on this island. It is my home. I left Paris a long time ago. There is nothing there for me now."

"And what is here that is keeping you? Your mother is getting married, you've graduated. These excuses will not work on me a second time. You're bright and young and beautiful. You should be in a city that sees you."

She doesn't answer. Her smile teeters at the edges, as if considering his words. *She can't be.*

"Tell me you'll think about it, *mon cher.*"

I grimace at the phrase of endearment he so comfortably uses.

"*Je vais y réfléchir,*" she says in perfect French.

I kick myself for not knowing enough to understand her response. They resume a more lighthearted conversation, Cyrus putting on his booming salesman voice at full charm. We approach the stables and dismount, returning the horses one by one to the waiting worker. I brush the dirt from my trousers and pat the dust off my shirt, then we take turns washing our hands in a freestanding basin by the stables. The water is crisp and refreshing, a much needed luxury after the sensation of horse beneath my hands.

"Shall we return to the office for an espresso? We can sign everything afterward," Katia suggests.

Luke follows, slapping the lapels of his suit jacket. Mia falls behind, trailing beside me.

"I'll be up in a moment. I haven't had a smoke since yesterday."

"I'll join you," I say, trying not to sound too eager.

To my surprise, Luke produces an unopened pack of Camels from the inside pocket of his suit jacket along with a flag of matches. He hands them to Mia and winks, running a knuckle down her bare arm before joining Cyrus and Katia.

When they're out of earshot, I take my place beside Mia and open my palm, requesting the pack. She hands it to me and I unwrap the plastic, popping open the top and working two sticks out. I light both in my mouth and hand her one.

"What the fuck was that?" I ask.

She rolls her eyes. "That was business. Nothing more."

"The only thing businesslike about that man was his suit."

She scoffs, taking a long drag from the unfiltered tip and grimaces. "These are terrible."

I nod and walk back toward the wooden gate. She follows.

We walk in silence, breathing in the distant scent of the ocean with the present scent of nicotine.

"Will you consider his offer?" I ask.

"You were listening?"

I shrug my shoulders as if to say *por supuesto, of course.*

She sighs, her slender shoulders, dark and bare, slump. "I don't know. He has a point. What is there for me here now?"

I outstretch both arms, waving at the land in a circle before walking backward. "You think this island doesn't see you, Mia?" I ask.

She examines her hands. "I'm not interested in being seen the way Luke sees me."

"And how does he see you?"

"As an investment. And not in a good way. As something to perhaps fuck casually on the side because I'm there and convenient. I'm not so naïve to not notice his little touches as advances in more than a professional way. But as a young woman in this industry—in any industry—I must choose my battles. I can handle him more than I could handle the kind of attention I'd get if I made waves. That's why I like it here. Tradition holds everyone on the island. Do you see anyone else wearing suits?"

My lips purse at the observation. She makes an excellent point.

"Everything was so fast in Paris. I like things slow, as they happen here. It takes time to make good relationships among the clients, and I enjoy that aspect of the business more than I enjoy the money it brings."

"It seems you have little to think about then, do you?"

She shrugs noncommittally. "Perhaps I need to grow up. Perhaps the fast paced life will do me some good for a while."

I try to imagine Mia in a suit, standing at the head of a conference table in Paris, pointing her delicate fingers in every direction and watching people follow. It's a turn on.

"I think you will be remarkable no matter where you are." I stop my backward gait. We are far from the main building now, towering trees surrounding us. The smell of horses and hay a close memory.

"I'm sorry for kissing you last night at the club," she says.

"Why?" I ask, stricken at the sudden change in topic. "I'm not. You used me to make a point. Unless it was only a move to make Matteo jealous—which I don't think is your aim—I'd be happy to do it again."

She takes a step toward me, the cigarette tucked between her lips.

"Two people know. How long before all the dominoes fall?" I ask.

She drags the last bit of smoke from the butt of the cigarette and discards it, stamping it with the toe of her shoe.

"No more can fall," she says. "I shouldn't have let Matteo confirm his own speculations. If he asks, I'll say it was a one off, that I was getting him back for his kiss on the beach. Simone we can trust—but Matteo," she shakes her head, "he will make this a problem."

I mimic her actions with my own cigarette and take another step toward her. "Isn't this already a problem?" I ask, placing both hands on her hips. I'll never tire of the honey reflected in her gaze. Something stirs inside me, and the panic from yesterday threatens to bubble to the surface. I tamp it down and swallow, my throat working around its own dryness.

"*Merde,*" she breathes, and her mouth is on mine, her hand a force at the back of my neck, bringing me down to her. I hold her steady at the hips, the crunching of our feet on the dirt road rough against the rustling leaves above our heads. What is that sound called? *Psithurism.* I commit the sound to memory. I commit the entire thing to memory, all taste and smell and sensation. Light penetrates my skin as the heat of her hand mixes with the warmth of the sun at the nape of my neck. She's flush against my chest as we find ourselves pressed up against one of the infinite trees. She is in my hair, my mouth, my mind. I'm infected with *Mia Cifuentes,* and

I would die a happy death if I could share with her the space between my veins. The life between moments like this. The air within the same room for the rest of my days.

My phone vibrates in my pocket but I ignore it. Nothing is more important than the taste of her—now. Even tainted with cheap cigarettes, she tastes divine. Her tongue flicks the sky of my mouth, and my already hard cock jerks in my trousers. Her back is against the massive tree trunk, her head tilted up at me to devour me further.

I untuck her blouse and unzip her trousers. "What do you have waiting for me, hmm?"

Mia smiles into my kiss. She likes when we play this game, whatever it is. I work my hand down her trousers and slip one finger between expectant, wet lips. Her head falls back, lashes fluttering. I kiss her hungry mouth and taste her pleasure as I move one finger up through her folds to circle her clit. She brings one leg up my thigh, and I hook her knee with my free hand, opening her more. Her right hand holds steady at the base of my skull while the other flies up to right herself against the wide trunk, sweat beading against my brow and back. Her hand slips, and I hold her up.

"Was that the same Luke?" I ask, my finger moving slowly against her hardening bud.

She opens her mouth to answer, but only a moan escapes. I kiss her again, taking the sound for myself.

"What?" she finally breathes.

"Your first."

Her brows crease in concentration before her lips break into a grin. "Does it matter? Would that give you an excuse to be angry with me?"

"I need no further excuses to be angry with you, Mia." I hold her lips open with my first and ring fingers and circle her entrance with my middle. "You vex me beyond belief," I say, slowly sliding into her, knuckle by knuckle.

Her hand grips my shoulder, trimmed nails digging into bare flesh. I breathe in the bite and dip my head to nip at the hollow of her neck, curling my finger inside her to massage the holy spot on her inner wall. Her hips come up to meet my hand, and I release her lips, running my thumb up to her clit, using both fingers to coax her pleasure nearer. She breathes my name like a prayer, and I kiss the fading mark on her skin. The mark I left. I want to leave more. I want to leave marks deep beneath her skin. As deep as she is under mine.

"No," she gasps.

I still and gently remove my hand from her trousers. The sun is beaming down on her beautiful face. If anyone were to stroll through the loose wood gate, they would not find us in the shade. They would find us under a spotlight, tangled in the mess of our predicament. Fallen leaves rustle against our ankles.

"No," she says again. "That was not the same Luke."

I release a strangled breath against her neck and laugh at the relief. I'm not sure what I have to be relieved of. Though the fact that this faceless first of hers is to remain a mystery—at least to my knowledge—makes this heat a bit more bearable.

"Would you have hurt him if he were?" she asks. Now fully balanced, she has both palms against the thin fabric of my button down. "For me?"

Genuine curiosity laces her question. The lust sobers from her eyes, and she tilts her head, waiting for my answer. I let go of her leg and graze a knuckle along her pointed jawline. "For you?"

Her head bows in a slow nod.

"*El mundo.*"

She narrows her gaze at me in disbelief before shoving my chest. I stumble back, the dirt crunching beneath my heels.

"What?" I ask. "Is that not what you were expecting to hear?"

She fumbles in her pocket for the Camels and lights another without offering one to me.

"You are open, like a book." The cigarette between her lips muffles her words. "You cannot think outside your classroom. Not everything is an equation that needs solving. Some pretty slew of numbers and letters that make sense only to those who look at the black board hard enough."

I shake my head, not entirely following what it is she is trying to say. Not understanding what just happened between the previous moment and this one.

"You are a romantic, Enzo, and that is a beautiful thing. But you see what you want in people. You treat people like variables in your equations, seeking to make sense of them without veritably understanding them as individuals."

"You're wrong."

"How?" She inhales a lungful of poison and clicks her tongue. "Both of us cannot make one good decision to save our lives. Should I go to Paris, should I not go to Paris? Do you tell the truth about Ana, do you lie to all of us to save face?"

"Stop." I raise both palms up in surrender, grimacing at the mention of Ana's name. "What do *you* want to do, Mia? Do you want to go to Paris?"

She sucks on the tip of her cigarette and impatiently stamps the heel of her foot into the dirt. "I don't know what I want when it comes to Paris."

"And when it comes to us?"

She looks up at the cloudless sky. A blue as bright as the waving water not far from where we stand. She shakes her head, pinching the top of her nose before cursing under her breath in French.

"I want peace," she says.

I take a step toward her, and she takes a step back.

"If we are on a time limit, does it matter what we want? It will expire." She pushes herself off the tree trunk and begins to pace, her blouse hanging loose around her unbuttoned trousers.

"What happened to everything we discussed yesterday?" I ask.

"Yesterday was a lifetime ago!" She stops her pacing and faces me. "Please tell me you feel the same as I do. I cannot take this, this..." her hands claw at her chest, "whatever this is."

I rub her arms and hold her steady. She's breathing as I was on the boat, short and frenzied. I tuck a knuckle under her chin and lift her lips to mine.

"We are condemned," I say, "and we will not go gently."

14

Mia

L uke's entire pack of Camels is not enough to quell the trepida-
tion flowing through me. Enzo leaves me in the field of trees at
my behest. His hands on me, in me, were too much of a distraction.
My legs shake with adrenaline, the unexpected horseback excursion
didn't help to still my hungry muscles. I bask in the intense sun
rays for as long as is tolerable. Punishing myself with heat both on
my skin as well as in my lungs. I haven't smoked like this since first
picking up the nasty habit. Stick after stick, each lit by the previous
one, passes through my shaking fingers as I contemplate the meaning
of Enzo's words. How they can ruin everything.

El mundo. The world. For me.

Nausea bubbles up within. Am I reading too much into it? The
meaning flows against me like silk. I take another long drag, pulling
myself deeper and deeper into my own internal pyre.

I can't feel this way.

The thought of Paris becomes more intriguing before I realize I
would be running. Not running to but running from.

The one thing I can admit with certainty is that I need not search
for another dance partner. Enzo's rhythm matches mine, having

not felt such music with another man before. Symphonies vibrating from the moment we met. His face fills my mind, fueling my anger. It's as though he's omnipresent yet elusive, and I long for the days before our first dance. Before I knew his face, his hands on my hips, his mouth on mine. When the days were as complicated as Simone would allow them to be.

Uncertain how to answer Enzo's last question, I crush the empty pack of Camels and attempt to compose myself.

I walk through the gate and make a mental note to ask one of the workers to tighten the loose latch. The back of Enzo's head comes into view as I approach the office building. He turns at the sound of my footsteps and points at my disheveled clothes. I tuck in my blouse and straighten my trousers, brushing out the wrinkles he's caused. If only ironing out the rest of our situation was as easy.

I pass him with a brush of my shoulder against his and he follows without a word. We climb the stairs and enter the office to find Cyrus, my mother, and Luke, sitting on the long leather sofa. Marco sits at Cyrus's feet, playing with his car keys. We interrupt their booming conversation, and they nod at our entrance. My mother is retelling a tale I've heard many times over with the same enthusiasm as if it were the first. Luke wears an indulgent smile, listening with perked ears. He laughs and raises his eyebrows on cue, which encourages my mother further in her performance.

The aromatic smell of espresso sobers my racing thoughts, and I make for the machine. Enzo leans on the edge of my desk, arms folded across his chest. He raises a hand to rub his face and lingers his fingers beneath his nose, thumb tucked under his chin in a pondering pose. His chest raises in a breath and his eyes flit closed.

Is he... Is he smelling me? *Traces* of me?

His gaze meets mine, and I don't need an answer; his hungry stare speaks for itself. Stubborn, stupid heat fills my chest, and I down a shot of espresso, grimacing at its bitterness.

"Why don't you head back to the house and get ready for the rehearsal dinner tonight, yeah?" I interrupt my mother before she delves into another rerun tale. "I have a few things I need to finish up here."

They stand, Cyrus and Luke shaking hands, making faithless plans to get together to watch the next World Cup. Cyrus collects Marco from the floor and pockets his keys while Luke kisses my mother on both cheeks and she returns the gesture. He gives Enzo a firm handshake before approaching me with outstretched arms. I smile up at him, and his blue suit envelopes me.

"*Pensez-y*," he whispers, *think about it*. I nod a noncommittal answer and exchange a set of cheek kisses.

Cyrus and my mother follow him out of my office. Enzo lifts himself from the edge of my desk and trails a curled knuckle down my bare arm, leaving a wave of gooseflesh.

I stand in my office alone. The sound of busy employees beyond the glass door. The idea of starting over in Paris as a new person with new goals dangles like a prize in front of me. The peace I so long for seems that much further away. Memories of the streets reel in my mind in a rosy hue. The smell of the city at night when it truly comes alive. Hearing the language my father used to speak to me. How can two countries both feel so much like home?

I arrive back at the villa in the late afternoon, my hair still damp from a refreshing shower that rid me of the lingering horse scent. Thank God for the private washroom in my office. Fresh flowers in crystal vases and linens drape every corner of the courtyard. The fountain spews happily, the sound creating an outdoor oasis. String lights create the ambiance of a starry night above a small stage in the courtyard's corner, large enough for a band of no more than four. Musical simplicity has always been my mother's preference. I marvel at the amount of work she was able to complete in just a few short hours.

The kitchen is full of people I only recognize from previous events we've hosted. Cooks and workers in unmistakable help-attire. I greet them before sneaking upstairs to change for the evening.

A faint guitar plays under the sound of dishes and erratic Spanish voices as I climb the stairs, my feet hesitating on the landing, the melody drawing nearer. Initially, I mistook it for a ringing phone, but the sound is more informal, less rehearsed. I round the corner at the top of the stairs and make my way down the hallway toward my bedroom. Enzo's door is closed, but mine stands ajar. I don't recall leaving it open.

An empty bedroom greets me, the bed draped in afternoon sunlight. I close the door behind me and undress, rummaging through my wardrobe to find another signature outfit. A chiffon dress in deep purple. The bodice is low cut, something a bra could never hide under. The skirt tapers at the waist, accentuating the lines of my chest and torso before billowing out around a generous slit along the left leg. Naturally, the back is open. I know some *Tia's* would share more than a few hurtful words of disapproval under their breath, but that has always been the case no matter what I wear.

I check my makeup in the vanity and pull my curls up and away, leaving a few small locks to frame my face. The sound of the guitar returns, this time quicker, as though the musician were being chased. Individual notes race after each other, creating a trilling cascade of music that makes me want to move. Both washroom doors adjoining Enzo's room to mine stand open.

My bare feet carry me into his space as the music grows louder with each silent step.

When we are not hosting visitors, I often use this room as an extension of my own. Clothes strewn everywhere, paperwork, notebooks, books across the bed and coffee table. I've entered this room time and time again as though it were a pocket of my own world, but now I'm an intruder.

Enzo sits on the lounge at the foot of the bed, his head bowed toward the guitar's hollow. His fingers dance along the neck of the instrument in a less than expert manner, yet the sound is exquisite, nonetheless. He's wearing a cream shirt that remains unbuttoned and black dress pants that appear too short for his long legs. He has his ankles tucked under the lounge seat and crossed. One foot balances higher than the other to give the curve of the guitar a place to sit upon his thigh.

I don't wish to disturb him. His brows are furrowed in focus, a line cutting through his forehead. His hair is damp, freshly washed, and soft as it falls around his temples in short, dark curls.

His hands are exquisite. The tendons strain, stretch, then relax. His left holds the neck steady while the right tickles the strings, each finger knowing exactly where to wait for the next phrase.

Enthralled in the spell of his music, my body moves.

Enzo lifts his head as the skin of my feet glide against the ceramic tile. He shakes the hair away from his face and appears surprised before the thin, concentrated line of his mouth is replaced with a weary smile. His fingers don't waver, the music uninterrupted. I move my shoulders through the next few bars. He leads me in this dance as he has before, without even a touch. As is our arrangement, he is the frame and I the painting.

I roll my hips, arms finding their rhythm above my head and down again, along my body. I glide my hands along my chest, my thighs, as the song builds in tempo. Engaging the muscles in my thighs and stomach, I flex and relax as one movement translates into another. The music flows over me like clear, warm water. Clean and absolutely filthy at the same time. His melodic language speaks to my rhythm. His performance for me is as much as mine is for him. He has charmed me like a snake out of its basket. I dance for him, my limbs removing themselves from my consciousness before returning again for yet another reel about my body.

My spine twists at the base as I twirl in place, gaining torque. I revel in the wind created by my movement, my skirt lifting to expose bare legs that hold me up with confidence. I catch the fabric in one hand and lift the skirt higher to show my feet move with increasing intensity. My hair falls out of its loose fastening, curls now draped over my back and shoulders.

I tilt my chin up to meet Enzo's gaze, as it's focused on me. Watching my every move, his shoulders peaked like a leopard preparing to pounce. His shoulder and forearm muscles tensed, his jaw clenched, creating an even sharper line from earlobe to chin. The cords in his neck work as he swallows. His dark eyes are like hot rocks placed in the palms of my hands. Painful at first, then wonderfully pleasurable as I melt into the sensation. Being watched in this way, I've never felt more powerful.

Previously, my movements were for my own pleasure. But now, he fuels them. I lean into the dips and curves a little harder, linger on a pointed toe a bit longer, and rapture in the way he watches me. I want him to watch me. I want his every glance. I want him to be consumed by the sight of me, to where he can no longer deny himself.

I want Paris. I want a life with music like his, to dance like this. I want all of it, and I have not the first clue what to do.

I roll my head back, closing my eyes in a blend of frustration and satisfaction. The act elongates my body, and a low rumble sounds at the back of his throat. Emptying my mind, I focus on the music. The steps my body takes toward him. I raise my skirt until the chiffon bunches at the thickest part of my thighs and place the sole of my right foot onto his shoulder. He surveys the precarious placement and lowers his mouth to kiss the top of my foot. I keep up the movement in my hips while balancing on one leg.

Enzo closes his eyes and rubs his stubbled cheek against my ankle. I shudder at the prickly sensation, pressing my heel into his shoulder.

He looks up at me. His fingers pause.

The music comes to an abrupt stop.

The room is now silent, with the distant sound of pots and running water another world away. My breathing grows shallow, my heart pounding in my ears with the anticipation of his next move.

He postures up, lifting my foot higher on his shoulder, and gently leans the guitar against the side of the bed. Removing the instrument reveals the tightness in his black dress pants. An animal pressed against the inside of a cage, hungry to be free and hunt. He holds my ankle with his left hand, fingers and thumb touch as they're wrapped around the narrowest part of my leg. I pull away, but he holds me steady. A doe with her foot caught in a trap.

A heady hint of fear heats me from within. Enzo's lips are on the top of my foot again, caressing back and forth before kissing his way toward my ankle. I've never danced like this before, never had this part of my body kissed before. The strength in my back threatens to give out, the muscles in my spine quivering with the unexpected pleasure. I attempt to keep my balance, my left leg holding me up with years of muscle memory. But his delicate ambush to my foot is deliciously unsettling, and he brings his other hand up to steady me.

His fingers graze the exposed flesh of my left thigh. Fingers that knead and pinch and move up, up, up toward the curve of my ass. Enzo continues with agonizing, slow kisses on my ankle and trails his mouth higher, his grip digging deeper into soft flesh. He licks from the top of my foot up to my shin in one long move, and I'm grateful for his steadying hand. I inhale sharply, my hips writhing, craving attention. A strange curiosity ebbs through me at this novel sensation of his mouth on my leg. Heat forges deep in my belly, along with both fear and absolute trust.

I don't fear Enzo. Though I do fear what he does to me. The addictive nature of his skin on mine. The way he makes me question myself and what I want. I fear what I would have to lose if I gained his company beyond our agreement.

Callused knuckles graze up my calf and stop at the underside of my thigh, my raised leg held in place by his broad hand inching closer to the bunched chiffon. Enzo resumes deliberate kisses up my shin, turning my leg this way and that to give my calf enough attention, until his tongue flicks the curve of my knee. He draws me nearer, my foot suspended behind his shoulder blade. Uncertain with this adjustment, my body surrenders control, enticed by the promise of *more.*

Orange evening light casts a spellbinding glow across Enzo's face. Between my open thighs, he devours me inch by agonizing inch. The sight of him is heady, desire building, and I realize it's been too long since I last touched him.

I palm his face and trail a finger along the line between his eyebrows to the tip of his nose. He tilts his head into my touch as I brush his full lips with the pad of my thumb, and he kisses me there. No man has taken the time to kiss my fingertips. To ready my body to take him so willingly, even with a game of stop and go. Enzo not only takes his time, he drags it out and lingers on the spaces of me I didn't know needed to be coaxed.

This tender attention he's giving me is something to be adored, yet I need more. I crave the rough and hard as much as the soft and slow.

"Have you decided?" he asks. I nod, unsure if I've just told an unspoken lie. "What will it be, then?" Fingers dig into my unfurled thighs. The bite of his nails comes and goes as he handles me. My thumb hovers below his lower lip, and I trail my fingers toward his throat, holding his gaze. I lower my head, leaning over as if about to share a secret.

"*El mundo*," I whisper.

His pupils dilate, and a grin breaks across his half sunlit face before he disappears beneath the chiffon and his mouth is on the panty covered mound of my pubic bone. He kisses me through the fabric, transforming the initial ticklish unease into something querying.

He makes me want to say yes and scream no. He makes me want too much too fast, leaving me frustrated with myself for succumbing to his words.

All thoughts of rationality cloud my mind, fogging in every direction, and all I can see is his face. Nips and kisses through my panties make the fabric grow sopping on both sides. His teeth grip the edge of the fabric and pry it away from wet skin, dragging the garment down until it resists on the curve of my ass.

"Move," he growls between clenched teeth.

I glance down at the mound of his head under my dress and hear his voice again, low and vibrating against the innermost parts of my thighs.

"My hands are busy." He pulls me in closer, my left leg growing weaker by the moment as it supports my full weight alone. "Move these to the side and let me see your pretty pussy."

I shudder at the command in his voice and move my hand to obey, reaching under my dress to show him what he's done to me. He chuckles at the sight before digging his nose between my folds and inhaling deeply. Flushed and mortified, I push at his head and shoulders, desperate for a gap between us. But he holds me too strong, my lower half at his mercy.

"Don't move." Each word wields so much authority, my mind and body struggle to relinquish control. Enzo presses the bridge of his nose against my exposed clit and breathes in again. His shoulders rise and fall as he exhales with a curse. My head tilts back, watching the shadows of dancing leaves through golden light on the ceiling. He repeats his command to stay still before his mouth claims me, and my mind threatens to split. My stomach clenches as he parts me with his tongue, his hands leaving marks on my thighs.

"So good, you're so good," his words of praise ripple through me, driving me higher and higher.

I struggle to keep the fabric away, to keep my leg steady as I raise the skirt of my dress and grip his hair at the roots with my free hand. And as much as he's bringing me to the edge, as much as I'm audaciously winding my hips against his mouth, I'm so empty. Utterly hollow, it almost hurts. A pull that starts from the middle of my belly down to where his tongue is now dipping and teasing my entrance.

As if hearing my unspoken thoughts, Enzo releases one leg and slides two fingers through my slit, not yet inside. He spreads my wetness fused with his until I am completely coated and slowly slides in one finger. I let out a seething breath as he follows it with a second. His fingers are blunt and wide as they spear me. The emptiness is quelled, but only somewhat. I need so much more as he fucks me with his fingers, my standing leg now shaking with the effort to keep me up. My mouth falls open, incoherent moans escaping me with every breath. I try to be quiet, to silence the scream building in the depths of my belly.

"Such a good girl, my Mia." His tongue flicks the hard bud at the top of my pussy, and he sucks hard, circling me in torture. His Mia.

His. The longing in his voice threatens to break me. The menacing idea that I could belong to him in more ways than this. His words, his fingers, his tongue undo me, and all I can hear is the sound of my voice as my leg finally buckles from underneath my weight, my every muscle seizing in the most delicious pain.

Enzo catches me, my limbs a scrambled mess. He slides us up onto the edge of the bed and eases himself beneath me, settling my knees on either side of his head. His hands run up my body and give my breasts a loving squeeze before holding me at the hips, bracing me as I'm seated against his mouth. The inside of my thighs is soaked, undisputedly inundating his face with my scent. I lift my skirt to see him deep in concentration as he devours me, his head bobbing back and forth, fingers digging desperately into my waist. I see the faintest glimpse of his tongue as it reaches the surface, playing with the hard bundle of nerves, then disappears back under to do its worst.

"I love seeing you like this," I say, repeating his own words back to him in a mouthwateringly possessive tone.

He chuckles into my skin and feels his way down my body, using his fingers to part me again. His tongue prevails against my clit, coaxing another climax from the pit of my core.

"Ride, love," Enzo says, muffled by my weight. "Ride my face, *cariño.*" Phrases of endearment swim in my head, encouraging my hips to undulate above his wanting mouth. I brace my hands against the tops of his thighs, and ride.

It feels so filthy to be moving like this, to use his face for my pleasure. To see him submissive under me in such a vulnerable position where I hold all the power as well as all the pleasure. But that's not entirely true, is it? He's the one holding me to him. He's the one commanding my every move. And he's the one building up his own pleasure as well as mine. We pass this fiery ball of power from one to the other in a continuous game, the line never truly solid in the sand.

I reach between his legs and cup the crotch of his pants, squeezing my palm gently against his hard cock. His hips jerk up into my hand and a devilish smile meets the corners of his eyes. He looks up at me and spears me with his tongue.

I see you. I raise you.

My head flies back with a sharp inhale, my climax advancing fast, and I quicken the tempo of my hips. "*Yes,*" I cry, because that's the only word I seem to remember. "*Yes, yes, yes.*"

A word with the power to change our entire lives. Yes. I want to say yes to Enzo in every thinkable way. I want to please him with every presented opportunity, every behest, every day we have left to spend together. Which, if we honor our agreement, is not enough.

My second orgasm rips through me, and I repeat the only word my mouth can form. His tongue persists, sustaining my climax and savoring it for himself.

Sundry thoughts reel as I come down from the high with a head-clearing epiphany. I can't imagine hearing the words in my voice—I can't even imagine formulating the entire thought, as it is too absurd. But what I can do is save the idea to be explored when my mind is sobered from such an overload of pleasure.

Enzo lifts me like a delicate vase, bringing his body upright to stand before me. His stare is wild with ardor and burns a hole straight through my chest. I find myself crawling backward at his advance, my feet now propping me upright at the edge of the bed. He pins me in one motion and kisses me. I taste the salty tang of myself on him, and my belly roils with the warning of another likely push over the edge.

His body hovers over mine, his tongue exploring my mouth with as much eagerness as it did my pussy. My fingers fumble to unbutton the top of his trousers, expecting him to protest as he had before, but he says nothing. He knows to trust me now. I unfasten the button and slide the zipper down, palming him through the fabric of his boxer briefs. His trapped dick begs to be set free, and I pull the waistband down, springing him forward. I raise my hips and widen my knees, ready to take all of him as I glide my fingers up his shaft and imagine him inside me. Imagine him spearing me as his fingers have. Hot privation demanding to be sated.

His mouth is on my neck, lightly sucking as he triggers nerves I didn't know I had in my lower back, my belly, and he raises his head to look at me, his breath jagged and shallow. "Condom?" he asks.

I blink. I've never been the one to provide them. Though I've been on the pill since before college, I've always been adamant about keeping myself clean, demanding any partner wear some layer of protection. It isn't until now that the thought of having to stop is possibly worse than the consequences. Lust and foolish need cloud my mind. Though Enzo may take pause and *think* for the both of us, I can't bring myself to care.

"Pill," is all I can breathe out.

"I haven't been with anyone since..." His words trail off, and I understand his meaning immediately. "She always supplied them." He explains. "I've never... without."

I kiss him, saving him from his own struggle. "Me neither," I say. My fingers flutter against the swollen crown of his cock, and I grip him in my small fist. The thought of him bare inside me is both terrifying and exhilarating.

"Are you sure?" he asks. I'm not sure if his words are more ambiguous than intended. My mind stalls at the question. I am sure. I'm more sure of this—of him—than I am of Paris. And so, I say the one word I know he will not refuse.

"Please." I lift my hips underneath him and shimmy out of my inundated panties. He's taken aback with recognition. He told me to be careful with that word, to be sure I meant it when said again. He sees my struggle and gives me the space I need before helping the garment off my ankles and flinging them across the room.

I suck my thumb before lowering my hand to his length and running it along his swollen head. Focused on me, his lashes flutter between closed and open, a snarl playing on his lips at the power I play. I fist myself around him and pump slowly, watching his shoulders tremble like a stuttering sentence. Scooting myself below him further, I hold his gaze as he braces both of his fists on either side of my head, then allows his hips only an inch of movement as he slowly fucks my hand between my spread legs. I splay them further, invitingly.

Enzo lowers his head and teases my lips with his, his breath a hot flurry of air. I lift my head to kiss him, but he refuses me, pulling his head away at the last moment just to dip down again and not-kiss my lips, my cheek, down to my neck. He breathes against my ear, his mouth and hard cock my only focus.

"Put me inside you, *cariño*," he breathes against my neck. I shiver at the gentle command, the authority in his voice before it deepens further, and my mind is swimming. "Show me how well you can take me."

Settled beneath his weight, I lift my hips to meet his cock as it's gripped in my hand. I run the blunt tip of him up through my wet folds and hear him seethe with the heated impact, smiling against his shoulder, wetting him thoroughly, running him up and down and up again before circling him around my clit. Using him.

His tongue leaves a hot trail from shoulder to ear before whispering another filthy order, "Now, *cariño*, before I do it myself." An intriguing threat, but the dominance of holding him at bay is too heady to pass up.

"Patience, Enzo."

He lifts his head to look into my face, and I squeeze him in defiance as I notch him at my opening.

"We've waited years, what's a few more moments of delayed pleasure?"

"We've waited long enough," he growls as he pushes in and stretches me around him. Slowly sinking, sinking.

I gasp a sharp breath in as my mouth opens in an involuntary *O*. I look down and see only the tip has breached my entrance, and he allows me to settle around his considerable size before grabbing the wrist that's holding his cock and pinning it above my head. "Like what you see?"

"I love it." The words are out of my mouth before I have time to think. The truth spilling out of me. "More," I command, writhing my hips as he has me pinned.

He leaves little not-kisses along my jawline and cheek before reaching my panting lips again. "Patience, Mia," he taunts.

I rock against him, forcing his tip to peek in and out in frustration.

Enzo kisses me hard as he slides home, a screaming moan travelling from my throat to his as his hips finally meet mine.

Full. I feel so utterly, gloriously full.

He doesn't move. The kiss deepens, my tongue running along the roof of his mouth, and his grip around my wrist tightens as hips against hips jolt wantonly. I sense the restraint in his bones, the hesitation in thinking we're not too far gone to reel it back now. To turn around and pretend we haven't walked, hands clasped together past the gates of hell. This feels too much like a blessing to be anything else.

I wrap my free arm around his waist and palm his ass, pushing him down and deeper into me. The back of my head sinks into the mattress as my back arches. "Fuck me, Enzo," I whisper licentiously against his open, wanting mouth. "*Please.*"

He snarls, almost angrily, and begins to move.

15

ENZO

THE DAY BEFORE THE WEDDING

M ia is radiant as sweat glistens off her skin, her dress a mess of purple chiffon hiked up to her waist in a wonderfully sordid display. I move inside her, her pussy gripping me with three years' worth of waiting. Vehement, exquisite thrusts rock her body beneath me and her mouth falls agape with words of *please* and *more* barely making their way off her swollen lips. Her plea so pure and undeniable when she turns on me with those eyes, glazed with the buildup of another release. I am a slave to her behest. She is scorching hot, holding me like a vise. I fill and deny her again in the same savory moment.

Her slight hand works its way beneath my dress pants and grips the skin of my bare cheek, fingers clawing my ass encouragingly with every advance. Aching, indecent moans slip from her, sounds I've heard before, but not this close. Not with her so deliciously tight around me.

She breathes in sharp, shallow inhales with every thrust, expelling sweet air onto my face as I hover above, keeping a steady rhythm, chasing both of our climaxes.

Her legs wrap around my waist, and she fucks me back, meeting my movements pound for heavenly pound. She gasps, *"Harder,"* her forehead coming up to meet my shoulder. I hold her down, whispering encouraging words into her ear as I acquiesce.

Ravenous lust overtakes me, and I pull at the straps of her dress. The fabric gives easily, and her breasts bounce free with my rhythmic thrusts. The sight of her is magnificent to behold. I flick her nipple with my tongue before taking her into my mouth and sucking, drinking in every bit of her arched back. I kiss one breast, then drag my tongue across her chest to do the same to the other. Her breathing shudders as I gently roll her nipple between my teeth. I release her pinned wrist, and she immediately threads her fingers in my hair, holding my head to her chest as I hold her by the waist, keeping her steady while I round my hips now up and down, circling deep inside her.

Mia's moans deepen into a cry. An evolved sound I've never heard and will give anything to hear again. Her pussy thrums, pulsing around my cock as I still myself and let her writhe, her body clamped onto mine, her legs wrapped around my waist, locked at the ankles, her hands clutching my face to her dampened chest. Tremors flow through her rippling muscles as her pussy slows, coming back down to earth with me. She brings my face to hers and kisses me hard before giving me a mischievous grin and bucking her hips unexpectedly.

She flips me onto my back, my dick feeling the air of the room again in discontent. Mia straddles me, and the view of her from this angle is angelic, her chest and cheeks rosy red, crimson burning, her heaving breasts already bearing the marks I've left on her soft, plump skin. Slight shoulders give way to slight arms that pull at my open button-down and force it off my back. Her dress is a mess around her waist, and I'm desperate to see her without it. I pull the chiffon over her head and hear the distinct sound of torn fabric. She complies, flinging the thing onto the floor, then kicks at my pants, and I wiggle them off along with my boxer briefs.

We are both naked in the golden light of sunset, and I sit up, drawing her close, caressing her arms and back with calloused fingertips, our kisses laden with unspoken desires, surpassing the boundaries we've set. She postures up and into my kiss, receiving every bit of it with a stifled moan.

Mia pushes me back down onto the mattress and braces herself against my chest. I hold her long fingers to me, letting her feel my racing heart.

"Watch," she whispers, her gaze traveling down to where our bodies finally meet.

I follow her gaze to the glistening mound of her pussy as it rubs eagerly along the length of my cock, watching the obscene image as I part her swollen lips, my size seemingly too big, too invasive for the space it needs to fill. Her wetness trails over me as she slips from the base of my balls to the very tip and back again. I glimpse the happy, enlarged bulge of her clit and place my thumb right above my dick. She meets my waiting thumb and smiles at the impact, continuing until I'm shaking with the need to be inside her. She displays her reign above me, allowing only what she wants me to feel, and it's more than I can stand.

My hands run up her stomach and squeeze both breasts, pinching her nipples. She bares her teeth as I run my grasp back down and around her plump ass, lifting it away from my dick, spreading her lips open with my fingers and tracing a circle around her opening.

She doesn't need a verbal command. My eyes on hers is enough to make her move.

Mia lifts her weight onto her knees and reaches between her legs to hold my shaft upright.

She lowers herself onto me, and we both watch, our breathing ragged as she struggles to take me in this position. Her brows pinched, I bring both arms behind my head and support my neck as I watch myself slowly disappear into her scorching, wet cunt, my position the picture of relaxation while a fire roils within my core at the feeling of her this deep. Her eyes roll back as she takes slow breaths, calming herself, adjusting to the invasion.

Her inner walls hug me tight in welcome, and it takes every morsel of my concentration not to rear my hips up and into her fully. No, this is her game now, but dammit, I want a *show*. I unlatch one arm from behind my neck and slap her hard on the ass. She squeals, her eyes darting open to look at me in delighted shock.

"No more playing. Be a good girl. Ride."

She smiles and obeys.

Slowly at first, unhurried and rhythmic, as she takes me in languid circles. I hold her warm cheeks, kneading them in my hands and guiding her hips wave after wave. She leans back, bracing her hands on my legs as she had at the foot of the bed. And like then, she's in control. She's calling the shots as I play servant to her pleasure. Her head falls back, dark curls tickling my knees, a long line of absolute art straddled above me.

Her tempo peaks, the motion becoming more frantic, and I watch and feel my way up her stomach from navel to between her breasts. Her pulse thrums below my thumb as it explores the shape of her neck and collarbone; my hands desperate to commit every inch of her to tangible memory.

As Mia rides my cock like it's her singular source of pleasure, as the most exquisite throaty sounds blanket the darkening room, as she's bathed in the light of the falling sun, sweat twinkling, the need to tell her overwhelms me. I want to say the words and I want her to hear them. Seeing her face light up in that beautiful yet subtle way that makes my chest go taut. I want her to know every secret I'm too much of a coward to say aloud. To grasp the depths of what's left unsaid. To remind me why I'm willingly pursuing the risk of heartbreak, no matter the price.

I've never felt such a desperate need to share what's inside. To feel something so completely, it must be verbalized. It must be understood.

I open my mouth, but all that breaks free is a choked, *"Fuck, Mia,"* as she props herself up, her hands now forward and pressed against my chest, and rides me up and down. Back arched, she pulses her pussy around me, ass bouncing against the tops of my thighs in one continuous motion that threatens to end our little session way too early.

The crack of my palms on both ass cheeks sounds loud, encouraging her to ride harder, faster. She does.

Mia's face is a blend of pain, determination, and ardent pleasure. She brings her head down and I meet her halfway, her cadence steady.

We kiss, frantic. Our mouths crash with another unrelenting thrust, and she holds my bottom lip between her teeth.

The tempo quickens still, and I can tell she's close as her rapid gasps brush my lips. I wrap one arm around her waist and hold her close. Steadying with my other arm, reaching up to hold her neck from the back as I drive into her. I match her beat for beat as her tits bounce against the top of my chest.

The sound of wet skin and foul moans fill the room, and I think the words as loud as I can, projecting them through my mind and into hers.

I'm in love with you.

It's on the tip of my tongue, threatening to escape.

Too focused, my mouth can't form the words.

Thrusting from underneath, I give Mia as much of myself as possible, and she seizes in my arms, her legs trapping me on both sides. Fingers in my hair and against my back dig into flesh, and I kiss the tops of her breasts, her neck, as she muffles a rich climactic cry into the top of my head.

We stay like this for a moment, unmoving, my hard cock still inside her, begging for a release of its own. I hear the beat of her heart slow, and she sits back to look at me, her fingers brushing the hair away from my face, and I do the same. We stare at one another, and a wave of understanding washes over me.

"Did you say something?" she asks between unsteady breaths.

I shake my head in answer. She kisses me lazily, ignoring her own question, then climbs off my lap and lays face down on the mattress beside me. With her hands underneath her chin, she gives me a devilish grin I'm compelled to kiss. Slowly, she lifts her ass into the air and wiggles it playfully.

I smile at her contemptible nature and rise to my knees behind her. "Hold on to the headboard, love."

She does, arching her back further and pressing her knees together. I raise my palm and bring it down hard against the soft flesh of her ass. The room cracks with the sound. Mia buries her face into the mattress and curses.

I have a perfect view of her quivering pussy from this angle. "You know how beautiful you look like this?"

I spank her again in the same red spot.

"You have no idea how delicious you look, *cariño*."

Crack.

"All spread open and wet, waiting for my cock, huh?"

Crack.

The skin on her ass rises in the shape of my hand, and I know she's enjoying every bit of this pain-pleasure cocktail as her body trembles, her toes curl.

"*Yes,*" she whimpers in a wet gasp, "*please.*"

"Good girl," I praise.

I run my finger through her folds and circle her clit, flicking it with my middle finger as I spank her again. Her screams are muted as I run my hand down her spine to grasp her hair from the root and pull her up.

"You like being punished?" I ask, lining up my dick just so, a fistful of her hair in my hand. She gives the tiniest nod. "Good," I say, and fill her in one sharp thrust.

Her back arches into a deep C, a silent scream on her lips as I hold her in place and fuck her hard and fast. My balls slap against her clit, and I run my other hand around her waist and rub her swollen bud to the tempo of my thrusts. Her moans become erratic and loud.

The sound of people working and the distant melody of background music are still audible, and the fear of being caught distracts me momentarily. We know our family won't be home for a while, but the thought of strangers hearing us fills me with heat. The fear turns into intrigue, and I quicken my hips.

What if someone tells Cyrus or Katia what they heard? Part of me wants to get caught. Part of me wants this game of hide and seek to be over, to let the truth come out and claim Mia in every way within these walls and in the sun.

But not today. Not now. And not like this.

With my hand wrapped around her mouth and her head at an uncomfortable angle against my shoulder, I nibble and bite at her exposed neck and shoulder as I drive into her relentlessly. She screams against my palm, her two hands gripping my wrists as her nails dig into my skin.

My sight blurs as my climax builds, growing hotter by the second. All I can feel, all I can taste, all I can hear is my Mia. *Mi mundo.* I love her.

My stomach tightens with the need to release, and I slap her clit once, hard. She lets out a final, long wail into my palm, her teeth grazing the flesh of my thumb. The inner walls of her pussy pulse and contract, trapping me inside her. We both ride her climax and I continue to thrust, dragging it out as long as I can before I push her down onto the bed and release thick ropes onto her ass and back.

Mia whimpers, her entire body trembling in the aftershock of both of our climaxes. She looks vulnerable and used as she gives me the most wicked grin. I spank her once again in the same raised red spot. She jumps at the impact, gritting her teeth as another wave of tremors makes its way through her body.

My head is swimming with the reality of what we've just done, and I climb off the bed and head to the washroom to grab a hand towel, running it under warm water and wringing it out before bringing it to Mia's still-shuddering body. Cleaning her well, I wipe down her spine and across both cheeks. Back in the washroom, I rinse the cloth thoroughly before throwing it into the hamper.

When I return to the room, Mia is laying on her side, her breathing now even, as though she's asleep, and I crawl into bed beside her, wiping damp hair away from her face and tucking it behind her ear, tracing the shell and finding the freckle I've thought of for the past three years.

She blinks up at me with content and something hinting at sorrow in her honey rimmed eyes. "You did say something."

I search her face, knowing exactly what she means, while having no clue at all.

"Me too," she says.

After a quick shower and some time to ourselves in our separate bedrooms, Mia and I come downstairs to join the party. She is wearing a different dress than the deep purple one that was flung heedlessly to the floor of my bedroom only an hour ago. This new dress is black and of a simpler style, yet elegant still.

Paranoid, it appears we have signs atop our heads projecting our secret to the world. To our relief, everyone appears too distracted with their own pre-rehearsal dinner tasks to notice us and our shameful faces. Cyrus and Katia have returned from their errands while we were taking time to clean up. Though some cooks present before Mia's arrival are avoiding me, and I am certain they must have heard her telling screams. I squeeze Mia's hand once in solidarity before releasing her into the kitchen, to the wrath of her mother.

Katia rattles off a slew of Spanish phrases of disappointment as they argue. It seems I have distracted her enough to forget to steam Katia's dress for this evening.

"*Lo siento*, Mama," Mia says, a slight edge of annoyance in her tone.

"It was me, Katia," I cut in.

Both women look up. Mia's face is warm.

"I didn't know what to wear for the occasion, and I'm afraid I've taken up too much of Mia's time. *Lo siento*, Katia. I'd be happy to help in any way I can."

Katia sighs dramatically as Mia's shoulders fall in relief. Katia pats my arm and gestures to my outfit. "At least something will look good at that table," she laments, before commenting on Mia's wrinkled dress.

I bring the back of my hand up to my mouth to hide a smirk.

Katia hands me two large empty vases and instructs me to take them outside and start arranging the centerpieces. I take them from her and exit the kitchen's glass doors.

The courtyard is a picturesque image of tranquility and celebration. Food festooned the table across a golden tablecloth. Multiple plates and silverware crowd each seat around two magnificent floral centerpieces. I feel I've been given a task meant to distract rather than aid. The fountain in the center of the courtyard spews in choreographed patterns, the sound of trickling water giving the space a peaceful ambiance, while string lights hang overhead, twinkling against a deep black sky. Reminded of what Mia and I have done, I imagine the darkness swallowing me whole. A demise worthy of my actions. Now, in the sobering night air, my mind clear from the lust and desire, and I don't regret a moment of it.

I do love her. Without the distraction of lust, I know it. The truth has its way of forcing itself against the interest of denial. It becomes too loud to ignore, refusing anything but honest acknowledgment.

Which is what I intend to do.

I need to tell her. It might be selfish, and it might be devastating if unrequited, but the realization is eating away at me inside, insistent upon its release. This will derail our plan and complicate things beyond repair, risking losing the short time we have left on this island.

But it must be done. Tonight. I will tell her tonight. Beneath the stars, with the moon as my witness, I will tell Mia that I love her.

Simone holds Marco in the crook of her arm, bouncing lightly while inspecting an array of loose flowers on a side table. She lifts a rose to Marco's small nose, and he inhales with a giggle. The two smile and Simone gives the rose a sniff as well before returning it to the table. Her smile shrinks as I approach, hanging awkwardly on her lips as she tries and fails to keep the judgment from her face. I place the two vases on the table and tell her I'm only here on Katia's orders. She nods and arranges the flowers from the table into the vases.

Simone puts Marco down, and he runs up to my knees, hugging them. I stagger and pick him up, not realizing until now how much time I've missed with him; how much time I've missed with everyone. He's so big now. Heavy, with gangly limbs. He thumps his cumbersome head onto my shoulder, and I bounce him lightly while handing Simone flower after flower. She smiles at me, though I'm sure she's more so smiling at her favorite toddler. Three more people

I've never seen before walk by with mystery boxes, while another three lay dance floor tiles. My eyebrows raise at the distinct wooden slats as they snap closed.

"Mia's one request," Simone says, answering my unspoken question.

I tilt my head at her, bonking it lightly on Marco's. Marco brings his mischievous toddler hand up to my face and grabs my nose. I cross my eyes at him and blow a raspberry against his forearm. He guffaws as though it's the funniest thing in the world. Simone and I laugh in turn, and he wriggles to be put down. I oblige, and he runs inside to tell anyone who will listen how funny *Tio* Enzo is.

"The dance floor," Simone continues, now with much less disdain in her voice.

I nod at the now mostly finished platform. "The woman can dance," I say, not knowing how else to fill the silence.

Simone's hands still midair from the corner of my eye. "It was you, wasn't it?"

I raise my head and meet Simone's wide eyes.

She looks at me like it's the first time she's truly seeing me. "The night Marco was born. It was you I pulled her away from."

A choked laugh escapes my throat. "Yes. I thought you knew."

She shakes her head. "This makes so much more sense now," she says, gesturing to my standing body like it's a problem she's just solved.

"What makes sense?" A hint of annoyance makes its way through my words.

She takes note and matches the attitude. "The years-long pining."

"What are you talking about?"

"Mia has been declining men since Marco was born, all because she danced with a stranger once and has carried a torch for him ever since. Come to find out, years later, it was *you* all along." Simone spits venomous words, emphasizing her disbelief.

Baffled, I twirl a flower between two fingers and gently place it into a vase before clearing my throat. "I didn't know who she was when I asked her to dance. If I had known..." I trail off, not sure how to finish that sentence.

"Nothing would have changed if either of you had known." Her words are sure and even, without doubt.

"How do you know?"

"I know my cousin."

"And me?"

She shrugs and picks up another rose, gently picking off stray petals and letting them fall to the table.

"I know you well enough to know you already regret the decisions you've made. You'd be a fool to repeat them."

Before I can ask what she means, Marco comes running out with his parents in tow. They've all changed into their dinner rehearsal outfits. Katia is stunning in a blush pink sundress, while my brother looks clean in his signature linens. Mia trails behind them, holding a gorgeous two-tier cake on a wooden stand. Though I've only been away from her for a few minutes, helped her step into the dress she's wearing now, washed her body, kissed and smelled the most intimate parts of her, I miss her still.

Katia claps her hands together, pleased with the arrangements Simone has put together. She looks at mine and frowns. My vase is haphazard and chaotic, with mismatched colors and varying stem lengths. The flowers appear to be thrown together without composition, resulting in a disordered display. Slight embarrassment flushes my cheeks.

"You should ask if they're hiring," Cyrus says, "though I wouldn't hold my breath." He gives a giant bellow of a laugh, and the table follows suit.

I laugh as well. It really is awful.

Footsteps sound toward the gate's entrance as Matteo walks in with a bouquet in his hand. "You waited for me," he says by way of greeting.

The arrogance in his tone has me stifling an eye roll.

Matteo goes around the table, greeting everyone individually. He kisses Katia on both cheeks, then Cyrus, Simone, and finally Mia. His free hand rubs against Mia's bare shoulder, and my jaw clenches.

Matteo hands Mia the flowers, and she takes them with a smile before placing them next to my sorry arrangement. We all sit at the impressively set table, Cyrus and Katia at either head while Simone and Matteo sit across from Mia and I. Simone places Marco in his highchair between herself and Katia. The reflection of the courtyard in the glass doors breaks as they open to a procession of cooks and servers dressed in sleek, all-black attire. They emerge, each with steaming bowls in hand as they place course after course before us. The first is a deliciously spiced *pozole* that makes my mouth water.

"*Que rico*, eh?" Cyrus remarks. The general hums concur.

A waiter places a laptop on the table where Simone and I left our discarded petals, connecting it to a hidden speaker system, and soon soft music pours through the courtyard, enhancing the milieu as gently plucked guitars sing melodies over a drum's calm heartbeat.

"This is lovely, *Tia Katia*," Simone says.

"I wanted us to have our own intimate banquet before everyone else has their fun tomorrow. I didn't want to be one of those brides who eats nothing at their own wedding. Tonight is for us." Katia raises a glass, her focus on my brother. He raises his in return, and the rest of us follow. Marco lifts a plastic sippy cup.

"To Katia and Cyrus," I say. "May you never again know the sweetness of solitude. *Salud*."

"*Salud*," everyone says in unison. We raise our glasses higher and drink.

Servers bring out the next course on large round dinner plates. They take our empty bowls in one hand and place the next course over golden chargers. Steaming racks of lamb sit in a reduction sauce with vegetables artfully arranged around the meat. We dig in, the sounds of forks and knives against china plates echoing across the stone walls that enclose the courtyard.

Simone and Katia discuss the dresses they intend to wear tomorrow. Katia asks Mia if she has yet to decide on one of the options she'd provided, and my ears perk up in intrigue.

"I have one in mind," she says, placing a piece of meat delicately on her tongue.

"From the ones I brought you the other day?" Katia asks.

Mia hums her answer, her mouth full. Katia clicks her tongue incredulously.

"We're going all out, yes? Full tuxedo? Like Bond?" Matteo asks.

"Yes," Cyrus answers. "No average Sunday suit. Black tie—non-negotiable. You brought a tux, eh *Lorencito*?"

"I did," I say, tasting the sweet char of a carrot. I cut another piece of meat off the bone and pop it in my mouth. Each lovely flavor combines and bursts on my tongue. I finish chewing and dab the corners of my mouth with a cloth napkin. "It's hanging in the wardrobe upstairs. I wouldn't show up to my brother's wedding in anything less than Armani."

Cyrus laughs at my sarcasm, an inside joke of ours no one else seems to understand. "Armani is what we would call the rich lads in school," Cyrus explains. His head whips back at me, "Unless you actually bought an Armani tuxedo?"

It's now my turn to laugh. "It's a good tux *hermano*, I promise."

He nods, the smile returning to his face.

The conversation continues without being directed toward me for some time. Mia leans in and whispers, "So, if not Armani?" she asks.

"Calvin Klein," I say, "just pretentious enough." I wink at her, and she smiles, her focus falling back to her mostly empty plate. I lean back and ask, "And what kind of dress will you be wearing?"

Mia places another morsel of food in her mouth and chews slowly. Her cheeks move before the muscles in her throat work, and she swallows. I'm reminded of being in the back of her throat, watching her swallow me down. My hand falls down my side and finds her knee under the table. I pull the fabric of her dress back and circle the flesh of her thigh with my thumb. She clears her throat and places a hand over mine before lifting both of our hands for the table to see.

"Let's dance, *si*?" she says, standing. In one swift motion, she guides me to the dance floor, and the rest of our small party joins.

The sound of chair legs scraping against stone tile fills the night air for a moment before the music grows louder and Mia is in my arms once more. I can't dance with her here, not the way I need to. Her jasmine scent fills my nose, and I long for her like another bite of delicious food.

We dance modestly, with the eyes of our family on us. I ignore the judgment in Matteo's stare as it sears on the side of my face. We face the other way for a beat, and for a moment, all I see is Mia under the canopied lights. Her bare arms and shoulders move in the twinkling glow, and I twirl her one way, then the other. Cyrus and Katia clap to the beat of the music, encouraging us. Marco claps as well, though not in rhythm with the drums, and Mia smiles at her little brother in adoration. She looks up at me, and for a moment my chest lurches. I want to kiss her, to pull her in close and inhale her sweet scent like no one is watching. But I can't. Everyone *is* watching, denying me the one thing I want most.

Instead, I pull her up to land on my hip. She doesn't miss a beat, and kicks one leg high into the air before landing on the ball of one foot expertly and twisting at the hips. Even Matteo claps at our theatrics. I spin her again, and she spins me in turn, we dance for judges rather than for ourselves, putting on a show that has nothing to do with character. The gate sounds again as the song comes to a close. I dip Mia low, and she tucks one leg behind mine, the other suspended, creating a long line from the tip of her outstretched arm to the elongated arch of her foot. I hold her inches above the dance floor, both of us breathing heavily, and place an innocent kiss on her cheek before pulling her up to her feet. It's a friendly enough kiss, but she looks on with awe all the same.

"Mind if I cut in?" Ana's voice hits me like a bat to the head.

16

MIA

THE DAY BEFORE THE WEDDING

At the courtyard entrance, a woman stands out of place in jeans and a gray hoodie. Her light brown hair sits above her shoulders, the top half swooped up in a knot, the rest ironed straight. A white suitcase behind her.

My brain fails to form a thought. I'm sure I've seen her face before, though I can't say where. Familiar and unfamiliar, her presence is unsettling, and all at once, I know exactly who I am looking at. There's a sudden loss as Enzo steps away from my fingertips.

"Hermanito," Cyrus calls from behind me.

The music drones on above the canopy of lights, and my head spins. An omniscient voice repeats her name in my head, waiting for the word to manifest in the surrounding air.

Cyrus clears his throat and speaks in a tone I know he practices when de-escalating certain transactional situations. "Ana called earlier today, when we were at the groves."

There it is. Here she is.

Why is she here?

"She had just landed on the island and wanted to surprise you for the wedding tomorrow. I invited her here tonight instead." Cyrus chuckles uncomfortably, and my mother lightly slaps his lapel yet continues to smile in Ana's direction. He raises his hands, palms up in innocence.

"I'm sorry if I've crashed your dinner," Ana says. Her voice is light and airy, like a twittering morning bird. She brushes a stubborn strand of hair away from her face and tucks it behind her ear, just for it to fall forward again.

"No," Enzo finally says, stepping toward the woman he was supposed to marry. He looks back at me, and I attempt to wear a polite smile, my hands behind my back. Everyone is waiting for his next move. His focus returns to Ana, and he takes another step closer.

It shouldn't hurt as much as it does, every step he takes toward her and away from me.

Ana takes his advance as a welcome and leaves her suitcase behind, closing the distance between them. She embraces him, her arms wrapped around his neck. Their bodies form around one another unquestioningly. A warm greeting with a sense of frank familiarity and intimacy.

My head spins faster and faster, my heart still racing from the exertion of our interrupted dance. Enzo gently takes Ana's shoulders and holds her at arm's length to look her over. He seems unable to help himself as he smiles.

She looks up at him with a returning wariness, moisture pooling in the corners of her eyes. "Hi," she says simply.

Baffled, Enzo shakes his head. "You're in Spain," he says.

She laughs and nods her head. "I am. Never thought I would be, but here I am."

Enzo rubs the sides of her arms. Her body stiffens at the excessiveness of his touch, and he removes his grasp to turn to the rest of the party. With his palm safely placed on Ana's back, he introduces her to everyone. First, she hugs Cyrus and Katia and comments on the vast loveliness of our villa. She shakes Simone's hand firmly, then Matteo's. They are both taken aback, as they are unfamiliar with Ana's somewhat unfriendly way of greeting. She shakes my hand next, and I meet the woman who let Enzo get away.

"It's lovely to finally meet you, Ana." I say before meeting Enzo's dark eyes, "We're very glad you could make the wedding after all."

"Oh," Ana looks back at Enzo, bashful, "well, yes, I'm glad I was able to come as well. I mean, it was all quite spontaneous and last minute, and I meant to surprise Enzo tomorrow, but," my gaze follows as Ana takes Enzo's hand in hers and rests her head against his shoulder. There is a possessiveness in the simple gesture, and jealousy winds me tight like a spring. Not just at the candidness in her behavior, but *his*. He's allowing her to touch him, stroke him, hold him, as though he's still in New York. As though he wasn't claiming me with his entire body earlier this same evening.

Anger floods me, and I do my best to tamp it down. I feel small. Insignificant. Rancor roils in my chest toward Enzo for making me feel this way.

"I couldn't resist when Cyrus suggested I drop in tonight," Ana continues, oblivious to the true nature of the man she's holding on to.

Enzo's gaze is on my face, begging me to look at him, but I refuse, ever stubborn.

"And who's this?" Ana crouches down to shake Marco's hand. An unnecessary hint of protectiveness washes over me, but I let it pass as Marco grabs her by both shoulders and kisses her on one cheek, then the other. "Oh," she gasps.

"This is Marco, our son," my mother explains.

Ana nods. "It's good to meet you, Marco." Her vowels sound harsh and foreign. Unsettling in our small world.

Marco twists his face at the mention of his name and giggles as Ana stands and takes Enzo's hand again.

"What are you doing here?" Enzo asks.

Ana blinks up at him, a bit hurt, and looks around, crestfallen.

"I got your message," she says.

Enzo shakes his head as Ana drops her voice, attempting to whisper, but the effort is futile. "The photo of the sky? From the plane?"

Enzo frowns at her and curiosity surges within me.

"You would always send me photos of the sky from wherever you were. It made me miss you so much, I had to see you again." She shrugs, her shoulders remaining high around her ears. She interwove her fingers, spinning a ring on one hand with the other. A simple band with a simple diamond.

A hole cuts deep through the middle of my chest, and I instantly, desperately, need a smoke. Behind me, Matteo watches the scene unfold with as much interest as I am trying to hide.

I make a peace sign with my fingers and bring them up to my lips. Matteo understands the universal gesture and fishes a pack out from his pocket, swipes the hair from his face in an expert twist of his neck, and lights two in his mouth, handing one to me. I take it and squeeze his hand once in thanks before bringing the stick up to my lips to suck in a sweet bloom of smoke.

Ana gives Matteo and I a side glance. Is she perturbed at our open-smoking-policy?

"That wasn't an invitation," Enzo says.

Ana's gaze flits back to him, and she takes a step back at the jab, shaking her head. "What do you mean?"

"I mean," Enzo runs a hand through his hair and turns toward the rest of us for help. He clicks his tongue and signals for a cigarette. The sadistic part of me wins over as I take a final drag from the half-smoked stick in my mouth and hand it to him. He pops it between his lips without hesitation and puffs.

Ana's eyes widen in overdramatic horror, and I stifle a smirk.

"That photo, it wasn't intended as an invitation, Ana. It was just a photo. I never expected you to get on a plane and fly all the way to Spain. We're broken up. What were you thinking?"

Tears well in her eyes, and all forms of sadistic thoughts subside, melting into the empathetic part of me that wants to hold this stranger of a woman so we may grieve over the unwanted heartache produced by the same man.

"Do you want me to leave?" she asks, tears about to break the surface. She swipes them away.

Enzo shakes his head. "No, no. You've come all this way, of course you can stay." Enzo looks to my mother and Cyrus, then to me.

"*Claro que sí*, of course she is welcome," my mother says in her velvety sing-song voice.

Ana wipes away more tears and smiles up at my family. A medley of emotions stirs within me, uncertain which deserves more attention at the present moment. Anger? Confusion? Heartache? The abrupt invasion has tilted me off my already spinning axis, losing control completely as this stranger makes her presence unavoidable.

My mother ushers us all back to the table, which is still abundant with food. She makes a plate to present before Ana as she is more formally welcomed. Shallow conversation of travel and weather and comparisons of our small city to that of New York clatter around the courtyard. The music continues into the night, and Cyrus asks my mother for another dance. She obliges and takes his hand. I excuse myself as everyone pairs off, escaping from the inevitable embarrassment of being the odd one out.

I race through the glass doors, weaving through the few cooks left, now cleaning their stations. Held back tears spring forward as I make it up the three flights of stairs to my bedroom, and there, in the silent stillness of my room, I keep myself from breaking down. Two narratives war in my mind. A voice of longing clashes with a voice of reason. Memories of Enzo beneath my dress, pleasuring me until I've come so hard I can think of no one but him. The words he thinks I didn't hear as his final thrusts brought him a similar pleasure.

I'm in love with you.

Life altering words I had been holding onto since they were uttered and have been afraid to repeat aloud. Did he mean it? Or was it cheapened by the actions clouding his judgment?

How could this work? How could any of it work despite what we think we might feel for one another? And now, with Ana's arrival, how do I know seeing her won't stir up some unresolved emotions in him? Emotions he *thinks* may be reserved for me but are, in fact, left-over from his time with the woman he once loved. What if, in light of her presence, I am left behind?

Don't be so pitiful, my mind scolds me from deep within. I knew heartbreak was a possibility when we started this. Perhaps not when I accepted a stranger's request for a dance one night, but surely between then and now. We both knew we were doomed from the start. So why do I feel as though it's *me* who is not enough?

If that is the case, fine. I still have Paris. My life there could be plentiful in experience, food, romance. I am not hopeless, I am not pitiful, I am *not* in love with Enzo.

Doubt creeps into the dark corners of my mind.

Mentirosa.

I run my fingertips through the roots of my hair and kick off my heels in frustration as I pace the length of my bedroom. Another pitiful voice makes its way to the surface as I kick myself for being so easily seduced. Humiliation runs over me in a frenzy of rash thoughts, and I have half a mind to pack for Paris this very minute. But I don't.

Instead, I rummage through my drawers to find the only thing that might calm the pounding in my head and find a half crushed pack of Marlboros. I take the pack outside along with a lighter. The ceramic tiles are cool and calming beneath my bare feet, grounding me as I sit by the ledge. Above the canopy of lights, the party down below seems like a world away. I see the tops of heads as they swish this way and that in the evening air, dancing to the light music.

Enzo and Ana are still sitting at the table. He stands, and I cannot bear to watch him dance with another woman. The moon hangs high in the sky, casting her knowing light onto the distant water as I close my eyes and drown out every other sound but the crashing waves, and light another cigarette.

17

ENZO

Ana's presence is a mirage of deceit. I reach out and stroke her cheek, her chin, making sure she's real. Unable to trust the natural ease of my arms around her, the acquiescence of her touch, when all I truly want is Mia.

Ana's scent conjures up forgotten memories of late nights and early mornings. The redolent scent of slow drip coffee on her breath, the medical grade soap she's used for years. I smell Ana, feel her warmth in my palms, and a torrent of emotions fog my thoughts, along with one life altering realization.

I don't know what to do.

What am I to do with her here, now? I took the time to grieve the loss of what we had—the potential of our future discarded. I admitted responsibility for the relationship ending, knowing I could not change myself to suit her needs. Accepting her decision to leave, I used it as a diving board to get on a plane less than a week ago and face my family alone.

Seeing Mia opened my eyes to the gift of freedom Ana had tangentially given me. Though, that wasn't freedom either, was it? By loving Mia, I've put myself in the same cage, albeit from a different perspective.

Ana's hands in mine feel familiar.

They also feel wrong.

She is mid-sentence, telling me of all I've missed in her life, and my body pulls away from hers without notice. I stand, my knees more sure than my heart.

"Excuse me," I say, and squeeze her shoulder.

A wan smile breaks across her face before I make my way toward the glass doors of the kitchen. I need space, I need a moment. I need Mia.

The sharp clicks of my dress shoes against the tiles match my racing heart as my feet move me forward. I nod to those in the kitchen and thank them under my breath to keep from running for the stairs. When I finally do race up the three flights, I find a ray of moonlight streaming from her open bedroom door.

I steel myself and walk into Mia's room. She's standing on the veranda, gazing up into the night sky. A lit cigarette sits between two long fingers. She doesn't see me walk into the room, doesn't hear my footfalls grow louder as I prowl closer to her slender, leaning form. Her dress falls with little effort across her shoulders and hips in a pool of fabric that teases the flame building in my core. She brings the cigarette down to the crystal ashtray sitting precariously on the ledge of the veranda and flicks off the stray ashes. Taking another slow pull, she closes her eyes, reveling in the small high I know it brings. Moonlight kisses the angles of her beautiful face, and my breath hitches at the sight. She is perfection, marmoreal, a living statue.

Mia tilts her head back, releasing smoke between pursed lips, and her eyes open, locking with mine. My presence in her room doesn't surprise her. Studying me, I know she sees the burning behind my eyes, yet she stares. Her lips part as she takes another drag. Breath held, she reaches out a slender arm for me, cigarette in hand. My feet obey her wordless command, and I am before her.

The low hanging moon is full, her light abundant as it shines across us both. Mia exhales, wind rustling through my coarse stubble. My eyes drift closed as the sweetness of her breath blends with the bitterness of the smoke. I tilt my head down to search her face, desperate to know how she is taking the derailment of our plan. She gives me nothing, torturing me without a word. She brings the cigarette up to my mouth, and I oblige, sucking on the tip, reveling in the fact that the same object touched her lips a moment before. Lipstick stains the white texture, the tip creased in its use. Our eyes remain locked as I desolately try to read what's behind hers. There exists the sensation that she can see right through me, penetrating to my very core. I am stripped bare before her, vulnerable and exposed and unequivocally hers.

Wicked eyes grasp my every muscle, my every breath. The moment stretches, and I feel myself grow hard. Heat ebbs its way down my spine while party noises from below coalesce with the music as it fades along with the evening light.

When did her hand start playing with my hair? Her wrist rests at the base of my neck, the ashes of the cigarette falling down my back, resulting in a sweet heat.

We stay there, sharing the deep silence, until she breaks it. "Do it, Enzo, before you lose your mind."

She raises her chin in challenge, bitter hate written behind the sweet drops of honey behind her lashes. I'm at her mercy when she looks at me like this. A twinge of fear flickers inside me at the idea of her abusing that knowledge. Fear and intrigue. Her fingers ghost across the back of my neck before cupping it with force. My focus falls to her lips, hands reaching for her hips. Our breath mingles for a moment as I stare back into those searing golden eyes. There's no hesitation in them. Only hunger. She darts the tip of her tongue out and flicks my upper lip. The smallest touch unravels my mind into a frenzy.

I crush my lips to hers, taking everything I've ever wanted. It doesn't matter how soon after we've been together. How mischievously inseparable we've been over the past few days. I want her more now than I've ever wanted anything, and I no longer care who I hurt in the process.

Even if it's Ana. Even if it's me.

Her tongue fights mine before taking over completely. She tastes like smoke and wine and the captivating unknown. Anything but soft. She is rough and fast. Her cigarette burns the back of my neck on its descent as we move against each other. I hiss against her mouth at the luring pain, and we hit something hard. A reflexive moan slips from her throat. I may burst from such sounds. When I open my eyes, she's pressed against the stone wall of the veranda. Lipstick smeared across her mouth messily, lips plump, skin flushed. She tries to hide her racing heart, steadying her breath through her nose.

I am not such a good actor.

Gathering her wrists from the back of my neck in one hand, I pin them to the stone above her. With a glance toward our outstretched arms, her lips curl at their edges. Defying me without the slightest hint of struggle. A leg raises up around my waist, her dress drifting to expose her thigh to the evening air, her hips curving to meet mine.

So tempting.

She licks her lips, tasting us. There is no question she can feel me. Let her. Let her feel what she does to me. My other hand grips her ankle and trails up her bare leg, kneading her calf, her thigh, the roundness of her ass. I stroke my thumb against her ankle, remembering her taste as I nipped at the angles of her foot before devouring her whole.

My grip grows forceful, digging my nails into the soft flesh there, taking every bit of her I can into my hand. She snarls at the thorns in my touch, her visage a pure liquid fire. She's livid. What she had been trying to hide before now comes forth in the crease of her brow, the rise of her chest. Upset with me, yet still, she lets me play. The vigor in my touch persists, claiming her waist, seizing a breast, possessing every inch of her. Her breath grows shallow and fast as she arches her back, feeding herself into my touch as her mouth parts, hips rising further, reaching.

Delighted in my ability to coax her from one extreme to another, I have half a mind to step back now, to see if she will beg. She wants everything I am willing to give her. I palm the flat of her chest, feeling the proof of her arousal in her pounding heart, and my fingers brush along her collarbone before wrapping around her throat. A small inkling of relinquished control I know she gets off on—as do I. My thumb pushes against her jawline, forcing her gaze up.

Possessive.

I've grown possessive of this woman. My brother's stepdaughter. I remember Matteo's lips on hers on the beach, Luke watching her at the groves, every man who has had her before me, and I wish to erase them all from her memory.

Of all the women I could have fallen into bewitchment, *this one*, this one makes me beg for mercy. This one makes me forget who I am, who I'm supposed to be, who I should be. I despise her. I hate her for making me like this. I loathe myself for blaming her for being so primal, bringing me down to such a basic need. Making me question everything I've ever known to be myself. With my hand wrapped around her throat, I no longer know who I am without her.

I am hers. And by God, I will make her mine.

18

Mia

The Day Before the Wedding

"Enzo," I sigh.

A war rages behind his eyes. He can't do this on his own. Take what we both want without some sort of blessing. I hold no such obligations. I've wanted him since the day we met. I had him earlier today, and want him still.

"I hate you," he finally says through gritted teeth. His hand wraps around the entirety of my neck, squeezing an inch with the inflection.

I smile at the constriction.

He tightens half a breath more. "You will ruin me."

I lick my lips and bite down on the bottom, responding to the eroticism of my hands and neck bound, my body at his mercy. Damp fabric clings between my legs, and I shift in his grasp, desperate for any form of friction.

"You never needed my help ruining yourself. You want to blame me? Make me pay," I challenge.

His grip tightens still, restricting blood flow now. I can't breathe, but I don't fight. I want to see this side of him. To see how far he will take me. I want him to break with me.

A low rumble of applause erupts in the party down below, and he turns his head toward the sound. We've forgotten where we are. Who we are. To each other. His grasp lessens, the fever in his eyes breaking ever so slightly. I stifle a cough, forcing myself to swallow as blood rushes back to my face. The ringing in my ears subsides, and low breaths steady me, maintaining a stubborn facade.

Ana's interruption has stifled our plan, yes, but it has not brought it to a complete stop. He belongs to her as much as he belongs to me at this moment. And I intend to use that to our advantage.

"Have you any idea what you do to me, Mia?" He shakes his head, his voice filled with both anger and longing.

My nose stings at the pain in his words, but I steel myself. My resolve to see this through must not falter. He sees us as unobtainable. Good. We are.

"You want to punish me, Enzo? To see me suffer knowing I can't have you? You want to see me beg?" I smile in defiance. "I refuse."

The music picks back up again from the yard, the twinkling lights casting a glow around my family as they gather on the dance floor. A breeze catches the curls framing my face, blocking my vision for a moment. Yet, I feel him still. All of him, all over me.

His hand at the base of my neck moves up to caress my jaw before his thumb brushes my lower lip. "Open," he growls.

I obey, and his thumb enters my mouth, brushing against my tongue.

"You refuse?" he asks in a whisper. "Shall I take what I want, then?" His thumb travels deeper into my mouth before he removes it and slides back in again. He repeats the motion. Every thrust threatens a gag, but I remain unmoving. The sensation pulls at my core as I remember my mouth wrapped around his cock. "What do you want, Mia?"

I close my lips and suck, trailing my tongue in circles around his thumb. *Reminding him.* I bob my head slightly, never breaking my stare from his. He rips his thumb out of my mouth like it's an open flame.

"Do it," I say, disregarding the question he already knows the answer to. "You can't hurt me any more than you already have. Standing there with *her* on your arm—so comfortable. So do it."

His expression twists in confusion and something like contrition.

I swallow before continuing my challenge. "If that's what you need to give us both permission. As long as she's here, nothing we do matters, right?"

He loosens his grip from my throat, his hand falling to his side while the other still pins me to the wall.

My back arches in response, longing for his touch as I release words of indignation. "You hate me? I despise you. How long have you deprived us both? It must have been quite the stretch of the imagination—fucking that mousey girl of yours downstairs and thinking of me. How many times did you kiss her just a little too rough and realize she couldn't handle what you could give? You don't think I recall our dance before I'm wet at the thought of you, riding my own fingers? I don't care if she's right downstairs, I can't take any more. How much longer can *you* last, Enzo?" I lift my leg up his inner thigh and dig my shin into the stiffness between his legs. "Take it."

His eyes drift close as I press the bone of my shin further into him. His other hand comes up hard against my jaw. I gasp as the back of my head hits the stone, biting the inside of my lip open as he grips my chin, forcing me to look up at him. An iron taste fills my mouth.

"*Wicked* little Mia."

"Yes." I exhale, licking the blood off my lip.

"Who knew you could say such filthy things without even blushing?"

"Not all women are like your Ana."

He pushes my head half an inch higher. "Don't say her name."

I laugh. "Too soon, *amorcito*? What did you do? Something she couldn't handle? Something like this?" I wiggle my wrists and he tightens his grip in response. I smirk at his enraged countenance, amused. "Did you scare her off with your little kinks? Couldn't get hard unless it hurt just a little, *si*? Must not have been enough, because here she is." I press my shin further into his groin, and he pushes back. "That's it, *Lorencito*," I taunt, coax, pushing him past his limit. "She may not have been able to handle you, but we both know—*I can.*"

A bead of blood trickles down to my chin. His face lowers to meet mine as he licks the drop and dips his tongue back into my mouth. My arms grow numb, the back of my head smarting at the impact, and my body goes limp with his kiss. Despite the force of the rest of his touch, the kiss is gentle. Exploring. Savoring.

He removes his grip from my chin and tugs at the strap of my dress.

"Be careful," I warn. "You've ruined one dress tonight already."

The music picks up pace as the party rages into the evening. The fury I possess toward this man who has me pinned against stone starts to burn.

I fight back, wrapping both legs around him, locking my ankles at the base of his back and bringing him in close. The hardness of him presses against the softness of me, and I grow furious with the desire to have him inside me again.

Enzo releases my arms, and they fall to brace against his shoulders, blood racing back toward my fingertips like a river of needles. The prickling sensation adds to the frenzy of pain and pleasure making its way throughout my body. I kiss him again, make him taste the blood he's drawn out of me, and he holds me strong, kneeling to the ceramic floor. My feet meet the cold tile as I right myself in his lap, straddled across him, and he kisses me with a fervor unlike before.

Enzo bends over me, arching me to accept his weight. Cold tiles lick my back and shoulder blades, and I gasp, my body shuddering at the sensation as goose bumps spread across my arms and neck.

He rises and takes his time to see what he's done to me, sits up on his heels, hands resting on his knees. "Lift your dress, Mia."

An involuntary smile gives me away, the responding rush at the command in his words. I lift my dress without hesitation, and he rips my panties off like an animal ripping into flesh.

"Spread your legs." His voice is raspy and decadent.

The taste of blood still in my mouth, I spread my legs wide, baring myself to him.

"Good fucking girl," he says before diving his head down and parting me with his tongue.

My back bows against the tile, my hand whipping to my mouth to stifle a scream.

"You're already wet enough to take me, wicked little *slut*. I just want one more taste..."

I hear the zipper of his trousers, then the head of his cock pushes into me and my back bows once again. This time, Enzo's hand stifles my scream as his palm holds my head in place, and he begins to rock his hips hard against mine.

My hair catches behind my head, bending my neck back uncomfortably. I grasp at nothing, my arms outstretched at my sides, flailing to find some form of leverage to relieve the pressure. Enzo grabs my hips and pulls me in, impaling me deeper, and this rights my neck as he kisses me hard and fast, his cock angling at just the right spot to coil me tighter and tighter.

Enzo breaks the kiss and lifts again, never breaking stride with his hips. He cups my jaw with one hand and smears my lipstick across my face. I gape at him, the creature he's become, and paw at his shirt. The need for his bare skin building higher and higher as I chase my own climax. He slaps my hands away and rips the shirt off himself, discarding it on the tile, postures up, and grabs both of my ankles. The stretch is uncomfortable at first as he widens my legs, holding me open in such an obscene manner, and humiliation engulfs me like an ocean wave. The noises escaping my throat send him into a frenzy as he drives deeper, harder. He's fucking me for his own pleasure, and I am enjoying every moment of his punishment.

"See what you do to me, Mia?" His words emerge through gritted teeth.

"*Yes*," I moan, trying not to scream.

"Look how well you take me," he looks down to where our bodies meet, and I follow his gaze, watching as he enters me with every rough infliction.

His thumbs hook behind my knees and push my legs down on either side of my ears. He has my arms pinned beneath my thighs in an extraordinarily humiliating position. Enzo rises off his heels and thrusts down. My view from this angle is even more apparent. The length of his cock disappears into me as I stretch to take him, swallowing him down, my walls contracting with every stroke. The sight, the constriction, his words laced with hints of sweet degradation, they all send me spiraling as the spring that's wound tighter and tighter finally snaps.

I scream, and Enzo's hand claps down on my mouth to muffle the sound in a panic. Over the music, the chatter, the clinking of glass and silverware, I continue to scream into Enzo's palm as he pounds, harder and harder. I finally stop, gasping for air as he releases me.

I'm given no time to recover as he lifts me up by the arms. Straddling, I take hold of his neck as I brace my feet on the tiled floor and rock hard against him. Hips lifted, I ride expertly along his length. His eyes roll back before meeting mine again, and he grabs the back of my head by the root of my hair, and my skin smarts. I dig my nails into his back, returning his violence.

He seethes, teeth bared. "Fuck me like you hate me."

"I do hate you." My hips roll harder as I fuck him back. I don't have to pretend. I don't have to act like this is fantasy. This is real. I hate him as much as I love him, and it is just dawning on me now how visceral the two sensations feel as they both roar to the surface.

I hate seeing him next to her. How easily he makes it for her to slide back into his arms like I was never there. It breaks and burns my heart at once.

The hardness of his brow softens as he watches me.

"No, you don't," he says. Enzo lifts his hips to match my stride, deepening himself inside me. He's kissing me again, his lips softer than his thrusts, which angers me further. He has no right to be sweet.

I claw at his back, leaving scratches for Ana to find later.

"Fuck," he cries out before pushing me back down to the floor. He gathers both my legs by the ankles and lifts them straight up. The angle is new, building a different cadence deep inside.

"Punish me," I challenge.

He chuckles, and then I'm bracing myself against his knees, holding onto them as the sound of skin slapping against skin fills the space of the veranda. My feet frame his face as he holds me by the ankles, trailing kisses along the arch of one foot, then the other, nipping at my ankles until he holds one between his teeth, and I'm writhing with an overwhelming awareness of my body. I've never been fucked so rough yet so tender at the same time.

Familiar pressure builds with a demanding need to release, his pace quickens, his breathing ragged.

"Come inside me," I say.

His eyes glaze over with desire as he looks down at me and shakes his head.

"Yes, Enzo," I stroke his bare chest, his stomach, and cup as much of his ass as I can before using the one word I know he won't deny. "Please."

Enzo throws his head back in a roar of moaning laughter. The pressure in my lower abdomen teeters on the edge of unbearable. He comes back down and caresses my neck, pulling the strap of my dress, allowing my breasts to tumble out. He palms one and rolls my nipple between two fingers. I arch into it.

"Are you sure?" he asks.

I nod.

He reaches for his discarded dress shirt and wads it into a ball, places it behind my head, and guides my hands toward his knees. "Hold on tight like a good girl."

I smirk and obey.

He doesn't make me wait long, his thrusts matching every breath, sending us both closer and closer to the edge.

"*More... yes... please.*" Words tumble from my lips, though not all syllables make their way out.

He holds onto both ankles in one hand, my thighs gathered in the other as he lifts my bottom half up to meet just the right angle. Unbelievable pleasure roils through me, a fire burning deep within, his rhythm unrelenting, and my mouth falls open in a silent scream, my eyes rolling back, the spring coiling tighter still. Two more thrusts and I'm there, my mind snapping again with the force of all our pent up anger and fears. Knowing better now, I gag myself with my hand, silencing a cry I want him to hear.

The walls of my pussy flutter and contract, spasming the rest of my body in a wave of pleasure that seems to go on for far too long. The pressure that's been building in my belly releases in a messy display. A final blow of humiliation, I've marked him as he's marked me.

Enzo comes hard and rough, a heady groan in his throat, then he stills, a low rumble vibrating my legs as they rest against his chest. He kisses my ankles once more before releasing them down on either side of him and lowering himself on top of me. I cup his face between my hands and bring his lips to mine.

In his exhausted aftermath, he lets me rule the kiss, tasting every bit of him I can manage. His body slackens as he falls into me with submission, and I hold him close, our arms entangled around one another. We stay like this for a dangerous amount of time. The space between lust and something else growing more precarious by the moment as our racing hearts calm against each other.

I ruffle his hair while he fondles my breasts, his hips idly rock against mine, the animalistic need sated for now. In our exhaustion, we kiss lazily, gleaning any last bit of remnant pleasure we can from the other. Enzo holds me tight and rolls us to our sides as he pulls out of me, and I feel him spill against the inner part of my thigh.

The lie we're both telling ourselves bubbles forward, and I find the courage to open my mouth and—

"Please, don't say anything," Enzo says.

I close my mouth, obedient as ever, still.

His knuckle strokes my cheek, and the fire behind his touch comes to the surface, burning my flesh. "I don't hate you, Mia."

I blink up at him and nod. He kisses me again with a brush against my lips.

"Let's go dancing," I say.

Enzo tilts his head at me, his gaze darting toward the edge of the veranda.

"We can go out the back gate."

There's a sense of doubt in his gaze, and I brush my lips against his again. "I know a place where we can pretend. Please?"

His beautifully swollen lips curl up at the edges at my magic word.

19

Enzo

The Day Before the Wedding

Faint music emanates from the courtyard as we sneak out the back gate of the house. The metal creaks, and we rush around the house and toward the gravel drive. Mia climbs into the driver's seat of Cyrus's convertible and fishes a spare set of keys from the folded visor. The car roars to life, and we skid off into the night.

I've abandoned Ana. I've left her alone in a house full of strangers to be with another woman. But Mia is not "another woman." She is Mia, *my Mia*. And I love her. Despite how much she enrages and challenges me, I cannot deny it any more than I can deny the sustenance of sunlight. Remorse twists in my chest and my fingertips prick with panic.

I don't know what to make of Ana's arrival. What cruel test could this be from heaven above if I am meant to choose between these two women in the presence of both? It was difficult enough returning to Ana and confessing the dance to her three years ago, now I must choose Mia over my past. Would I be a decent man if I left Ana entirely, after she's come all this way to try again? She's a woman I once had the intention of sharing my life with. One I thought I could love for the rest of my days. Or would that decency eat away at me for not exploring the possibility of a happier life?

My head spins, the night air cool and calming against my cheeks. I look out into the night sky and watch the stagnant stars as we speed by the Spanish coast. Searching the archives of my mind for a semblance of peace, I find Mia's hand on mine, prying my white knuckles loose and placing herself in my grasp. Her focus fixed on the road ahead.

We ride under the light of the moon toward an unknown town before pulling into a dark lot full of small cars, motorbikes, and scooters. The booming bass is loud enough to hear through the dark building, and Mia parks far from the entrance, nods at the bouncer, who lets us in without question. We have no coats to check and walk through velvet double doors to a nightclub teeming with half naked bodies. Strobe lights hover above, giving the illusion of a stop motion film. The music is deafeningly loud, the bass shudders my bones, and Mia's hand guides me through the crowd and onto the dance floor.

This is no place for spectacle. No place to be seen and admired. This is a place to hide. The strobing lights and loud music drown out any other form of self, any identity you might carry with you in the light of day. It washes who you think you are away from your mind and lets you coast above your own ethos.

With the ease in which Mia falls into her role here among the sea of strangers, the telling nod to the guard at the entrance, I gather she's been here before. Perhaps when she's too overwhelmed, when she risks overflowing, she comes here to let herself run along the brim of her mind and wash herself away in anonymity. This club is as much a sanctuary to her as her veranda.

Mia's body sways against mine and I sway back, feeling her without reservation. There is no one here to see, no one to judge or make their disapproval known. Nothing else exists here but our two bodies and the music moving them. Though we've danced before, the pace of this is different, unambiguous as we move to a simple, repetitive bass. A heartbeat this room full of strangers can sync in rhythm with together.

Thoughts, doubts, guilt, names, occupations, they all leave my head as the contours of Mia's body and the humidity of the room flood my senses. Nothing in the world matters now but this. Her. In my arms. Thick air in my lungs. Her back is against my chest, and we move as one body toward the climax of a song I've never heard before, exchange no words, no glances, no kisses. Just our rhythm in the strobing light. And it is here I find clarity.

If I am to call myself a man worthy of the woman I hold in my arms, I must free myself of all other ties. I've kept Ana knotted in a place within me I've ignored for far too long. Untangling her from me will not be easy. How can I release her in a way that won't break her entirely?

Mia turns in my arms and lays her head against my chest. Her body quakes. Is she crying? If she is, the music drowns out her cries. Her tears hidden in the dark. She stills in my arms, her shoulders shuddering, and I hold her as we stand still in an ocean of undulating bodies, lost at sea together.

Mia and I return to the villa to find the courtyard dark and empty. The house is quiet, our every step seeming too loud. My ears ring with the aftermath of the club, my eyes adjusting to a source of constant light. I hold Mia's face and kiss her ardently before we both retreat into our separate rooms. I expect to see Ana waiting for me in mine, but the room is empty. The bed made, my clothes strewn out exactly where I'd left them.

The tamped down misgivings from earlier now boil to the surface. I should go find Ana and end this torment now before it eats at me any longer. But the stillness of the house makes me think better of it, and I ready myself for a night of fitful sleep.

The next morning, Mia and I allow the other time in the washroom to shower and ready ourselves for the big day ahead. I awoke many times during the night with harrowing dreams I cannot recall. When the sun finally breaks through the glass doors, I sit up in bed and watch as it rises higher in the sky. The house stirs with signs and sounds of life, and the smell of coffee wafts up to my room, its enticing clarity pulling me from my bed.

I come downstairs to find Ana and Mia sitting side by side at the kitchen island, mugs in their hands.

"Oh!" Ana says, getting up from her stool.

Mia smiles, watching Ana eagerly pour me a cup of my own, bringing me the mug and rising on her toes to kiss my cheek. My arm instinctively holds her waist at arm's length.

My attention drifts to Mia, but she's focused on the depths of her mug.

Ana clears her throat. "I didn't want to disturb you, so Katia showed me to another room for the night. I hope that's all right."

"*Claro*—yes," I stammer. My mind is hazy with confusion. "Where are the bride and groom? Still here I hope?"

"Upstairs," Mia finally speaks. "The florists and caterer will be here soon to start setting everything up. Luckily, the dance floor is already in place." Her voice mimics Katia's melodic tone.

"Mia was just telling me about her new job in Paris," Ana says.

I look up between the two women. "Was she?" I ask. "I thought you were undecided on that front?"

Mia shrugs as she stands, the stool making a terrible scraping noise against the wooden floor. She brings her mug to the sink and rinses it thoroughly. "I only just decided last night. After the wedding, I assume you two will be returning to your lives in New York. Simone and Matteo have the speakeasy handled, and I can manage remotely if needed. Cyrus and my mother will have each other, and Marco does a well-enough job taking care of them. There's nothing left on the island for me." She uses the same inflection she exuded at the grove when speaking to clients on the phone.

I want to yell, to scream at her for being so naïve.

"Can you imagine, Enzo?" Ana says, "A life in *Paris*? You're living the dream, Mia."

Mia nods, scrubbing her mug under steaming water. "I grew up mostly in Paris, Ana. This would be more like going home."

"Going home or running away?" I ask.

Ana looks up at me, her excited smile wavering at my discretion.

Mia turns off the tap and dries her hands on a hanging dish towel before turning to face me and Ana. "Perhaps a bit of both," she says. "Excuse me, I should go find my mother. I think she's getting married today."

Mia leaves through the glass doors across the courtyard to Cyrus and Katia's wing of the villa.

"Still, *Paris*," Ana says. She releases a droning sigh and clicks her tongue. "It's not New York though." Ana downs the rest of her coffee and places her mug in the sink.

I rinse it with the same effort Mia had with hers. "Right," I say. "It's not New York."

20

Mia

Wedding Day

Having spent my formative years in the fashion capital of the world, I pride myself on maintaining a sense of self untouched by the pretentiousness of Paris, holding on to my individuality amidst the glamor and allure. My taste is, of course, rooted in such inspirations. All art is a form of imitation, including fashion. Most evenings, the sunset displays the same shade of pink as an Hermès scarf. My adopted shades and preferences, though darker now, have always come from my mother's influence. Her sense of individuality in a sea of mimicry stemmed from both necessity and talent. Our need for clothes brewed an opportunity for expression, and therefore creativity. My mother always made a day out of thrifting. Finding unique pieces in second-hand stores with the potential to bring out her eyes or my complexion. We would return home with our spoils and tailor each garment to our own bodies. Creating piece after piece in her image.

Which is why when I see my mother in a wedding dress she's designed, in a color so elegantly red and stunning, with a signature all her own, I begin to cry.

"*Mi hija, mi hija*," my mother gathers the dress's train in her hands and approaches me, wrapping me in her arms.

As with most tears, the ones that tip over the edge are rarely the ones found when the sobbing begins. My shoulders tremble, my vision blurry as I cry into my mother's embrace. She holds me, cooing Spanish words into my hair and stroking my back in the most Katia way.

"*Qué pasó, mi vida?*" She pushes the hair from my face, framing me in her hands and forcing me to look into her eyes, searching through the pain, the exhaustion of hiding, through the years of pretending.

A heavy sob escapes me again, as I can no longer bear the weight on my own. She sees me and understands. I don't have to say a word. She holds me to her chest again, and I collapse into my mother's arms, and she catches me, as she always has.

We fall in a pile of lace and silk on the floor of her bedroom. She strokes my hair and back silently, letting me purge the tears I've been holding back. She doesn't ask for an explanation. Heaving sobs steal the breath from my lungs, forcing harsh bouts of air in and out as my body processes the simple act of breathing.

When I find my breath, my sight finally gaining clarity, I tell her about Paris. About the decision I had come to while dancing in that club last night. Where the music was so loud, I could finally think.

I tell her how Luke has offered me a life I've never known before. A life away from her.

I confess my falling in love with a man I should not want and spare the most telling detail of his identity. I acknowledge the ignominy of it all. How I can't bear to be parted from him, yet the affair itself has gotten out of hand, and I must end it. The idea of being a second choice or met with hesitation is not something my mother raised me to accept. Therefore, I appear to be destined for heartbreak. And the secret I have been so desperate to keep no longer matters.

In this moment, I've redirected my mother's attention from herself on her wedding day back to me. That disgrace makes me shut my mouth and rise back to my feet.

I wipe the tears from my face and help her up as well. Fluffing out the train of her dress, I quickly fumble for the fastens down the side of her waist. She stops me with steady hands.

"I will not ask you who he is. I know you would tell me if you felt the need. But please, *mi hija*, do not live your life for me. You think I can't live without you?" She raises one eyebrow at me, forcing a laugh between my dulling sobs. "If Paris is what you want, go. Live your life. You have given more than enough of yourself to this family."

Silent tears stream down my face at the meaning behind her words. She is letting me go so easily, I don't know whether to feel inspired or wounded.

She wipes the moisture from my cheeks and smiles. "I will always be here for you to come home to, *mi vida*. Now go, clean yourself up. Only the bride is allowed to cry at her own wedding."

I steady my breathing, steeling myself for the day to come. When I awoke this morning, I had every intention of keeping myself solid for my mother. Of being the rock upon which she may stand. And now, after falling into her familiar arms and realizing a girl sometimes needs her mother, I feel even stronger for it.

Avoiding the courtyard, I make my way through the second floor toward my wing of the villa and into my bedroom, grateful Enzo is nowhere to be found. His presence bombards my thoughts too viciously for any string of rational thought. As for Ana, it would be easier to detest her if she were less than decent. In truth, she is as formidable as a young woman should be. Polite enough, smart enough, nice enough, pretty enough. She is enough. And what woman would I be if I were to intentionally sabotage a relationship that stood on its own before I entered the picture?

I'll have Paris regardless of where Enzo finds himself in the world. But the thought of him in that city with me adds an extra layer of sweetness to the fantasy. Yesterday, he asked me what I wanted, and I had replied with "peace." I can't have both. Can I?

Locked in the washroom, I splash cold water on my face. The shock snaps my racing thoughts into place. Agitated breaths finally even out into some semblance of calm, and I look into the swollen eyes of my reflection in the mirror, finding a broken image of myself.

I turn toward the large porcelain tub and run the tap, dumping calming salts and gels into the water, then strip off my sleeping clothes and step into the brewing bath, determined to emerge with a made up mind.

21

Enzo

Wedding Day

The courtyard teems with guests as they arrive in casual suits and cocktail dresses. Crisp evening air warms with the presence of mingling bodies, and the trickling fountain lulls under the hum of fraternized conversation. I stand by the glass doors of the kitchen with a flute of champagne in one hand and Ana by my side. She is wearing a knee length pastel blue dress I've seen her wear a dozen times before. It is simple, safe, and so very Ana. Her hair is swept half up, half down, as it always is. Her face is bright and happy, yet the sight of it brings me no joy.

A sea of strange yet familiar faces pass by. Some I recognize from Marco's baptism, others I know I've seen in the offices at the grove. None, though, recognize me. A foreigner at my brother's wedding, I stand with a straight spine and a friendly smile. Matteo passes us, and I regard him with an upheld glass. He shakes his head and smirks at me, taking a sip from his own flute without returning the gesture.

I swirl the bubbly liquid in my flute and long for a past full of different choices. One where I wouldn't be so out of place here today.

The twinkling lights above flicker, signaling the start of the ceremony. I down the rest of my champagne and place the empty flute on a passing waiter's tray, the crowd making its way around the courtyard through a pair of iron gates and toward the back of the villa.

Rows of white clothed chairs sit atop a small hill that overlooks the island's coast. An altar frames the ocean view at the hill's peak. Flowers adorn every corner of the scene. Gardenias and jasmine blooms vine their beauty across the back of every chair as well as the length of the aisle. The sun is resting just above the horizon, waiting for the ceremony to begin.

I escort Ana to her seat and stand at the back, waiting for my musical cue.

A serene quiet falls upon the guests, the hum of their conversation breaking into waiting anticipation, then the squeaking of iron against iron introduces my brother, looking as clean and presentable as I have ever seen him. The smile on his face speaks of years of patience and deserving happiness.

I will not cry.

Cyrus claps my shoulder with a firm hand and brings me in for a hug. I hold him close, smelling the strong cologne I know he saves for special occasions. The same cologne our mother gifted him when he was first old enough to wear such a masculine scent.

I hold my brother at arm's length and look him over, making sure every hair is in place, every piece of his tuxedo perfect. "You're ready, *hermano*," I say.

He nods. "Finally."

The music begins, and my brother leads the way. I trail behind, his lone groomsman and best man wrapped in one. We take our measured, rehearsed steps one at a time to give the expected theatrical pause, making our way to the head of the altar, and I take my place behind him. The music rests for a moment before transitioning into a soft and elegant procession.

Little Marco skips around the side of the house with a basket of flowers in one hand and a box in the other. He fumbles with the box, cradling it in the crook of his arm as he flings flower petals down the aisle. The crowd oohs and ahhs at his theatrical display, encouraging him all the way down. He meets his father at the head of the altar and hands him the box of rings. Cyrus kisses his son on the top of his head and ushers him to go sit with Simone. He obeys, placing the basket on the outer side of the aisle as instructed.

The screech of the iron gate sounds once again, and I hold my breath as Mia rounds the corner and waits at the end of the aisle.

The sight of her hits me like the sweetest arrow through the heart. Of course she's wearing the dress. *That dress.*

Feelings of banishment, of unworthy frustration cloud my vision. An emerald dress, so dark it's almost black, shimmers in the setting sunlight. It sways around the curve of her hips, and I remember the feel of her in that dress, between my fingers. Without seeing the lacing back, I know it exposes soft, freckled skin waiting to be kissed. The slit along one leg teases at a glimpse of thigh.

She wore this dress on purpose. For me. I can't help a smirk as I keep my eyes on the woman I love.

Her gaze lowered to the bouquet of white gardenia flowers in her hands, Mia makes her first step down the aisle. The music gains momentum, and her head raises at the cue. She smiles at the guests on either side of the aisle and nods to Simone, who is now holding

Marco up on her lap. Her soft gaze flits from one guest to another and back to the front of the altar before meeting my waiting glance.

Her smile fades by a fraction, replaced with a ghost of sadness that stabs me where I stand. As she slowly progresses to the rhythm of the music, I imagine her walking toward me every day. Approaching my outstretched arms at every hour, waiting for her to fill the void in my chest and sway to the music of our lives. She makes every step look like a dance, expertly shifting her weight from one foot to another, elevating such a banal practice into perfection.

Her eyes lock on mine for the rest of the journey down the aisle, maintaining as she takes her place on the opposite side of the altar. Our attention breaks when the music transitions once again, accompanied by the telling squeak of the iron gate.

Katia emerges from the side of the villa, an absolute vision in the most beautiful shade of red. Her dress fits to her body like wine in a bottle, perfectly complimenting her every move. Cyrus beams, tears flooding his eyes before quietly breaking the surface. I fetch a handkerchief from my breast pocket and hand it to him. He thanks me over his shoulder with a small chuckle.

"That's my wife," he says with a giddy schoolboy's voice.

I squeeze his shoulder before returning to my place, hands clasped behind my back.

Katia doesn't look at her guests, the setting sun, or the patient officiant. She looks through the ether and into my brother's eyes, as though every answer to all her life's questions lie behind them. A deep longing thrums through my very bones, an ache I've grown more accustomed to this past week. No woman has ever looked at me the way Katia is now looking at Cyrus, and I must stifle a sting of my own as tears threaten to breach. All I've ever wanted, presented here in a simple glance. And I am but an outsider, looking out from a room I've locked myself in alone.

The side of my face pricks, a sense of being watched. Ana's eyes are on me, her brows furrowed in concentration, the corners of her mouth pulled down. She shifts her gaze down and away from mine. The space in which I once would have flown to her side to fix whatever might be the cause for her upset is now occupied. By distance, by time, and by Mia.

My Mia. With proud tears streaking down her lovely face. Wisps of curls dance in the light evening breeze, tickling the roses in her cheeks. She shifts in place and lends her mother a hand as Katia approaches the altar, then the music comes to a close, as everyone is now in place.

The officiant is a tall young woman with a beautifully tailored yet feminine suit. Her voice booms across the grassy hillside, meeting every corner of the field with minimal effort. Spanish tradition and the roles of men and women in each other's lives lace her words on love and marriage. A true native, her accent is thick and loud. Ana must be lost in a sea of Spanish words, but when I look out into the rows of guests, my gaze falls upon her empty seat. A hint of unease flicks inside my chest. I can't leave my place to go see if she's alright.

The sun lays itself down beyond the horizon just as Cyrus and Katia recite their vows and kiss for the first time as husband and wife. The guests applaud and whoop happily, standing to greet the new couple as they walk back down the aisle, hand in hand. I join the crowd in their applause, wearing a bold grin. Mia cradles her bouquet in the crook of her arm and claps her hands enthusiastically, tears twinkling in her golden eyes, cheeks flushed with emotion, and with the brightest, most genuine smile. She's never looked more beautiful.

On cue, I approach Mia and offer an elbow. She takes it, and we follow the people we love most in this world as they stride toward the rest of their lives. Her warmth is comforting in the curve of my arm, a reminder of all I have to lose by the end of this day.

We return to the courtyard, where music and fresh trays of food and champagne greet the waiting guests. Tables with gorgeous floral centerpieces surround the spewing fountain beyond the dance floor.

I search for Ana with Mia on my arm and only find unfamiliar eyes looking back at me.

Guests roam aimlessly at first as they find their seats and settle in for the evening. The smell of freshly baked bread and rich red wine wafts through the crowd, scents indicative of any night here on the island, and I breathe the aroma in deep, a hint of jasmine and coconut catching my attention.

Simone's voice breaks my reverie, her song a velvet blanket wrapping every guest in the richest of melodies. She sings in front of a small four piece band atop a narrow stage at the west end of the courtyard. The evening is timeless, effortless. A memory for all in attendance, akin to a dream.

Simone introduces the new couple in Spanish. The crowd applauds again as Katia and Cyrus enter the courtyard and take the dance floor. Cyrus spins Katia onto the hardwood in an elegant twirl, catching her by the small of her back and into a two-step with the beat of the music. Their figures intertwine with ease, limbs beginning and ending each movement with fluid grace.

I lower my head toward Mia and whisper, "Care to dance, Mia?"

She beams up at me before looking around.

"We're the best man and the maid of honor. It would look even more suspicious if we *didn't* dance." I take her long fingers in my hand and hold them out, guiding us both onto the dance floor.

The movement is ordinary, practiced, yet my heart races as though it's the first time. With that emerald dress on her slight frame, I may as well be living in the very same memory.

We begin with a simple waltz. Her hand in mine as I lead, twirling her this way and that as her dress catches the wind with each step. Her lithe legs flick between mine, her weight never leaving the balls of her feet. By now, Mia and I have danced in more ways than an innocent waltz. My body has grown accustomed to hers, molding itself to fit around her in an unwilled, possessive way. I almost don't notice myself pressing her chest closer to mine, the slip of my hand as it falls from the widest part of her shoulders to the narrow curve of her lower back.

Mia squeezes my hand in hers, bringing my attention back to the present. I ache to kiss her, to bring her lips to mine and taste the evening on her skin. To forget the misgivings and surrender to the simple need to kiss and be kissed.

We move to the sound of her cousin's voice, while bodies surround us as the guests join our lead and enter the dance floor two by two.

I don't know when, but the space begins to crowd, leaving us little room to move through our unrehearsed steps. Heat creeps up my spine with the rapid onset of bodies, and her gaze pierces the deepest parts of my mind, infecting my every thought with the way she feels in my arms. Our bodies weave through the crowd, both hidden and exposed among family and friends. Where I craved recognition before the ceremony, I now find solace in the ability to go unnoticed by the majority of the guests' watchful eyes. Tomorrow they'll be asking about the stranger who danced with the bride's daughter.

Mia clears her throat and brings her temple to the hollow of my neck. I rest my cheek atop her head. She smells like rain in June, like the bouquet she's been holding all day. Like Mia.

"So, you've accepted Luke's offer?" I ask. She moves to lift her head, but I hold her close. "No, keep dancing."

"Yes."

"Why?" A question I've been meaning to ask since hearing of the news this morning.

She lets out a deep sigh. "Does it really need explaining, Enzo? There's nothing left for me here. But there's possibly a whole life waiting for me in Paris."

"There is life waiting for you, no matter where you go. But if Paris is where you see yourself living, you must go, Mia."

Her arms relax in my embrace as she lets out a breath on our next turn.

"Won't you grow lonely alone in a new city?" I rub idle circles on the bare skin of her back.

She shakes her head beneath my chin. "I enjoy a little solitude. I may grow homesick but never lonely. I am not like you, Enzo." She looks up at me, and I must resist the urge to press my forehead to hers. "Which is why you should go back to New York. With Ana."

My legs cease mid spin, causing Mia to fumble. My heart flutters in my throat.

"Your life is there, Enzo. With her. She came all this way for you. Surely she still loves you."

I shake my head. "I'm not in love with Ana, Mia. I'm—"

She places a hand on my chest. "We agreed to play this game until the wedding, and now—now it's time to return to the reality of both of our situations."

"Bullshit," is all I manage to say.

Mia looks from side to side, as we are now the only stationary couple on the dance floor.

"I don't think even you believe that, Mia. This may have started as a game, but we both know it is much more than that now. Don't cheapen us like this." I clutch her hand to my chest, desperate to tell her how I feel.

"I'm not. Enzo, please." That word. I cannot resist the pleading in her voice.

My legs reluctantly move with the rhythm of Simone's song once again as my world falls apart. Mia's decision to go to Paris is one thing, but her banishing me is another entirely.

I don't know what I thought would happen at the end of this week. I pushed all probable outcomes out of my mind, trying my best to etch every precious moment to memory, purposefully forsaking the life I must return to. Forgetting my lonely apartment in the city, the stressful job I've devoted years of my life to in a world that doesn't understand my language, my food, or my music.

"Whether I return to New York or move to an entirely new city such as Paris, I no longer care where I go, as long as I am dancing with you, Mia."

Her bottom lip falls slightly open, eyes trained on mine. My nose stings with the onset of tears, and I look up into the twinkling lights, begging them to retreat.

"Enzo?" Ana's voice startles the both of us out of the moment.

"Ana, my apologies," Mia says sweetly. "It seems I've stolen your date. Please, have the next dance."

Mia separates herself from me. She brushes her lips against the stiff collar of my dress shirt and leaves behind, a whisper. One that will carry the weight of all I've ever lost, before every trace of her is removed from my touch. "*Mi mundo*," she hums so low I may have imagined it. Two words spoken as a secret in my mother tongue. Pain shoots from the base of my spine through my chest as my heart shatters.

Mia regards Ana with a polite nod before leaving for the kitchen's glass doors. I take Ana's hands and place them where Mia had hers. The warmth of her still lingers on my skin. I glimpse the back of Matteo's head as he follows Mia, navigating through the crowd and into the kitchen.

I'm too broken to be enraged with jealousy. Too disappointed with my own choices to think of the comfort he may be giving Mia at this moment. Comfort from my own inflictions. Comfort *I* should be giving her. Now and always.

Ana's arms are stiff, her posture wrong, her steps jagged. She wears a pained smile as she tries her best to be what she is not. The feel of her in my arms is a stark difference to having held Mia only moments before. My throat grows dry, scratching as I swallow.

"Is she all right?" Ana asks.

"I don't know," I say, afraid a thread has unraveled from the fabric of my life with no hope of weaving it back together.

Every part of me screams to run after Mia. My body aches to hold her against me for as long as it takes for the world to quiet down, for the storm to calm, for the sun to set. Yet here I am, swaying beneath a summer night sky with the woman of my past and the deepest sense of displacement.

Ana shifts her weight awkwardly from one heel to the other. "Could we go somewhere to talk?" she asks.

We stumble off the dance floor and inside the house. I usher Ana through the kitchen to Mia's study on the second floor, switching on the corner lamp and gesturing for her to sit in one of the lavish reading chairs. Sitting opposite her, I try to breathe deep against my constricting lungs. The white noise of the party comforts me slightly, knowing there is somewhere to run to if need be.

Ana fiddles with her fingers, a twitch I know all too well, and a sparkle of light catches my attention. The ring she stopped wearing for months before she had ended it. A ring I thought I'd never see again and was happy to be parted with. She twirls the thing around her finger and clears her throat.

"I know it's strange, me showing up here like this. We didn't really get a chance to speak last night, and I understand your disappearance. It took a lot for me to get on a plane. And an international plane at that. You know how bad I am with flying." Ana runs her palms up and down the cotton fabric of her dress, avoiding my eyes. She clears her throat again. "I am sorry for what happened between us."

"Why would you be sorry?" I interject.

She looks up at me, puzzled. "Because I couldn't..." She shifts in her seat. "I couldn't be what you wanted. But it wasn't just that. I wasn't willing to step outside of my comfort zone. To explore the things you enjoyed. I was too selfish, too naïve, too in my head. I—" her hands fumble at the tops of her knees. And then, she says the one thing I was hoping she wouldn't say, "I want to try again."

A headache forms between my temples, and I pinch the bridge of my nose to alleviate it. "You shouldn't have to change for me, for anyone. That's not how relationships are supposed to work."

Ana shakes her head vehemently. "No, no. It's about compromise. I wasn't willing to compromise then, but I am now."

"Well, I'm not," I say, my voice harsher than intended.

"I don't understand." Her voice is small and timid, and I want to shake her for being so vulnerable. The room is plunged into silence, a slight vibration tickling the soles of my feet from the distant music. "You've met someone, haven't you?"

I remain silent without denying or defending myself as she arrives at her own conclusions.

Ana sits back in her seat, her hands held tight across her stomach. "I was afraid of this. Of waiting too long. I wanted to try again soon after you left, but I—"

"*You* left *me*, Ana. You ran away," I snap, flooded with an exasperated unease.

Her nostrils flare, anger budding. "Could you blame me, Lorenzo?" I always hated the unseasoned way she'd say my name. "I was your student. You were the mysterious professor. I didn't know any better, but you should have. You're enigmatic and absent minded while still being overly romantic. How does that even work? You were suffocating me and abandoning me at the same time."

"Then why are you here?"

"Because I love you, you idiot," she yells, quickly bringing her voice back down to an appropriate volume. "I was wrong, okay? You know how hard that is for me to admit? I was wrong to shame you for the things you wanted. I just wasn't ready to give them to you." She spins the ring on her finger again. "But I think I might be ready now."

We sit in silence. The moment heavy. Every word that comes to mind is too harsh, too insensitive to say aloud. I don't want her here. I don't want the confusion she brings and the complication of her presence when I was just beginning to find a new path for my life to take. She is an image in my memory I had been successfully blanching, and here she is now, forcing me to look back rather than forward.

"And what if I have met someone else?"

My words hit her almost physically. She blinks up at me in pain. "Have you?"

I give a noncommittal shrug.

Her forehead creases with hurt at the idea, and she shakes her head, then her eyes widen with a sharp intake of breath. "It's Mia, isn't it?" She lowers her voice, dipping her chin. "Enzo, she's your niece."

"Mia is as much my niece as you are my wife." I regret it the moment it's released. But she spoke with such disgust, such prejudice. I run a hand through my hair and lay my palms facing up in an attempt to appear unthreatening. "I'm sorry you've come all this way for nothing."

Ana stands, her hands in tight fists at her sides. "No," she says with more determination than I'm used to hearing from her. "I did *not* come all this way for nothing. You loved me once, Enzo."

"I did. I *loved* you. And I always will, in a sense. But I am in love with another, and I am sorry it is not you." Every word pours out of me as a sentence of its own. The punctuation in my voice a determinate to my resolve.

Tears pool and spring free, running down her narrow face. She swipes at them and takes a step toward me. Ana's fragile nature fractures her attempt at appearing vexed. She takes in a shaky breath and averts her gaze, unable to meet mine. She turns in place and looks about the room. "So, that's it? I'm too late?"

"I'm afraid so." I could sound more tender, drain the disdain from my voice at the even larger mess she has now caused by showing up here the day before my brother's wedding. I could. But I don't. "You left me for a reason, Ana. Nothing's changed. You made the right choice for both of us. Why come all this way now?"

"I've already told you," she says with a whine. "I'm ready to give you what you want now."

"And you expected me to wait around until you were ready?" The words aren't fair. She shouldn't have to bear that guilt. But the cruel reality is that I did wait, just not for Ana.

She shrugs, new tears spilling free. A wave of anger washes over me at the sight. Anger at Ana for seeing me as a pawn in her life, fervently waiting to be of service, self-loathing for allowing her to see me in such a light, and frustration toward Mia for proving her right.

I steeple my hands under my chin and wait for her answer. Fear crosses her face, and she blinks more tears before wiping them away with the back of her hand, saying nothing.

"I think you should go home, Ana."

She shakes her head defiantly. "I have no place to go."

"I didn't ask you to come."

"You did. You did ask. You knew what that photo meant. Now here I am, giving you what you want, and you toss me to the side?"

"I may have asked you to join me on this trip when we were still together, something to look forward to as a desperate last chance effort in hoping this might bring us closer. But you *left*, Ana. You left me to come here alone, and I did."

The ring keeps spinning on her finger before she sits back down in the seat across from mine.

"Does she do what you like? What I..."

I raise a hand to stop her.

"No, I want to know. I can't imagine a woman enjoying the things you do. Does she?"

I laugh at her incredulous words, remembering the judgment she would throw at me when I held her just a little too firm for her liking, when I whispered things in her ear she couldn't bear to hear. There was a time the shame she gave me stuck to my skin, cold and uncomfortable like wet clothes. When I thought something must be wrong with me to want more than what she was willing to explore. She made me think of myself as a monster for simply wanting a bit more excitement in our lives. But now, everything has changed.

"That is none of your business," I say, holding up a finger to interrupt her coming interjection. "But it was never a problem with *me*, Ana. I know that now. Your condemnation for my desires had nothing to do with me."

She looks at me, disgusted.

"Judge all you want. You say you want to try again, but I don't believe you. How can I when you still look at me the way you do with such discernment?" I shake my head and stand. "I hope you find someone who can express their love in a way that makes you comfortable, Ana. But it is not me. It never was. One of us was always going to resent the other for not being what we needed. But I refuse to be humiliated any longer." I raise my hand and gesture for the door, but she doesn't move.

Instead, she sits with her arms across her chest, studying me. "Did I really make you feel so ashamed?"

I lower my hand and nod once.

Her face softens, tears welling in her eyes once again. "I'm sorry for that."

"It's in the past now."

"I thought I could... try? Try harder, I mean. I tried before, but I just couldn't." Her voice breaks, the words falling flat as I kneel to her eye level.

In truth, what I requested from her was rudimentary for most, not even aligned with what some would classify as kink or fetish. But it was too much for her all the same. A simple rough touch was too triggering, and I never pushed her save for the one time. The *last* time. I bring her into my arms and let her cry silently into my chest.

After some time, I hold her head away from me and wipe the tears from her face. Ana's gaze flits from my eyes to my lips and she arches her head up to meet mine with a kiss. My first instinct is to flinch, to reject her touch. But I don't. Instead, I let her kiss me.

A whimper escapes her, a sound I haven't heard in months. I see Mia behind closed eyes. It should be her I'm consoling, her lips I should be devouring. A pang of regret splits my chest and I drop my hands away, breaking Ana's hold. I step back.

"Please," Ana says, standing up too quickly. The word holds no magic coming out of her mouth. It falls to the stone floor between us, and I have to look away from her pleading stare. "I don't want to be alone anymore, Enzo."

I run a confused hand across my face and scratch at my stubbled cheeks. I want to shut out the light, shut out the uncertainty and wait in the dark until things make sense again. But I can't run away; can't face anyone, including myself, with the choices that have brought me to this moment. As certain as I may be about loving Mia, the realization of Ana's words dawn on me.

I don't want to be alone either.

Returning to New York with Ana would be a remedy for loneliness. To return to my life as it was before and discount my time here as nothing more than a summer dream. I made it work with her before. I could do it again.

Ana strides toward me and tentatively places her hands on my waist, bringing our middles together. Confidence and hesitance both fumble in her movements as she grabs the lapels of my jacket and pulls them over my shoulders. She lifts herself up on her toes and kisses my jaw, trying her best to coax me into loving her again.

She claims she wants to try again. Would it be cruel of me to test that? To prove her wrong?

I shake the blazer off and let it fall to the floor. As wrong as it feels, I need to know. I hold her shoulders and kiss her again, harder this time, experimenting with her newly willing nature. Her neck cranes and I can sense the struggle behind her kiss. She presses her eyes closed, causing them to crease at the edges.

There is a wrongness in her hesitance that stops me flat in my tracks. A feeling of force that makes me sick to my stomach at the thought of coercing something from Ana that does not belong. Pulling something out of her that doesn't come naturally. I can't bring myself to be what she needs just as much as she can't force herself to fit into the mold of my desires.

Despite her being here, despite her words, nothing's changed. We are the same people we've always been. And where we may have prolonged our relationship in the past, it inevitably ended for a reason. What reason do we have to believe a different fate awaits us now?

The sting of a goodbye pierces my chest. I've never been fond of endings, though some grow more welcomed in hindsight. Ana's goodbye resembled that of my mother's. Unforeseen yet understandable. I never questioned if it was my fault because I already knew the answer was yes. Accepting that reality hurt most, more than the loss of either woman in my life. But now, faced with the potential loss of the evening, I am consumed by profound devastation.

Mine and Ana's shared fear of isolation calls to a place deep inside me that longs for compassion. And so, the least I can do is stave off that loneliness for the both of us just a little while longer. I break our second kiss and give Ana the only thing I have left to give.

"Wait for me at the airport tomorrow, you shouldn't have to fly alone," I say before leaving the room with the purpose of finding Mia to say goodbye.

22

MIA

WEDDING DAY

Matteo's hands are all over me. His words are reassuring and sweet with a scornful edge toward the cause of my flustered state. We stand in the low chandelier light of the formal dining room, a space rarely used. His fingers run up and down my arms, caressing my bare skin and leaving a trail of goosebumps in their wake. He interprets this as attraction, bringing his body close to mine.

The pain of letting go, the need of a warm body to fall into, surpasses the need to set boundaries. I let him hold me as he's done a million times before, his large arms enveloping me with ease, his warmth a needed comfort in the moment.

"He's leaving tomorrow, Mia. You never have to see him again," he says. Words he thinks should bring me solace only damage further.

The thought of never seeing Enzo again, of never lying with him as we have this week, shatters my stoic facade into a million pieces.

"He's clearly been playing with you, bringing his girl here to flaunt in front of us all. What a prick. I should never have let him get so close to you, Mia." Matteo talks and talks, words tumbling out of his mouth that have such little meaning compared to the truth of my own reality.

His broad hands run up and down my spine like hot coals, and I rest my head against him, closing my eyes as the sound of his voice vibrates his chest. The will to correct him floats undisturbed within me. I allow him to bash Enzo verbally, letting him bear the abhorrent burden on my behalf.

Glasses clink outside, followed by the sound of a zealous crowd. Cyrus and my mother must be kissing. I'm missing it.

I sniffle, wiping away the few silent tears I've allowed to escape, and lift my head from Matteo's chest. In his face, I find a "what if" I have mentally explored countless times before. I see through the pretense of his brutish act to the soft core of him and wonder why I can't seem to feel more than a familial love for someone so right for me. Why that insatiable, primal desire within me seems to be drawn to men I have no business involving myself with.

I smile weakly up at him, and he brushes away another fallen tear. "Oh, Mia," he says.

I laugh at the pity in his tone, disgusted with myself for allowing anyone to see me so assailable. He holds my chin delicately on the knuckle of his forefinger. "I would never make you feel this way." His voice is low and sure. "A day would never go by without you smiling," he says, brushing my cheek with the pad of his thumb. "I'd make sure of it, Mia."

What happens next is almost too fast for me to comprehend. A wild succession of events that begins with his lips on mine. An unwelcome sensation of being kissed too soon after saying goodbye to the man I believe to be the love of my life. Matteo has kissed me before. Whether on the beach, by a drunken dare, or to say goodnight. But this kiss is different, prominent, with meaning behind it that suggests much more than a Farewell-for-Now.

Alarms blare inside me, and I push at Matteo's chest, forcing him to break the seal of our kiss. "What are you doing?" I ask, annoyed at the smile on his face.

A blur of motion crosses my vision, along with the crashing sound of flesh and bone. Funny how one's mind makes sense of the sound before comprehending the situation fully. Like hearing a car crash, you don't realize you're involved until your view is upside down and glass shatters around you. The picture becomes clearer.

Enzo's fist. Matteo's jaw.

The force of the blow sends Matteo sprawling into one of the dining chairs, the legs screeching dramatically on the stone floor. Matteo finds his footing and barrels toward Enzo, tackling him to the ground. The dining table shakes, and a glass vase crashes to the floor in pieces. I shudder, shock resonating in my bones. Fine wine glasses hanging from the bar on the other side of the room jostle. The two are on the floor in a brawl of well-dressed limbs. Matteo lands his fist into Enzo's face. He returns the attack, throwing his palm up into Matteo's nose. A defining crunch, followed by a yelp of pain, and the blood on both their faces snaps me from my awe.

"*Basta!*" I yell, dumbfounded.

They don't hear me, transfixed on destroying the other, their fists continue to make contact against face and body. Matteo's dress shirt rips, his face covered in blood as it drips heavily from his crooked nose.

"Oh my God!" Ana appears beside me, standing with her hands over her mouth. "What's going on?" she asks, out of breath. "Make them stop!" She lunges forward to pull the two men apart.

I catch her wrist and pull her back, shaking my head. "You want to end up with a broken nose, too?"

She looks back at the two men, then brings her body close to mine. I let her, needing someone to hold, myself.

Matteo spews Spanish curses around a bloody mouth, throwing further promises of violence. Enzo remains silent, defending himself and landing counter blows of his own.

Another body is thrown into the brawl, and I take a moment to register who drags them away from each other with such little effort. Cyrus pulls Matteo off Enzo and hauls them both to their feet. His outstretched hands meet both on their chest, Matteo's now bare, his shirt hanging in tatters off his broad shoulders. Their fists clenched and ready.

"*¿Que esta pasando?*" Cyrus asks, but no one answers. "What is going on?" His voice is fearsome and furious, making me flinch.

Ana clutches me tighter, just as frightened.

Matteo and Enzo breathe heavily and stare each other down, their chests heaving. The click of my mother's footsteps approach from behind. She lays a hand on my shoulder, and I turn to see her bewildered demeanor.

"Speak!" Cyrus yells.

We all flinch.

"*Ella no te pertenece,*" Matteo barks, looking at Enzo in a rage, then to me.

She doesn't belong to you.

"What did he say?" Ana asks.

I shake my head, grateful for her ignorance.

Matteo looks back at Enzo, who has now given up the aggressive guise. He runs a hand through his tousled hair. Sensing the slight release in tension, Ana lets go of me and approaches Enzo. A pang of envy splinters me at her open ability to approach him. She lays a shaking hand on his shoulder, and he gives her an apologetic look.

"What's going on?" she asks, lost.

Matteo takes this as an opportunity to move toward me. Stunned, I stay in place as he wraps his arms around me. My breath is shaky, the smell of his sweat and blood strong. I feel small in his embrace.

"*Lo siento, Mia*, I'm so sorry," Matteo says, kissing my temple. The confused countenance of Cyrus and my mother tip me over the edge.

"Let go," I say softly at first, but Matteo doesn't hear me over the roaring in his ears. "*¡Suéltame, Matteo!*" I yell, pushing his bare chest away.

Enzo's posture tenses, and I brace myself for the possibility of another brawl. Matteo loosens his grip. A crowd of peering eyes appears from beyond the open corridor, and the music ceases abruptly. Simone begs the crowd to return to the dance floor. They don't move.

"What's the meaning of this, *hija?*" My mother's voice is calm and assertive, bringing up memories of being reprimanded as a child.

I step away from Matteo and meet everyone's staring faces around the room without a word of explanation. Ana clings to Enzo, and he has one arm held lightly around her waist for support, the other cradling his side. Red scratches mark his face and neck, and blood coats the swollen, split skin of his lower lip. I press my tongue to the small cut on my inner lip. An infliction made with pleasure, where his are born out of brutality.

Enzo takes a sturdy step away from Ana and confesses for the both of us. His voice is sure and strong, and I love him despite the mess he's caused in my home.

"*Lo siento Katia. Lo siento hermano,*" he says, facing them with regret. He then looks to me, his brows tight and the whisper of a smile across his beaten face. "*Estoy enamorado de Mia.*"

I'm in love with Mia.

His words hang in the air among the silence. The room grows heavy, my lungs constricting against struggling breaths.

Matteo advances, and I place a palm on his chest, shaking my head. He settles on his heels obediently. Ana's head swivels between Enzo and me as I plead for him to stop.

"Come on," Ana says to Enzo, "let's get you cleaned up." She apologizes to us before taking Enzo from under the arm and nudging him around the dining table.

Enzo's figure disappears through the arched doorway, and the rest of the room turns, expectantly, to me. Frozen in place, the instinct to run tingles between my toes, and I listen to it, turning for the kitchen. Matteo reaches for my arm, but I pivot out of his touch and push my way through the crowd of guests. Simone stands on stage and nods in my direction, trying again to bring the crowd's attention back to the dance floor.

I run for the iron gate, leaving the wedding I've ruined behind.

23

Enzo

Wedding Day

A deserved bite of pain jolts me back as Ana touches a warm washcloth to my cut lip. She tends to the scratches on my face, knowing—without knowing what exactly happened downstairs. The penitence of this entire week eats me alive as tears cloud my vision.

Ana clicks her tongue and takes my face in her hands. I can't look at her. Not with the indignity and pain I've brought. The humiliation she must feel, tending to wounds caused by fighting for another woman.

Ana finishes cleaning the cut on my cheek and lip without a word and stands. She takes her supplies back to the washroom, and I hear the tap running as she wrings out the used washcloth, then returns to the room and takes a deep breath before finally breaking our silence.

"I am not so blind to not see what's going on here. What I've walked into." She shifts on her feet with a newfound resolve in her visage I hadn't seen before. With her shoulders pushed back, she appears taller somehow. "I will be on that plane tomorrow. With or without you. And although I appreciate you not wanting me to fly alone, I'll understand if you don't show up." She shifts her weight from one leg to the other again and clears her throat before continuing. "Enzo, I don't want to be anyone's choice out of sheer convenience rather than undeniable preference. I believe we were once the latter to one another. But now..." she trails off, her gaze falling toward the floor. "I'm afraid we may now be the former."

Ana closes the distance between us and bends down to bring her face to mine. She kisses me softly on the lips, careful not to disturb the wound she just cleaned. "You've been smoking again," she whispers. It's not a question or an accusation. A simple stated fact.

Ana stands again and nods once, agreeing with her own statement before walking out of the room. The determined clicks of her heels fade as she makes her way down the corridor toward the stairs.

I lay myself back on the bed and wince as pain shoots from my side. Matteo must have bruised more than one of my ribs in his attempt for Mia's honor. I close my eyes and press the heels of my palms into them. The coolness of my skin soothes a pounding beginning to take shape, exhaustion takes over, and my mind slips into darkness.

Pain wakes me. Sharp and piercing. Small hands jostle me out of sleep, and I reach out to stop them. They feel foreign and delicate. I clutch my ribs and register a voice in the room.

"Enzo. *Mon dieu.* Enzo!"

My mind finally breaks through the fog, and I open my eyes to see Simone kneeling on the edge of my bed, her hands on my shoulders as she shakes me again.

"What?" I try to choke out, my throat clogged.

She doesn't wait for me to fully rise. Her hands are moving frantically around her face as she's rambling a slew of words in French and English. I hear Mia's name within her blubbering words and finally put my hand on her shoulder. Her voice screeches to a halt.

"In English, Simone. What's wrong with Mia?"

"She's gone!" she yells, climbing off the bed and pacing the floor. "I saw her run after that little show of yours, and I've been trying to call her ever since with no answer. She always answers me. *Always*. No matter what she's running from, she knows not to be so stupid as to not tell me where she's going."

I rise to my feet, my mind spinning with the rest of the room.

"I'm sure she's just off trying to clear her head."

"No." Simone snaps, pounding two steps toward me and pointing a long nailed finger in my face. "You. This is your fault. What have you done to my cousin? You've made her stupid with your empty words and hollow affections. You may have been born here, but you are just as American as they come. Arrogant, self-absorbed, narcissistic. You think everyone is meant to serve you, that this is just a holiday. This is my home, *my family*. Mia is my family. And I will not let you play with her like this any longer. You've ruined *Tante* Katia's wedding. You've broken my cousin's heart. You've disturbed the peace of this island for long enough. Help me find Mia, and then I think you should leave."

I stand, stunned and chastised. Where contrition had consumed me into unconsciousness, I am now numb to her lashings. Aware of the validity of her disdain.

"Okay," I say. "I think I might actually know where she is."

Simone's eyebrows raise, and she opens her mouth to say something, but closes it again and looks up the length of me. She gestures toward the bedroom door. "Lead the way."

Everyone is gone. The courtyard is an organized mess. Chairs on top of bare tables strewn across the stone, the silent fountain eerie and foreboding. The numbness in my chest flutters when I glance at the empty dance floor.

Simone throws me her car keys, and I climb into the driver's seat.

"Why didn't you ask Matteo for help if you hate me so?" I ask as Simone puts on her seatbelt.

"Matteo might think he's right for Mia, but he's less qualified to make her happy than you are, if you can believe that."

I try not to take her words too harshly. There's a compliment in there somewhere if I dig deep enough. I say nothing and pull the car onto the narrow streets of the island.

We ride in silence, the windows down. Crisp air fills my lungs, clearing my mind. Knowing some of Mia's secrets, I have an idea of where she may have run off. If I'm right, there may be hope yet in attaining a morsel of atonement. I drive from memory, unfamiliar with these streets but confident in my mental map.

"I don't hate *you*," Simone says, focused on the road ahead. Her profile is as stunning as every other angle of her sharp face. Dark, arched brows, arms folded across her chest. "I just hate what you're doing to her."

"For what it's worth, she's doing the same thing to me."

Simone shakes her head, a judgmental smile curling her upper lip. "I heard what you said in the dining room. We all heard, even outside."

I grip the steering wheel with both hands, breathing evenly to keep the numbness from returning to pain.

"You love her."

A truck whips by, shuddering the frame of our small car.

"Yes," I say simply.

"*Mon dieu,*" Simone shakes her head again with a light chuckle. "We better find her. I refuse to ruin my aunt's first day as a married woman by making her a childless mother."

"What about Marco?"

"Oh, right. I count Marco as mine. Daughterless, then."

I laugh, to my surprise, and the lightness in my throat breaks through the bleak reality of our quest, my shoulders slowly coming down from around my ears.

We pass the turn for the speakeasy, and Simone turns to me in question but says nothing and sits back in her seat. I drive, enjoying the roar of the wind in my ears. Simone gives no indication of knowing where we're going. We turn into the dark car park and see a row of familiar motorbikes and scooters.

"Where the hell are we?" Simone says with a hint of disgust. She curses me in French not-so under her breath. "I can feel the bass from out here. No class."

I park and climb out of the car, opening Simone's door and helping her out of the passenger's side. We approach the entrance and I realize we might have to put on a show to be able to enter. I drape my arm across Simone's shoulders.

"What do you think you're doing?"

"Go with it," I say. I fake a confident head nod toward the large bouncer. He gives me a once over and then eyes Simone from head to toe. He nods back, opening the door for both of us.

I didn't expect it to be that easy.

"Eww," Simone whispers.

I remove my arm once the door closes behind us, and she rubs her shoulders, unsettled by the blinding, strobing lights and booming music.

I cup my palm around my mouth and try not to yell too loudly into her ear. "Check the ladies' room."

She nods and turns, arms out in front of her like a blind woman, the grace and mystique gone in an unfamiliar environment. I head toward the dance floor, half afraid of what I might find.

Bodies crash into me from every direction as sweat beads at the base of my neck, the air heavy and difficult to push through my lungs. I raise my arms and try to weave through semi-conscious dancers, a blur of limbs blocking my vision every other second in stop motion. I try to focus on faces, looking for Mia's in a sea of strangers.

I turn in place and yell aimlessly into the crowd for Mia, but the bass of the music instantly drowns out my voice. Dozens of ambiguous faces come in and out of focus, requiring significant effort to keep from falling dizzy.

Frustrated, I grab every shoulder in reach, searching for my needle in this haystack. Body after body, it's a fruitless attempt. The room spins, my ears grow hot, and an overwhelming sense of hopelessness settles in my throat.

What if she's not here? What if I misjudged her character and don't know her as well as I thought? What if we are strangers, still?

I call her name again, desperate. A few eyes meet mine, but none rimmed with honey.

Then, a flash of green. Between the intermittent darkness and blinding light of the strobes, I zero in on a woman in a green dress. There are hands around her waist, touching her body in an intimate display not meant for such a public space. Groping and moving, the hands wrap around the woman's frame and hold her close as they both move clumsily to the beat of the music.

I try not to blink, and catch the woman's face. My heart sinks on the dance floor. Mia is dancing with a stranger. This is not so out of character—I should know. She told me herself, this is what she prefers.

Pushing through the crowd, my eyes trained on the figure in green, I pull Mia from the arms of the strange man. Fabric tears as the strap of Mia's dress comes loose. She flings an arm up to catch the strap before it exposes more skin, and I pull her into me to further shield her.

The man is upset at first, his vacant arms scrambling for something to hold on to, but he quickly turns and finds another figure willing to press themselves against him and continues his mindless movement.

Dazed and off balance, Mia's feet find the ground as she rights herself before turning to yell at the asshole who ruined her favorite dress. Recognition dawns on her lovely face, and her brows crease in horror. She looks down at the ruined fabric and shakes her head. Words tumble from her lips, but I can't hear them. I make out the shape of a "no," said over and over again and hold her close. Her body vibrates as she confesses into my chest.

We sway in a sea of bodies, having come back to the same spot, yet everything's changed. Overwhelmed by relief, numbness settles back in its place again. The jealousy and rage brewing at the sight of her in the arms of another quickly vanished when the honey in her eyes melted into mine. She is safe. Everything else can wait. The sunrise, tomorrow's plane, the inevitable loneliness in returning to my life in New York; it all can wait.

I kiss the top of Mia's head and wrap an arm around her waist, guiding her body against me. We don't dance to the blaring music. Instead, we move to the song in our souls. A slow and steady melody with nothing to prove and nowhere to go. A couple enthralled in an amorous sway, mismatched movements to the music around them.

We settle into a relaxed and repetitive rhythm. Her arms trail around my neck and tickle the hair at my nape, a shiver running down my spine at her touch. I keep the straps of her dress in one hand, mindful of the consequences of letting go, as my fingers trail up and down her spine. Sweat slicks her bare skin. My thumb fits into the divot of her spine, and I relish the warmth of her beneath my touch, remembering what the rest of her body feels like, what she tastes like. I didn't know the last time would be the last time. Unaware of the significance of our last encounter with one another on the terrace. If only I'd known, I would have savored it more. Committed to etch every moment to memory. A treasury of reveries to fall back into and reminisce on a time where I was the most selfish, the most careless with my honor. The most in love I had ever been.

Mia lifts her head to mine and kisses the edge of my jaw. The softness of her lips soothes the racing thoughts pounding in my head. Glimpses of her come into view, and I fumble to tie the strap of her dress secure again. I place both hands on her shoulders to get her full attention and mouth Simone's name. She nods, understanding, and I point toward the exit of the club, her gaze following. She nods again and takes my hand, then we push our way off the dance floor, toward the exit.

We see Simone yelling at a security guard who is trying his best to hear her over the pounding music. Mia grabs Simone's shoulder and she whips around in a mess of hair. Her demeanor falls from rage to relief as she recognizes her cousin and hugs her tight. The security guard shrugs before walking back toward the bar. Simone looks up at me over Mia's shoulder and mouths a thank you. I nod once, knowing better than to take her word of gratitude as full forgiveness. But in this moment, I'll take what I can get regarding the mercy of the Cifuentes women.

The three of us head for the door, the music drones on behind until it fades into the night, our ears ringing with the aftermath of the bass, and my eyes take a moment to readjust to a continuous source of light. I open the back door for Simone and Mia and they both climb in. Then I drive us home on shaking legs, checking to see Mia's reflection in the rearview mirror as she lays her head on her cousin's shoulder. They both gaze out the window at the coast as it flies by.

This isn't how I thought I would spend my last night on the island. I had imagined either a quiet night of reflection after seeing my brother marry the love of his life or a night with Mia, after realizing how deeply I wanted to spend every waking moment with her. Perhaps part of me thought I could have both.

We pull into the villa's drive and I open the door for them. Simone takes the keys from my hand. "Thank you," she says again, though I'm not sure if she's thanking me for finding Mia again or for simply handing her the keys. I'm too tired to give it more than a passing thought.

"You're welcome," I say.

Mia purrs a few words in French and Simone gives a quick response. The two kiss on both cheeks and say their goodbyes. Simone points an accusatory finger at me before she gets in her car and drives off.

When Mia turns to me, I expect a sunken visage. Something I may have to soothe after knowing how we both destroyed the day. Instead, she smiles.

"I wore the dress for you," she says.

"I know."

Her eyes drift shut, her smile widening into satisfaction. The moon brightens her face, lighting the path in front of me, and she takes my hand and guides us up to our rooms.

Outside our doors, Mia turns to me and places a kiss on my palm before saying, "We are both making the right decision."

I lift a hand and brush a hair away from her face, cupping her ear. My thumb finds the freckle there, and I brush against it slowly.

"You love me, Enzo?"

"I can't help it."

She smiles again and steps away. I watch as her hand comes up to the broken strap of her dress, and she easily undoes the tie I secured, letting the dress fall to the floor, revealing a naked Mia before me. Watching me, she steps out of the dress and back, falling into the darkness of her bedroom before closing the door.

24

Mia

The Day After the Wedding

The sun's heat bears down on me through the open shades of the balcony doors. I try to savor it, stretching the seconds between sleeping and waking for as long as possible. Not ready to face daylight just yet, my head pounds behind closed eyes. The drunken memory of last night swims in my mind as a dreadful recount.

I groan and squint in the brightness of my bedroom, laying naked above the sheets of my made bed. Clothes and shoes strewn about the room from yesterday's chaos. I reach for a glass of water on my bedside table, my throat parched raw. The liquid tastes faintly of dust, but I choke it down anyway, hoping to quell the persistent dryness.

As I rise, my head beats like a drum. I rub my temples with both thumbs and try my best to transition into full conciseness, standing on boneless feet and heading for the washroom, desperate for a shower and a toothbrush.

Enzo's door is wide open. Instinct tells me to cover up, though at this point I'm not sure it matters. The room is quiet, the bed empty and made. I step into the light to find it pristine, no evidence of his lodgings for the week. His clothes, guitar, phone, laptop, coffee mugs, suitcase—it's all gone.

He's gone.

A dream from which I may as well wake.

The cold tiles of the washroom floor sober me, and I close the bedroom door.

I turn about the room in a blur of involuntary motions. Picking clothes up off the floor, ripped scraps of paper and pens. I straighten the contents of my wardrobe and vanity before turning on the shower.

A faint image pokes at the edges of my memory, but I can't seem to pinpoint it. The noise of the water is deafening, bringing my focus back to the present as the mirrors soon steam, and I can no longer see my reflection. The water burns as I accept the punishing bite of heat against my skin, and I tilt my head back, allowing the water to soak my hair and face, shame and heartache dripping off my body and washing down the drain.

A note. I remember reading a note. *Writing a note?* I squint my eyes tight as the water rushes over my face. A piece of paper in my hand is the only image that comes, but that's as far as my mind is willing to recall. I click my tongue in frustration. I must have been more drunk than I thought.

When I emerge from the steam wrapped in a towel, hair dripping down my back and shoulders, my newly tidied room is not empty as expected. My mother sits on the edge of the bed, patiently waiting with one leg crossed over the other, hands held prim in her lap. The morning sun lights her profile, and I take in her glow as a wife. She smiles up at me, and I try my best to twist my mouth into a smile in return. But all I can manage is a quivering lip.

An onset of tears sting the back of my nose, and my vision blurs, the sight of my mother muddling as I begin to cry. She stands and we slowly make our way toward each other. With my face in her hands, she examines the mess of her precious daughter. She clicks her tongue and presses her thumbs into my wet cheeks, vigorously swiping away my tears as new ones spring forward to replace the banished.

Fear consumes me. The fear of being a disappointment. Of failing her. This fear has shaped my life choices, guiding my every step. It is woven into the fabric of my being, shaping the person I've become. And I don't know whether to thank my mother for this fear or resent her for it.

The spiraling ceases for a moment as she rests her lips against my forehead and kisses my thoughts away. "*Lo siento, mi hija.*" She releases my face and tilts my chin up to look at her. "This is my fault."

I blink in confusion and shake my head. Brows creased, I step away. My mother shakes her head as well, dismissing my reaction.

"*Sí.* Yes. I raised you with no home. No father. No school. No country. I set you up to be just as lost as I was from the start. And I am so sorry." Her voice cracks on the last word and shatters my heart to pieces. My mother releases a light chuckle, choking back tears of her own. She twirls one of my curls around a finger and continues. "I was selfish. You were always an extension of myself. You never complained, never made a fuss about always uprooting our lives to jump from one city to the next. You seemed to enjoy it as much as I did. But I was running. And you had no choice but to follow."

I try to listen to her words, to soak in the meaning of what she is trying to say. I try to envision my childhood as something resembling structure. A faceless man carrying me atop his shoulders. A school I returned to, day after day to learn alongside children my own age.

I can't see it.

"No, Mama," I say, and hold both of my mother's hands within mine. "I was not just following. I held your hand, and we ran together. I didn't have the things most children have growing up, you are right. But you were never selfish with me. You did your absolute best, and I never doubted your decisions because I trusted you. I still do."

My mother releases a blubbering laugh and swipes fresh tears away from her face, a smile breaking through the surface.

"I wouldn't change a thing about my upbringing, Mama. We had proper adventures. I lived a hundred lives others would only dream of before the time I turned twenty. And I owe all I know of culture, of the world, to you. Your tenacity, your spirit, it lives on in me. We slept on trains, we fed people on the streets during Christmas, we visited shrines and tribes and beaches. We climbed mountains. My school was the world, and you were my teacher. In all things." The words pour out of me.

My mother brings me to her chest in a crushing hug, squeezing the breath from my lungs.

I hold her back as best I can, my arms pinned to my sides. "You have not failed me, Mama. I have failed you."

She breaks the hug and holds me at arm's length. An arched eyebrow tells me she doesn't approve. "If what you say is true, and I have taught you all you know, falling in love with the wrong man would be expected." Her words slap me across the face like an open palm. "But what if he's not the wrong man, *hija*?"

Breath catches in my chest.

"He's your brother-in-law, Mama," I say, astounded at her blasé tone.

She waves a hand in the air. "People marry their cousins every day. There is no blood between you."

"What about Marco?"

"Marco is a product of Cyrus and myself. You and Enzo have nothing to do with that."

It's hard not to laugh. The stress of secrecy, of keeping my feelings for Enzo so hidden in the face of possible disappointment and betrayal, of disrupting my family, it all lifts in an instant.

"I *was* selfish, Mia. Now it's your turn."

My mother leaves to finish packing for her honeymoon. I dress and run cold water over my face to relieve the tension building behind my eyes. The smell of coffee wafts up into my bedroom. An almost sour smell I'm not used to. I gather my curls into a cotton shirt and wrap the sleeves around my head to dry.

Downstairs, the sour aroma is too strong to ignore. I step into an empty kitchen and find a full pot of lonely black liquid sitting on the island. Movement catches the corner of my eye through the glass doors.

Ana is sitting alone in the courtyard, a mug cradled in both hands, her suitcase and purse in arm's reach. I see her reflected in the lone coffee pot in more ways than one.

I pour myself a cup and take a quick sniff. The pungent scent threatens a gag. I step through the creaking glass doors with bare feet onto the stone steps of the courtyard. The dance floor and decorations still lay draped in every corner, forgotten after the absurdity of the night.

Ana turns at the sound of my steps and tries her best to give me a wan smile, a look of shock crossing her features when she sees the mug in my hand.

"Oh, please don't drink that. I clearly don't know what I'm doing," she says.

I place the mug down on the table and take a seat across from her.

"Have you seen Enzo this morning?" she asks.

I shake my head. "No. I was going to ask you the same thing. His things are gone from the room."

She nods, taking in each bit of information as pieces to a puzzle.

"When is your flight back to New York?"

"This afternoon, we should be on the same plane." Ana studies her mug, brows pinched, lips turned down into a frown. "I've made a fool of myself, haven't I?"

A breeze rustles through the courtyard, whipping her fringe away from her forehead. I gently unwrap the cotton shirt from atop my head and shake my fingers through my roots. The wind breaks through my hair in the most delightfully refreshing way. I know this will break my curls, but the sensation is too lovely to pass up.

"I think we've all taken turns playing the fool this week, Ana. At least you were brave."

She gives me a quizzical expression.

"We have all acted like cowards. But you came all the way here, on your own, searching for something meaningful. And in the absence of the one thing you were hoping for, you've managed to retain your dignity."

"Dignity?" She scoffs. "I'm humiliated. I'm the discarded ex who's come to ruin the wedding."

"No. The wedding was ruined before your arrival. That was mine and Enzo's doing."

"So, it's true," she says after a beat. "You. And Enzo."

I say nothing.

"Do you love him?"

I say nothing.

"He's never punched another man in my name before." Ana takes a sip from her mug and makes a twisted face. "Ugh, that is horrid." She laughs, bright yet sad, and I join.

I nod in silent answer to her previous questions. A gesture understood without need of further elaboration.

"Don't waste him like I did. Whether you choose each other or not." Ana shifts uncomfortably in her chair. "It took some months of separation, but eventually, I realized what I had after seeing what else is out there." Another gust of wind swirls our hair toward the sky. Ana swipes at her fringe, annoyed, then places her mug on the table and stands with a sigh. "If you see Enzo, could you please tell him I've gone to the airport early?"

I shield the sun from my eyes with the back of my hand and nod.

"He is in love with you, Mia. Don't be a fool, like me." Her words are warm, yet there's still a subtle undercurrent of resentment.

A taxi driver honks their horn once from the drive. Ana gathers her things and nods in my direction before turning on her heel toward the villa's front gate.

I search the entire grounds for Enzo. There's no trace of him to be found other than the marks he's left on my body. Ana's words ring in my ears, a warning I fixate on.

I use all the strength in my knees to pull open the rusted door of the detached garage. The hinges screech in pain as I yank the door up and over my head. The weight of it catches on the other side and slips up and out of my grasp. Sunlight beams through the dusty air. I cover my nose and mouth with the neck of my shirt and gaze over the contents of the garage, not knowing exactly what it is I'm looking for until I see it.

Then, there it is. The only items in the room that aren't covered in a thick layer of dust and dirt.

Enzo's luggage.

I still for a moment, wondering if he might pop up from behind the stack of boxes in the corner. After a moment of silence, I approach the luggage and find a discarded tarp laying on the floor. I turn in place, and it finally clicks.

Cyrus's old motorbike is missing.

25

ENZO

THE DAY AFTER THE WEDDING

I t takes more than a few attempts to get the motorbike started. Once the old beast is humming, I pull out of the drive and onto the narrow highway. Strong winds threaten to topple me over, but I lean into every turn and cut through the air like a mighty ship. Muscle memory takes over where doubt had crept in, and dust billows from the back wheel. The sea breeze lifts my lungs, and for a brief moment, I forget who I am or what I've done. On this motorbike, on this highway, riding along the coast of this island, I am no one.

Wind whips around my face and through my hair. The sound of the engine and the rush of air fill my ears, white noise drowning out my thoughts, hurtling down the highway toward an uncertain future.

I pull the motorcycle into the car park of a dingy liquor store and make my way inside with a sense of resignation. This trip has opened old doors of addiction I've long since put to bed. I grab a pack of Marlboros and a lighter from the counter. Outside, I slide two cigarettes out of the pack and tap them against my hand, tucking one behind my ear and placing the other between my lips. A flick of the lighter ignites the tip, and I inhale as the smoke fills my lungs.

For a moment, everything fades away. The burn of smoke swirls in my mouth, and a warm buzz takes over my mind. The wind picks up, carrying my exhale up toward the sky where it dissipates into nothingness.

I close my eyes and see Mia's face as it fades into the darkness of her bedroom. Moonlight bouncing against her exposed skin. The image of her in my mind may very well be the last I see. At least for a long time to come. The importance of that moment hadn't dawned on me until now. The frankness in her movements, a distraction from an oblique farewell. It didn't feel like a goodbye.

I inhale another lungful of smoke and wonder if this is what I'm destined to repeat. A life of almosts, never quite courageous enough to break the surface of what I truly want. I suck the first cigarette down to my fingers and use it to light the second. Nicotine washes over me like a much-needed respite.

As I breathe in the salty air, I allow the loss to take me over completely. The loss of Mia, Ana. The loss of myself. Who am I without being tied to another? Fickle and unsure, I finally see what Matteo sees when he looks at me. I may very well not know myself without the accompaniment of a woman. A lone note without a melody.

What awaits me on the other side of today's plane ride brings me no excitement, no hope toward the future. I may as well run off to Paris myself. Give the head of my department my resignation and be done with a life that has no give and only take.

I picture a life here, with my family. With the sounds of home on my tongue. The quiet life this island would bring in contrast to the never ending cyclical days I've been living on the other side of the ocean. Yet, if this trip has shown me anything, it's that I don't belong here anymore. Unfit for this unit, however much I long for it. I may be Cyrus's brother, but I'm a stranger to this way of life now.

I sigh, utterly conflicted.

It's time for a new beginning. A chance to start over and be someone else. Perhaps Mia is right in running away to Paris and leaving everyone who has molded her behind. Or maybe it's too late for me. She is young, bright, and ready for the world. It would be enough just to watch her unfold. To see her run toward her choice.

A beat-up sedan pulls into the car park and comes to a stop next to the motorbike. A man emerges from the car and regards me before approaching the store door. He looks me up and down and gives me a stern nod. I nod back politely and continue the last bit of my cigarette before crushing the butt under my shoe. The man keeps an eye on me from inside the store, and I soon recognize him as one of last night's guests. A sudden urge to run overtakes me.

The wind has died down now, the air calm. It's time to go.

I mount the bike once more and head back toward the villa. No point in delaying the inevitable. I have a plane to catch.

Wind whips around my face and through my hair. The roar of the engine and the rush of air fill my ears again, white noise drowning out my thoughts as I fly down the highway toward an uncertain future and say a silent goodbye to the island. The ocean air in my lungs soon to be exchanged for the sweet smog of New York City. I turn left onto the gravel drive of my brother's estate and approach an already open garage door. So much for discretion.

I cut the roaring engine and dismount the bike, walking it back into the garage. My luggage remains untouched in the corner.

"It's yours if you want it."

I almost lose my grip on the bike when I spot Cyrus leaning against a lopsided table on the far side of the garage.

"I haven't ridden that thing since Marco was born," Cyrus continues. "I'm glad it got a chance to see daylight again."

I lower the kickstand and lean on the bike for support. "Shouldn't you be on some honeymoon by now?"

Cyrus brushes the tabletop, and a wad of dust circles into the air. "We leave in a few hours. There are still things that need to be put right before we go. Katia has her daughter to think of. And I have you."

"What's that supposed to mean?"

My brother wears a tired smile. The kind you reserve for a toddler at the end of a long day. In an instant, I am his baby brother once again. Reduced to longing for the comfort of his words.

"It means I have you, Enzo. I know you. I know everything there is to know about you, whether you're under my roof or on a different continent. And I've known this whole time."

I stare at him, mouth slightly agape, unsure of what he means exactly by his last statement.

"I knew from the expression on your face the day Marco was born. You looked at Mia sleeping in the corner of the room, and I just knew. And I get it. Believe me..." he runs a hand through already disheveled hair. "I completely understand what it's like to love a Cifuentes woman."

He knew.

I rub my face with nicotine hands, trying my best to rub away the knowledge of my sheer transparency. "How much do you know, exactly?"

Cyrus raises an eyebrow at me, his smile finally breaking past his eyes. "You two were not exactly discreet."

My knees give out from underneath me. Pure embarrassment crimsons my face as my brother releases a bellowing laugh that would put Ricky Ricardo to shame.

Cyrus crosses the garage and envelopes me in a hug I've been needing to collapse into this entire week. I hold him back, unable to suppress the laugh that breaks through my chest as well. Because of course he knew. Of course I can't hide anything from my older brother. But wait.

"What about Ana?" I ask. "Why invite her to the rehearsal dinner?" He releases me.

"Because she was already on the island, and you weren't taking her calls."

I can't be mad at him. I can't be anything but exhausted.

He gives my arm an extra squeeze before letting go. "What time is your flight? I'll drive you."

"Soon," I say. "I already have a car on the way. I thought for sure you'd be off the island by now."

"What about Mia?" Cyrus asks.

I open my mouth, but nothing comes out. There are no words.

Cyrus nods. "You were never one for big goodbyes. Hence, stealing the bike."

"I obviously had every intention of returning it."

Cyrus nods again with an extra lull to his neck. "Yes, and you had every intention of sneaking off before anyone knew you were already in the air."

The crunch of tires on gravel tells me my ride is here.

"I would be selfish to take any more of her time now, Cyrus."

He squeezes my shoulder. "You are both grown and both stupid. You'll find your way."

The driver of the black sedan hops out and calls my name with a question. The three of us load my bags into the trunk.

Cyrus places a hand on my cheek and gives it an affectionate slap. "Thank you for being my best man, *hermanito*. Let me know when you land, *sí*?"

I tell him I will and hug him goodbye.

The villa is tinged orange through the car window, and I watch as my home for the last week fades from view. Masochistic thoughts creep up like a ghostly mist as they had at my arrival. I allow myself to think of Mia, imagining a life that could be if I were to stay. Seeing her face light up as I walk through the gates. Her arms wrapped around my neck as we stand in the sun, greeting each other in the open courtyard of our home.

26

Mia

The Day After the Wedding

Running into the empty speakeasy, I find Matteo behind the counter organizing a new shipment of bottles. He wears his bruises proudly, his face half purple from Enzo's returning blows. A small smile breaks across my face at the memory, followed by an overwhelming feeling of guilt.

"Mia?" Simone calls. She signs a clipboard and returns it to a delivery man. "You look awful. Did you run here?"

We've caught Matteo's attention, but he ignores me still.

"I'm looking for Enzo. Have you seen him?" I ask, trying to steady the trembling in my voice.

"No. Not since he helped me find you last night. You should be in bed. How are you not hungover?" Simone asks.

"I am. I don't know why I thought he'd be here."

"Because you met here?" Simone says. "Your *quixotic* nature had you hoping he would return to the place where you two met."

Dumbfounded, I blink at my cousin.

She sighs. "You're hopeless."

"How did you know that?"

"Know what?" Matteo's voice is much closer behind me now.

"Mia and Enzo met here. The night Marco was born," Simone answers.

"Yeah, always thought that was weird. Why did you dance with him like that? He's practically your uncle."

"I didn't know who he was at the time." I try to defend myself. To defend the me that fell for a stranger's query, ignorant to the significance he'd have in my life.

Matteo scoffs, judgment laced in his tone. "That's some bullshit. You really didn't know he was Cyrus's brother? Mia, we all knew who he was the moment he approached you that night."

Simone's hand jumps up to counter him, but I don't give her a chance as I turn on Matteo in a rage.

"No, Matteo. I didn't know. And neither did he. It wasn't until you and Simone pulled me off this dance floor that I thought he might look familiar. I didn't recognize him until Marco's baptism. So I can do without your higher-than-thou attitude. In fact, it's getting quite tired at this point. I rejected you. Get over it."

His steel demeanor melts, and I know I've hit too low. But I'm too furious to take it back now.

"For the record, I only put the pieces together this week," Simone says in an attempt to diffuse the tension.

We stand in a beat of silence. When he says nothing, I storm off and up the stairs.

My eyes take a moment to adjust to the harsh daylight. For a moment, everything is white, shapeless. The door to the speakeasy bangs behind me.

"Mia," Matteo calls.

I keep walking.

"Mia!" he calls again.

"I don't have time for this, Matteo."

"Wait, please."

I close my eyes and silently count to ten.

"I'm sorry, Mia." He places a hand on my shoulder, and I finally turn to face him. His apologetic countenance makes me regret my choice of words a moment ago. "I'm sorry for waiting so long to see you as I do now. And I'm sorry for forcing myself between you and him. It's just... I thought I knew what was best for you. And I see now how insulting that is. How much of a fool I've been. I love you. I will always love you. You are my family first, always. I know now that I will always soar beneath your radar."

His words should sting. They should come with some sort of reverberation within me, and yet, they fall like leaves in the back of my mind. Sorrow pools in my heart for not feeling toward Matteo what I do for another. We would make a good match. But I am not his. He is not mine.

"I hope you catch him in time." Matteo places a soft kiss on my cheek. His smile makes the swelling in his eye more profound.

I touch the unbruised part of his face in thanks before running back toward home.

I finally come to a slow stride through the courtyard and into the kitchen to find Marco helping Cyrus wash dishes in the sink. Marco is standing on one of the bar stools, soaked and smiling.

"You're still here?" I ask.

"Ah, Mia," Cyrus says, too nonchalant for my liking.

"Have you seen Enzo?"

He lets out a sigh that ends in a small chuckle. I'm slightly annoyed.

"He left, *mi hija*." My mother is carrying an embarrassing amount of cups and dishes from upstairs.

I rush to take a few from her cluttered arms. "When?"

"A driver came to take him to the airport a little over an hour ago."

My thoughts fumble over themselves. Question after question arises, though I already know the answers to all of them. I knew the answer when I saw his empty room this morning.

I love him. And he's gone.

Tears threaten to breach, and my vision blurs. My mother puts down the contents of her arms and takes the dishes from mine. She holds me as I sob softly into her chest. I've needed her comfort more times today than I have in years. On a day that is supposed to be about her and Cyrus's new life.

I feel selfish.

I feel stupid.

I feel abandoned and loved at the same time.

Marco's wet footsteps slap on the floor before he holds my legs. He looks up at me with an oblivious smile that makes me envy such innocence. He makes me long for a time where all I needed was a sink full of water to make me happy. I pick him up and hold him close. His little hands wipe the tears from my face, and he gives me a sloppy kiss on the cheek.

"Better?" he asks.

I kiss the top of his head.

Marco reaches for our mother and she takes him from my arms.

"I think I need to go lay down for a bit," I say.

Maybe I'll go back to the club tonight to drink and dance the heartache away. But first, I need sleep.

I trudge up the stairs and back into my messy room. Wind from the open veranda doors ruffles the sheets, cooling me as I lay down and close my eyes, tears trailing down toward my ears. I make no move to wipe them away. All at once too tired, my body too exhausted to do so much as lift an arm to shield my face from the sun pouring in, my breathing steadies, and I fall into the soft nothingness of sleep.

27

Enzo

The Day After the Wedding

C lacking heels and rolling suitcases echo off the walls of the small island airport. Muffled announcements from the intercom system roll overhead in a Spanish rush. There is a sterile glow about everything, making it difficult to distinguish one face from another. I search for Ana as I approach our gate. Rich coffee stings my nose, and I remember the espresso she made that morning.

The strap of my laptop bag slips off my shoulder again, the weight catching in the crook of my arm. I haul it back up, annoyed. Fumbling with my bags, I weave my way through the crowd, my legs moving me forward on their own. The hour before a flight is usually when my anxiety is at its peak with the anticipation of what's waiting on the other side, unknown. A sensation that is temporarily abated when the wheels of the aircraft lift. Time stops. For the duration of the flight, I have no one to answer to. My anonymity reduced to a seat number.

The thought of a drink once I board the plane lessens my nerves slightly. A book to keep me company may help keep my mind off the past week. I make my way toward the airport bookstore, and that's when I see her.

Ana is in front of a row of brightly colored book covers. A pastel paperback in her hand with a cartoon couple on the front. She pulls a strand of hair behind her ear as she reads the back of the book before placing it back on the shelf.

"Ana," I say.

When her eyes find mine, I see tears welled in them. With my next breath, her arms are around my neck. The weight of my laptop bag pulls at the crook of my arm yet again, and I let it fall as I hold her.

"You came," she sighs into the crook of my neck.

I don't respond. I don't know how to. How do I tell her I didn't come for her? How do I manage to break her heart time and time again? And how could I avoid it now?

I grab hold of her hand and guide us toward our gate.

We make our way through security in an awkward silence before boarding the plane. Our seats are nowhere close to one another, but Ana's natural docility persuades the woman sitting next to me to switch seats with her. She makes herself comfortable, an appeased smile sitting prim on her face.

Much of our section has now settled, waiting for the plane to taxi, when a voice on the intercom announces an unexpected delay. I figure I should respond to a few emails while we wait and pull my laptop out of its case to get it set up. A folded sheet of paper whips out with it and floats onto my seat, waiting to be acknowledged.

"Oh, here." Ana picks up the paper and unfolds it. She reads whatever is written, lashes fluttering as she darts from one end of the paper to the other. Her smile stiffens without falling entirely.

"What is it?" I ask.

She hands me the piece of paper and looks out the window. Men in orange vests are hauling luggage to the underside of the plane. I grab the piece of paper, my heart now pounding in my throat.

I want you more than I want peace.

I only saw her handwriting once, but I recognize it all the same. Letters crowding one another, as if written in a hurry. Each word bleeding into the next.

"It was Mia the whole time. She's the woman you danced with when you were last here."

"Yes," I answer.

Ana is still facing the window, her hands fidgeting in her lap. A life with Ana would be peaceful. But the crinkling paper in my hand brings Mia closer in my mind

I'm not sure if peace is what I want either.

Ana twists the ring on her finger until it's released and cradles it in her palm before offering it to me.

"Go," she says.

I gape at her. The reality of what she's saying takes no more than a heartbeat to register in my mind.

"No," I say. "That will always be yours. I can't imagine anyone else wearing it."

She looks down at the ring and back up to me. "Are you certain?"

I'm not sure if she's asking about the ring or about the silent decision we both know I've just made.

"Yes." I say without hesitation. "Please, keep it. I bought it for you alone."

She twists it back onto her finger before trying her best at a sheepish smile, then stands to pack my laptop back into its cumbersome case.

Ana places her palm on my cheek, tears springing from her eyes.

I kiss her cheek and taste the salt of her sadness on my lips before gathering my things and making my way back the way I came.

28

Mia

The Night After the Wedding

The music and muffled conversation of the speakeasy is a needed respite after the events of this week. I draw another cigarette from the pack on the table and place it between my lips. A stranger's hand presents a lit match before me, and for a moment, I hope.

A man with blond hair and a mischievous smile holds the offering. I place the tip of my cigarette to the flame and puff out a small cloud of smoke. He shakes the match and tosses it into the ashtray on the table.

"*Hola, bonita.*" The stranger drapes himself across the seat beside me, spreading himself as far as he can. His accent is undoubtedly British.

I mouth off a cascade of Spanish in the hopes it will scare him away.

It doesn't.

"Fiery. I like that," he says, leaning in even closer.

I roll my eyes and try to show my disinterest as obviously as possible without being rude.

"You sound almost as beautiful as you look."

Any other night, that wouldn't have worked on me. But tonight, drowning in my self sorrow, I smile. And hate myself for doing so.

"*Bailar*?" he asks with an off "r."

"*Sí,* oh-kay," I say with an exaggerated accent.

He'll return to his friends back home and tell them how he danced with an "exotic" woman, I'm sure of it.

He follows me to the dance floor and pulls me in too close too soon, unable to read the movement of the music. He grinds himself against me, and I let him. I let him pretend to lead as he wedges one of his legs between mine almost crudely.

"I have a room not far from here." His breath is hot against my ear, and I recoil instinctively.

"*No entiendo,*" I lie.

"That's so hot." He moves to kiss me, and I shove him away. "Bitc—"

I slap him before he has a chance to finish his monosyllabic insult.

The anger in me erupts, and I am cursing him in every language I know. He looks at me in horror, mouth agape, as though I'm casting a spell he'll suffer for generations.

A hand grabs my shoulder. Simone pulls me off the dance floor and back toward our regular private booth. "I can't have you assaulting the clientèle. Distasteful as they may be."

The blond boy stalks back toward the bar, where Matteo refuses him, before leaving. Matteo winks at me. I mouth a 'thank you' in his direction.

Simone sits me down on our favorite chaise lounge and puts a drink in my hand. She takes a seat across from me to watch in the high tower over her kingdom. The music switches from a fast paced flamenco to a slower samba.

"Why aren't you up there tonight?" I ask, the fire of my anger still burning.

"I will be later. Once there's more of a crowd," she says without looking away from the dance floor. Surveying the patrons as they trickle in.

I pick up the pack of Marlboros and light one for myself. Sweet smoke cushions my mind, and I calm, releasing a breath, closing my eyes, listening to the tantalizing sound of the new guitarist on stage.

I love this song. I want to dance. I want to drink. I want to forget everything about this week and start over. I want to go home and start packing for my new life, away from every mistake I've ever made.

But for now, I can be here with my cousin, giving her hell and support at the same time.

A light gasp brings my attention to Simone. She is alight. A clean smile across her striking face, her focus held on something behind me. She looks to me, and laughs.

The confusion clears when I hear Enzo's voice.

"Care to dance with a stranger?"

Epilogue

P aris in winter is magic. The air is crisp and fresh, with the sound of crunching snow underfoot. The Eiffel Tower stands proud in the distance from our small flat. During the day, it flickers in the sunlight, a dusting of snow covering its metal structure. The lights make it even more prominent at night. As evening falls, the streets glow with a dazzling display of Christmas lights and decorations. The markets sell everything from mulled wine to handmade ornaments, trees along the streets adorned with sparkling orbs, and festive music fills the air.

I open the French glass doors onto the veranda overlooking the narrow cobble road beneath. Cars and scooters pass by as a pink cast of sunlight dims over the horizon and the lights across the city flicker on.

Mia wraps her hands around my waist from behind, her cheek pressed against the center of my back. I hold her arms in mine.

Two musicians with instrument cases in hand make their way down our street and set themselves up right in front of our building.

"Right on time," Mia says.

The performers unload their instruments, and the guitarist tunes his strings while the violinist tightens her bow and rubs a block of resin across its hairs.

The music starts in a jolt of urgency, as if they were late for their own street performance. I take Mia's hand and twirl her across the veranda and back into my arms. My hand curves under the strings of her laced top, feeling the arch of her back in my palm. Her nose brushes mine, and I kiss her ardently on the balcony of our flat.

Her curls tickle my cheeks, and I brush them away from her face, kissing her again, guiding my tongue toward the sky of her mouth. She moans into me, and my grip tightens at the sound.

The fireplace cracks in the corner, its heat escaping through the open veranda doors, our bodies moving together as they did that first night, from one note to the next, finding one another in the rhythm of the music. Her confidence never falls, whether we're being watched by a club filled with strangers or alone in our home.

I bunch the fabric of her green sleeping shorts in my fist to reveal a bare thigh. Her hands snake up underneath my shirt. Finely trimmed nails on my back elicit a shiver from my spine as she pulls my shirt from over my head, and I tug her sleeping shorts down toward her ankles. The strings of her top easily spring loose as we undress one another, the snow and music trickling in from outside.

"Do I know you?" I ask.

She shakes her head and smiles. "No. We haven't met."

Mia's eyes melt into mine like honey in tea. Naked, she lifts herself onto the tips of her toes to kiss me again before bringing me down to the floor with her.

We fit as we always have, allowing ourselves the satisfaction of one another after years, in a city where no one knows our names.

A city that, when asked how we met, we answer with the truth. We met as dancing strangers.

Fin

Author's Note

This process consumed me. My every waking moment was spent in Spain while writing this novel. I had the time of my life at my desk.

Nothing compares to the thrill of reading a good book. The feeling of being so immersed in a story the words on the page fall away and you're surrounded by the setting, the characters, the mind of the author. It's quite an intimate exchange, yet we do it every day.

Witnessing your own story slowly come to life is something akin to free-falling. Time seems to take a breath while you wait for wings to burst from your back and catch you before the ground does. There's a chapter in all our childhoods where stories come naturally. We play make believe and come up with interesting scenarios to pass the time, flexing our imaginations into impossible shapes. I believe all children start out as artists, and it's heartbreaking to know that for most, given the opportunity, we would have stayed that way.

For the longest time, I refused to call myself an author for fear of insulting those who've completed the task of writing a novel from start to finish. For the writers who bled their fictitious truth on the page to share with the world, fearlessly. I've taken that leap, cut myself open, and it's the most exhilarating feeling, I can barely describe it. This is my first completed novel; however, it's not my first story.

I struggled with the concept of writing for this genre, making up excuses as to why I should stay away from contemporary romance and the ease with which the words come to me when writing in this form compared to others. Then, I found Mia and Enzo. Characters I've subconsciously woven myself into. From Mia's freckled ear to Enzo's fear of flying—I give myself to these characters as they've given themselves to me in this little dance.

I enjoy books of all genres, for why limit the possibilities of escape? Every story is an exit from this world, a portal to another. And this world, though beautiful at times, can be cruel. Especially to those whose minds are spelled against them. For me to build a portal from which others can escape... Well, that feels like something to keep writing about.

As my mother would tease me as a child, as she teases me now when I can't seem to stay quiet in her presence: "You have so many stories." I'd like to thank you for being here, and I hope you return in the future. I have so much more to tell you.

Stay lost, keep reading.

Nadia Samar

ACKNOWLEDGEMENTS

Writers are often depicted as lonely. They lock themselves away, immersed in fantasies of their own making. Though no truer words have been written, the journey can also be quite collaborative. Above all, it's intimate... and terrifying. After writing the last word of a manuscript, the truth finally dawns on you—people will read it. Is there anything more harrowing?

Like most first-time authors, I turned to the internet for help during the tireless endeavor of developmental edits, line edits, copy edits, all the edits. All the rewrites, reworking chapter structures, you name it. And I was fortunate enough to find a handful of people willing to believe in my little dancing story enough to help. From friends like Brian Brathwaite with his dirty mind and delightful disposition to more structurally helpful friends like Nathaniel Loscombe with his knowledge and advice, I thank you. To my beta readers, Rebecca Sampson and Ella Luking, your feedback in character development, story structure, tweaking the plot to better serve the characters opened my eyes to issues I would have otherwise never seen. To my editor, Marni Macrae, I feel so fortunate to have found you. Though we've never met in person, I now consider you a friend. Your notes and feedback were invaluable. You polished this book, giving it your time and attention to where it now shines. I can't wait to work with you again on my next project.

To my co-workers and lab-mates, thank you for putting up with my constant obsession.

Okay, now for the individuals I hope never read this book yet helped me write it all the same. Though I kept the spicy elements vague, I still sought advice and validation from my family.

My husband, Pablo, has a knack for story development. I trust his judgment in conjuring up scenarios or roadblocks that can make a story that much more interesting. And though I wrote this novel alone, he was almost always in the room, kindly looking away from my screen to give me the privacy I needed to finish. Thank you, my love, for just being there (and for tolerating the emotional turmoil I put myself through).

My sister is the poet in our family. She introduced me to writing at a young age. I remember barging into her room and finding her on the floor in her closet with an open notebook nearly full to the margins. Lines and lines of devastating words written in pristine handwriting. She had always been a force—magnetic, pulling people into her orbit with her beauty and style. But her words had a bite. I remember hearing her practice before performing on stage. There was a sense of pride in anticipating the audience's reaction, knowing their applause was real and earned. Being six years my senior, I had always looked up to her, sometimes stealing the spotlight as younger siblings often do, though she never seemed to mind standing by my side. When I found myself playing the piano behind her performances, she happily shared her stage with me. And for that, thank you, Maymay. Thank you for your relentless encouragement. Even when it felt like life's rejections were personal stabs to the heart, you pulled the dagger out and placed it in my hand, teaching me how to wield a pen instead. (Insert our secret sister handshake here.)

For my mom, I hope you never read this book. You taught me the joy of reading, the magic, the possibilities, the absolute fun. You never denied me when it came to books. Growing up, you were the fun one, the adventurous parent. You still are. You take life by the horns while tickling its neck, laughing at fear. You're the one I want to laugh at everything with. You taught me to not take myself too seriously yet still strive for the very best possible outcome from life. Thank you, Mama.

Where my mother is the kite, my father is the string. He wrote scripts. His stories were wild and intricate, different and specific. My sister and I got our writing bug from him. And though I'd never care to share this story in particular with him for fear of utter mortification, he's always steered me in the right direction. No matter where I find myself now, I will always remember his words, the wisdom he radiates. I've been told by a number of strangers how lucky I am to be his daughter, and I believe them. Maybe that's why I have an affinity toward strangers. They tend to tell the truth.

Finally, to every single viewer and supporter of the Neverland Book Club. I am so happy you're here. I wrote this with you in mind.

Stay lost, keep reading. I'll keep writing.

Nadia Samar lives with her husband, Pablo and her black cat, Hades in Los Angeles, California where she hosts the Neverland Book Club on YouTube.

She graduated Magna Cum Laude with a degree in Biology and has since worked in one of the top IVF clinics in Southern California as an Embryologist.

Her passions include classical music, literature, fine cinema, and the *filthiest* smut she can find.

Nevertheless, Nadia enjoys reading all genres and encourages readers to stay lost, and keep reading.

Follow, subscribe, and visit nadiasamar.com to be notified of upcoming projects.

youtube.com/neverlandbookclub

instagram.com/neverlandbookclub